Copyright © 2024 by B. M. Light.

All rights reserved.

This book or any portion thereof may not be reproduced or used in any manner whatsoever without the express written permission of the author except for the use of brief quotations in a book review. This is a work of fiction.

Any resemblance to actual persons, events, or locales is entirely coincidental.

Ebook ISBN: 979-8-9902554-0-1

Paperback ISBN: 979-8-9902554-1-8

Cover Design by B.M. Light

Everyone Has Secrets

B.M.Light

Dedications

I would like to thank my editor, Chrissy for taking the chance to read my first novel and for keeping it real and giving me tips on how to make my story even better. I do not think I would have been able to branch out like I had if it were not for your help.

I would also like to thank my mother who always told me that if I had a dream, do not give up on it. To keep reaching for that goal, no matter who or what tries to beat you down. Finally, I'd like to thank my beta readers, Kristy C and Kaiidth from our Discord Server. You both were the first ones to read this book and gave me your honest feedback and I wanted to take a moment to personally thank you both.

And to my 15-year-old self. If I could, I would give her the biggest hug and tell her all the trial, the errors, and the many, many rewrites were *finally* worth it. We **did it!** We made our dream finally come true.

To anyone with dreams, one day you will get there, I know it. Just keep reaching for the stars.

Chapter 1

Taylor

"The snow has finally stopped falling in the mountains of Salt Lake City on this beautiful September Sunday evening after a day and a half of precipitation. Crews are working hard to clear the roads for school Monday morning." A local news reporter says from the TV in the living room. "So far, the following schools are on schedule: Lincoln High, East High, and Woodlawn High schools. As more schools open, we will be sure to give you the latest."

As I'm leaning on the couch with my forearms across the back, I lift the remote to turn off the TV, shutting out the rest of the news drivel when my mom, Kathy, comes in the front door fresh from work. She's in her mid-forties, with short chestnut brown hair, and she has blue eyes that seem to sparkle when she smiles. When I look at her, I know I look just like her. I have the same hair and eye color as she does. Total mini-me.

"So, school is on for Monday, Taylor?" Mom asks as she takes her coat off and hangs it up on the coat rack.

"Yup, so much for another snow day." I moan. "How's the hospital doing since this last snowstorm so far?"

"Pretty good. If you want, you can come by to help with the files again after school sometime this week." Mom says while untying her snow boots and tossing them in the mudroom to dry.

"Okay, just tell me when and I'll be there." I say with a smile.

We say goodnight, and Mom heads to my little brother's bedroom to check on him before going into the master bedroom to join my father, who is already asleep, while I go in the main bathroom to get my shower.

As I let the hot water cascade over my body, I find myself thinking about what my parents have taught me from their careers. My dad has an auto repair shop, and my mom is an EMT/nurse at the local hospital. So, I know how to do simple things on cars like oil changes, tire changes, and maybe try to figure out why a car won't start, but I can't drive a stick to save my life.

I also know the difference between a mild to a severe injury, and how to stabilize someone until help can get there. I start to think about how their lives are so normal. So run of the mill. But my life? It will never be the same. It's all because of a year and a half ago and me not minding my own business. I was trying to help a friend that I thought was in trouble. I shake my head to clear my thoughts.

I don't want to live in the past anymore, even though I have a scar on the right side of my stomach, which is a constant reminder every time I look in the mirror. I shove those thoughts to the back of my mind, let the memories go down the drain and I finish my shower.

***

Monday morning comes all too quickly. At six O'clock AM, my alarm goes off, and I get up and I start to get ready for school. I walk out of my bathroom in blue jeans and a navy long-sleeve shirt. I am still towel drying my shoulder-length chestnut brown hair when I hear my computer beep with a notification, and I walk over to it. I noticed the video request is from my best friend Alexis aka, Lexi Smith.

I click the notification and I continue to towel dry my hair as I sit at my desk waiting for the feed to load. I then see her sitting cross-legged on her bed and her blonde hair up in a high ponytail. She has a big smile on her face that reaches her light brown eyes.

"Hey Lexi, what's up?" I ask. "How's Cali treating ya?"

"Hey! Nothing much going on at the moment. And It's amazing! I just wish it was more play than work. Ya know? Adulting sucks, and no one tells you beforehand. What about you?" Lexi asks, twirling her hair around a finger.

"Don't tell me that. I have another year before I'm an official 'adult' after graduation." I make air quotations around the word *adult*. "I was told it was fun, don't ruin that for me. I'm just getting' ready for school."

"Oh, well, I'll make it quick then. I hear you'll be getting a new classmate today!" She says with excitement. "But I would be careful if I were you." Lexi says with a hint of seriousness in her tone, all excitement disappearing in the blink of an eye. Her poker face gives nothing away.

"How do you know that a new student is coming to school?" I ask in shock, while cocking my head to the side.

"You know I have my ways! Just watch your back. I gotta go." Lexi says back to her normal excited self and cuts off the feed with no further explanation.

Well, isn't that nice, she says to watch my back, and leaves with no explanation.

I'll see if I spot any warning signs today. I say to myself.

So, I finish getting ready and go down to the kitchen where my dad,

Tom, has some breakfast ready. I see him in a red 'kiss the chef' apron and with his messy blonde hair and sleepy brown eyes, he looks all the more comical.

"Good morning, Dad." I say as I grab a waffle off the stack that's cooling on a plate behind him on the island.

"Good morning, Honey. Have a good day at school. Drive safe." Dad says.

I take a bite of the waffle while I get my backpack from the storage bench/coat rack near the front door. I wave to my dad as I close the door behind me. I notice that my light blue, 2010 Ford Focus Sport has already been cleared of snow and is ready for me to hop in and drive off. So, I take a moment and I go back in the house, walk back into the kitchen, and I throw my arms around my dad's waist.

"Thank you for clearing my car off, Dad."

"You're welcome. Honey," Dad says while he gives me a kiss on the top of my head.

"Drive safe," He says again.

I walk back out the door, and I toss my backpack in the passenger seat, and when I walk around to get behind the wheel, I notice the roads are clear in my development. I just hope they won't freeze over before I get home later.

Traffic is a little slower than normal, but I arrived at school with little trouble, thankfully. I pull into the parking lot, and I park beside a white 2013 Dodge Dart that belongs to my friend, Tina Flagg. I grab my backpack from the passenger seat, and I walk to the main entrance of the school; where I see a red 2018 Ford Mustang that belongs to Macy and Casey Green. The captain and co-captain of the school's cheerleading team, who happen to be identical twins, but their style choice is the only thing that makes them different. We all have been friends since we were little, so being cheerleaders wouldn't change that between us at all.

I start to think of how we used to be a group of five and now it's just the four of us. I know the girls miss Lexi just as much as I do. Every time I do think about the five of us, I can almost feel that searing heat on my side again, the memory creeping up like a ghost. I take a deep breath and try to push through the memories that seem to be plaguing my every thought all of a sudden and walk through the doors of the school. I see familiar faces from last year, but also some new faces too, but I give them all a subtle nod or a small smile as I make my way through the bustling crowd. Then I see Tina and the twins waiting on me beside my locker, and I quicken my step to meet them.

"Hey, girl!" Macy says, while tossing her long blonde hair over her shoulder and gives me a wink with her bright blue eyes.

"Hey." I say to all three girls while unlocking my locker.

"Did you have an issue getting here?" Tina asks while pushing her glasses up on her nose.

The light gold frames make her brown eyes shine even more, and she tucks a piece of her short, black hair behind her ear. "Nope, no issues. I just hope I can say the same when I go home." I say.

"I hope we all can," Tina says. "I hate driving in the snow."

We hear the warning bell shrill throughout the hallway, announcing it being close to the top of the hour, and we stand in front of our first class while we wait for the teacher to get there. Just as I settle my back against the cool brick wall, I hear Casey squeal and grab my shoulders. Casey, who is the exact opposite of her twin sister, has her brown hair in a pixie cut style with the ends frosted in a light blue, but she has the same blue eyes as her sister.

"Ohmigod. Look at that hottie!" Casey says in a rush as she points down the hall.

I look at him, and my breath does catch a little. He's five-eleven and has dark brown hair that in a certain light almost looks black, and when I see his eyes, I can almost say I could fall in love with them. They are the most gorgeous green eyes I've ever seen. He's also very fit, but he's not all muscle.

I see another guy walk up to him, and they do the one-arm hug thing that guys do. It takes me a moment, but I realize who the other guy is Mark Stone. We don't talk much, maybe just a "hello" in the hall, but that's it. His dark hair and dark brown eyes make him seem a little intimidating. So, I've never gone out of my way to talk to him.

"You should go say hi," Casey says.

"Yeah, watch me." I say, rolling my eyes.

"Okay, we are." Macy says as she crosses her arms over her chest.

"Girls, no, I don't need guy drama." I whine.

"Oh, it's not that bad," Macy says.

"He's coming over!" Casey squeals.

I watch him walk toward us, but I get the feeling he's looking at me, or I could be imagining it.

"Hello, I'm Bryan. It's nice to meet you." He says as he waves at our group.

"Hello, I'm Macy; this is my sister Casey; this is Tina. And *this* is Taylor." Macy says, pointing to us in turn but pushing me forward just a tad.

I just give her the evil eye when I hear the emphasis she put near my name.

"Hello, girls." Bryan says just as the principal of our school walks by us.

"Oh hello, Mr. Evans," Mr. Snow says cheerfully.

He is a somewhat overweight man with a mostly balding head, but what hair is left is pure white. His last name is now just an unintended joke.

"I see you've met a few of our best students. Miss Sparks, would you mind showing our new student around?" Mr. Snow asks.

"Uh, sure." I say, shocked that I am being made to show him around. I mean, I'm sure Mark could do it. But I'll use this to my advantage now, remembering that Lexi said we would be getting a new classmate.

"Great!" Mr. Snow says.

Well, it looks like I will be getting to know who Bryan Evans is.

"Well, Bryan, looks like you'll be my shadow for a while."

"Yes, so it seems." He smiles at me, and I find myself smiling back.

Maybe Lexi was wrong; maybe Bryan was exactly what I needed.

"What's your first class?" I ask.

Bryan takes a piece of paper from his back pocket, and he opens it as he hands it to me.

"Looks like math. The girls and I have math too." I say as I look over the creased paper.

"Great," Bryan says with a smile.

The final warning bell sounds, and we head to our first class of the morning with the thought bouncing in my mind: *He looks like a decent guy; maybe this is what I needed after all.*

Chapter 2

Taylor

To me, it's stupid to do math first thing in the morning, and I audibly groan as we all take our seats with the rest of the class. Tina sits at one of the desks in the front. Macy sitting next to one of the jocks on the football team near the back of the room, and usually Casey and I sit beside one another, right behind Tina but Casey gives me a wink and takes one near the back and I watch as Bryan sits in the desk next to mine. I groan internally at her and sit next to him while rolling my eyes.

"Not much on math, huh?" Bryan asks with a hint of amusement in his voice.

"Especially this early in the morning." I whine.

"It's okay. I say it's always best to get the worst class out of the way first." Bryan says while taking his black notebook out of his matching backpack and setting it on the desk.

"I guess. So where did you move from?" I ask getting right to it with questions.

I've never been one to ease into things, and that may have been my downfall when I poked my nose where it didn't belong over a year ago.

"I just moved back here from Fillmore. I was staying with some friends there." Bryan says.

"Oh, I've been in this town all my life. I would love to see other areas of Utah." I say with a smile.

"That's cool. It's nice to be able to say you grew up in one place." Bryan replies with a sad smile pulling at his lips.

"Why did you move back here now?" I ask.

"I moved here to live with my grandparents." Bryan says.

"Oh. So, you're helping to take care of them?"

Bryan actually laughs at me. I glare at him as he puts his hands up, showing me his palms. "No, they are very capable of taking care of themselves. I'm just staying with them." He says with a chuckle. "I decided to come here and spend some time with them and finish high school here before heading out to college."

"Oh okay. I just thought that maybe they were getting up there in age and they needed help." I say.

"It's okay. Mark made a joke of taking care of the old fogies when I told him I wanted to move back here." Bryan says. "Now, for him, I almost decked 'em."

I laugh at him this time. If something is up with him, it will shock the crap out of me. He's nice, funny, and charming. "So how far back do you and Mark go?" I ask while pushing a stray piece of hair behind my ear.

"Basically, you could call us brothers. If you see him, nine chances out of ten you'll see me," Bryan says.

"So, you go back to diaper days too." I say.

He smiles, and I know I'm right. Sometimes I'm glad I'm right. His smile lights up his face, making his green eyes dance with joy.

"What about you and your friends?" Bryan asks, propping his elbow on the desk and resting his cheek on his fist.

"Same," I say plainly.

"Well, we have some things in common." Bryan replies.

"Yes, we do." I reply, and for some reason, I feel a blush creep up in my cheeks.

We almost don't hear the teacher come in, but when we do, we stop talking and get ready to take notes. I don't want to be yelled at on the first day back after a snow break. I feel a foot kick mine under the desk, and I look over to Bryan, and he has that infectious smile again, like he can sense my thoughts. I look from his eyes to his mouth, and suddenly the thought to kiss those lips crosses my mind. I mentally slap myself, because I usually never think about that kinda stuff with a practical stranger, but the feelings that are already fluttering my in gut toward Bryan feel right somehow. I try to push them away, build the walls around me and focus on the teacher.

After math class, Bryan and I have History and Chemistry together, then we have lunch. Once the girls and I fill our lunch trays from the cafeteria, we invite Bryan to sit with us at our normal table near the front of the cafeteria near the main entrance. He follows us to our table in the corner, and he sits where his back is to the wall, like he's watching out over the entire cafeteria for any sign of trouble.

As I sit to the left of him, I see Mark come around the corner, and he sees Bryan sitting at our table and walks right over.

"Hey man, how ya doin'?" Mark asks while leaning on the edge of the table, hands splayed in front of him.

"Pretty good. These girls are very good at showing me around." Bryan says while looking at me.

"I'm glad. So, anything *else* going on?" Mark asks.

The emphasis he puts on the word 'else' goes unnoticed by the other girls, but not by me. I take a bite of my meatloaf like I didn't hear a thing.

"Nope," Bryan says flatly, his eyes still locked on Mark.

"Are we doing anything after school?" Macy asks the rest of us as she takes a bite of her lasagna.

"No, we need to get home, Macy, before the roads refreeze. Maybe another day." I say.

"If you want to party, Bryan here is a real party animal." Mark says with a grin.

"Oh no, I'm not! If anything, you're the party animal." Bryan scoffs.

"Maybe, but girls, still, if you want a good time, come with us," Mark says with a wink.

"We just might take you up on that offer, Mark." I say, trying to call his bluff. I find it weird that he all of a sudden is wanting to 'hang out'. Maybe he's just being nice.

"Good." Mark says while finally taking a seat across from me and next to Tina. "I'll be waiting for ya." He flashes a cocky smirk, and I have to suppress the urge to roll my eyes at him.

We all quiet down a bit to eat, but a few minutes later, Mark again is the first to break the silence.

"Hey, weren't you a group of five?" He asks while looking right at me with a slight smile on his face. Like he knows something about us, about me, that I didn't know he would.

"Yes, we were." Tina says softly.

"What happened?" Bryan asks, looking from Tina then to me.

I feel the girls look at me to elaborate, and I take a breath before I speak. "She... moved away....her parents got a better job." I say while picking at the food on my tray.

"I heard you got into some trouble before your friend moved away." Mark presses again with a smirk on his face.

"Mark, stop being an ass." Bryan scolds.

I barely hear Bryan's words. I can almost feel that burning phantom pain from the three-inch-long scar on my right side, and I swear I hear a faint gunshot in the distance.

"You heard wrong." I say, simply taking a sip from my Coke. Complete dismissal.

We hear the bell ring signaling the end of lunch, and Tina pulls me aside as we are taking our trays to the conveyor belt near the cafeteria kitchen.

"Tay, you need to stop downplaying yourself." Tina says, setting the three trays down and watching them disappear into the square hole in the wall.

"Tina, no one can know exactly what happened, you know that. I promised." I whisper as I empty the trash into the can before placing my own tray on the belt.

"I know. You're right; I wish you weren't right though. You did a good thing, Tay." Tina replies with sadness in her tone.

Tina puts her arm around my shoulders, and we walk out of the cafeteria. I would still do anything for the three girls around me. And I know they would do anything for me in return. I feel like these girls are my sisters. Since I'm a big sister to my nine-year-old brother Cody, I'm glad I have sister figures in my life to give me variety.

The school day ends with what seems like mountains of homework to do, but at least I don't have to deal with Mark and his pressing questions anymore. I'll take homework over that any day. People who ask too many questions can be dangerous to well-hidden secrets.

***

Bryan

"Dude, why did you have to be an asshole in there?" I ask as I approach my truck in the parking lot, pulling the collar of my leather bomber jacket closer into my neck.

I don't have to look behind me to know Mark is on my heels. I toss my backpack in the back of my black Ford F150 and turn to stare Mark down.

"Hey man, you would do the same thing if you had a gut feeling about something. So don't give me that shit." Mark says, and he leans against the front fender, his right foot resting on the tire.

"Not every person you meet has something to hide, Mark. You taught me that, remember?"

"I haven't seen you this riled in a while. You like her, don't you?" Mark says with a smirk on his face.

"No, I don't. I don't have time for stuff like that. I have more important things to deal with unless you forgot." I snap.

"Hey man, you gotta loosen up a bit." Mark begins as he puts his hands up in mock surrender. I glare at him, but then all aloofness leaves his eyes as he says, "We will find what we came here for. I know it."

"That's the plan, man." I sigh. "That's the plan." I rub the back of my neck with my left hand. "I'll catch ya later." I give him a smack on the shoulder, and he walks away from my truck and gets into his Charger with a wave.

As I am driving to my grandparents' house, I can't get that new girl, Taylor, out of my mind. Something about her calls to me, but I don't know why. Part of me wants to say to hell with the plan that Mark and I have and actually act like a normal nineteen-year-old guy and go after a beautiful girl, but deep down I know I can't. At least not yet, but maybe soon.

Chapter 3

Taylor

When I get home, I see my nine-year-old brother, Cody, sitting in the living room watching cartoons on TV. If I am the spitting image of our mother, he is the spitting image of our father. Blonde hair, blue eyes and still has that cute baby face. He was worried to death about me when I got hurt, and he tried to help Mom take care of me. I remember telling him I wanted him to draw me some pictures and that would make me feel better. That way he had something to do and be out of Mom's way at the same time.

"Hey, Taylor!" Cody says with delight when I walk in the door.

"Hey Cody, what did you do today?" I ask and I bend down at the waist so I can look at him at eye level as he comes out of the living room to greet me.

"I went to James' house, and we played in the snow. And when we were done, his mom made hot chocolate!" Cody exclaims.

"Hot chocolate sounds good." I turn my attention to the kitchen when I see Dad walk in with a smile on his face.

"Hi Taylor, are you hungry for anything special?" Dad asks while looking in the fridge to figure out dinner.

"I don't know. What do you plan on fixing?" I ask as I rest my arms on the bar that separates the living room from the kitchen.

"Chicken and dumplings." Dad replies, taking the pack of chicken thighs out of the fridge that he set there this morning before he went to work.

"Oh, sounds great."

Cody goes back into the living room and sits in front of the TV, and I go upstairs to start on my homework while Dad is busy with dinner. I am just about to pull out my history homework from my backpack when I hear my iPad beep. I open it up, and I see a video request from Lexi. I open the notification and wait for the feed to load.

"Hey Lexi, what's up?" I ask.

"Just checking in." Lexi replies while twirling her blonde hair around a finger.

"Well, I did meet *the* cutest guy today." I say with a smile.

"Spill." Lexi demands, scooting closer to the screen.

"He's kind, charming, and is absolutely the tall, dark, and handsome type."

"Wow, he does sound nice." Lexi replies. "What's his name?"

"His name is Bryan Evans." I tell her while pulling my notebook and history homework and lay it on my desk.

I expected Lexi to say something. So, at her silence, I look up from my papers and I notice a look of 'oh crap' floods her face. "Is something wrong?" I ask, my stomach dropping like a stone.

"Oh...no. The name just sounded familiar, that's all." Lexi says, trying to hide the waver in her voice, but I pick up on it anyway.

"But I thought you said that I needed to watch my back because of a new student going to my school?" I counter trying to call her bluff.

"I would still watch how close you get to him." Lexi warns me. "You don't know him at all."

"Okay. But you wouldn't lie to me, would you?" I ask, lifting a brow.

"Taylor Allison Sparks! You know I would never do that." Lexi exclaims, putting a hand over her heart in mock insult.

"Just checking." I croon.

I end the conversation, now deciding that I need to get to know who exactly Bryan Evans really is. But first homework. Nothing I can do about him anyways right now.

"Taylor! Dinner!" Dad yells from downstairs about an hour later.

"I'm coming!" I yell back and put my completed homework in my bag.

Before I leave my room, I hear a car door slam out front. I go to look out my window, but the black F150 isn't in my driveway, it's across the street. I stare out the window and see a familiar face standing by the truck in a black leather bomber jacket. My heart jumps in my throat the same time my stomach drops to my feet at who is standing across the street from me.

Oh, the hell *with it.* I think as I open my bedroom window and stick my head out.

"Hey, Bryan!" I say, waving down at him.

Bryan turns around and looks genuinely shocked to see me. "Hey, Taylor." He yells back with a smile on his face as he grabs his backpack out of the bed of his truck.

"Hang on a sec." I call as I put my bedroom window down and I race to meet him outside, not even bothering with a coat. "This is better, at least the whole street won't hear us." I say as I walk across the street to stand by his truck.

"Yeah, you're right." Bryan replies with a chuckle.

"I'm guessing that's your grandparent's house." I say, pointing behind him to the white, two-story colonial with blue shutters beside three windows on each floor.

I see an inviting porch that is large enough for the swing and two white wicker rocking chairs that occupy the space.

"Yep, so we're neighbors," Bryan says with a smile as he points to my house behind me. The two-story home with gray siding and black shutters blending in against the trees on my side of the street.

"So, we are." I say, trying not to let my smile show.

A gust of wind suddenly picks up around us, and I shiver against the cold. I see Bryan's gaze darken, like he should have noticed my coatless frame sooner.

"You should get back inside. I'll see you at school tomorrow." Bryan says, his voice taking on a rougher tone.

"Okay. See ya tomorrow." I walk across the street and walk back inside and shut the door with a silent click. I see that Dad was standing by the window watching me the whole time.

"Who was that?" Dad asks while eyeing Bryan through the window as he is finally walking up the few steps to the porch and walking inside. Almost like he was waiting for me to be safe behind my own door before going in his.

"It's a new friend from school, Dad." He looks at me with a look that says *okay, but I don't like him already.* "Dad, relax. He's just a new student that I was showing around school today."

"Okay, okay." Dad says as he walks back into the kitchen and fills my plate with the steaming chicken and dumplings.

After Dad, Cody, and I all finish dinner, I help Dad clean the dishes while he picks up the kitchen. After that, I grab more homework and work on it at the kitchen table as Dad sits and watches TV with Cody. After about two hours, I shut my final textbook as Mom comes through the door.

"Taylor, I tell you, I think you jinxed me. The hospital was full of people who were out driving last night." Mom says while hanging her coat on the coat rack/storage bench near the door.

"I'm sorry." I say as I go over to her, and I give her a kiss on the cheek. We both go in the kitchen, and I fill her plate for her when Cody comes running down the steps and wraps his arms around Mom's waist.

"Hi, Cody," Mom says.

We all sit in the living room while Mom finishes her meal, and we watch the latest reality game show on TV.

"So, anything exciting happen today?" Mom asks.

"Taylor met a new boy at school," Dad says.

"Really, Dad?" I ask in an annoyed tone.

"I saw the way he was looking at you," Dad says.

"Oh, come on. He's just being nice, Dad." I say, rolling my eyes.

"Okay, so tell me. What's his name?" Mom asks, taking the heat off me and Dad. Knowing he can be a little overprotective sometimes.

"His name is Bryan, and he moved back here to spend time with his grandparents across the street." I say.

"You know, I feel bad. We never introduced ourselves. But they aren't out much, so I didn't want to bother them." Mom says.

"Yeah, I've only seen the man maybe twice." Dad replies.

"Well, you will have to invite Bryan over one day for dinner, Taylor." Mom says.

Sure, so Dad can try to scare him off. Great idea. I think to myself.

"Maybe." I say aloud.

Chapter 4

Taylor

It's been almost two weeks since Bryan arrived at school, and he seems to be getting along well. We haven't had that much time to talk in these last two weeks, so I decided that during free period today, I'm going to find him ask him some questions to get to know him a little better. I find him in the library, and I see all kinds of old newspapers spread across the table when I walk up beside him. I try to look at what he's reading, and I get a glimpse of a familiar middle-aged man with thick black glasses and a receding hairline. My stomach drops at the image of this man and panic wants to fill my blood but make myself shut it down.

"Hi, Taylor. How are you?" Bryan asks as he closes the newspaper with that man's face on it.

"Hi. I'm good." I say, feeling kinda awkward suddenly.

Now that I saw that picture, I just want to hide for the rest of free period. But I remind myself that the past doesn't repeat itself.

"Did you want to sit?" Bryan asks while pointing to the chair next to him.

"Oh yeah. Thank you." I say with a small smile. He gets up and pulls the chair out for me to sit down and then helps me scoot it in. "You working on anything exciting?" I ask while pointing to the newspapers and notes that are covering the table.

"Not really. This is just personal research. What about you? What are you doing here?" Bryan asks.

"Homework. I need to finish up one more assignment before class today." I say, which isn't a total lie. I do have a paper that I need to make final edits on.

"Oh Okay. Anything that I could help with?" Bryan asks.

"No. It's just my history paper that I need to make final edits to."

We work in silence for a bit, and I decide to finally break the ice between us." So, tell me a bit about yourself. I know you're from Fillmore. What other things define Bryan Evans?" I ask. "What are your favorite hobbies?"

"I don't really have a lot of downtime for hobbies. I hang with friends, with Mark. We go to the air rifle range a fair amount for paintball wars." Bryan says.

"Oh, that's nice."

"Actually. There is one thing I do that not many people know of," Bryan says quietly.

"What would that be?" I ask.

"I like to draw and paint." Bryan says softly.

I look at his hands and I notice that while his nails are trimmed; he has calluses on the inside of his palms and a few tiny scars on his knuckles. I can tell they are absolutely hands that have seen some hard work, but I wouldn't have thought that a delicate thing like painting could come from them.

"Wow. I never would have taken you for the artsy type." I say.

"Not a lot of people would." Bryan says. "I tend to keep my biggest secrets to close friends."

"Oh. So, does Mark know you paint?"

"Yeah, but he thinks I could use my spare time in a better way. Like hitting the gym more." Bryan says.

"Nah, don't listen to him. I'm sure your paintings are great." I say.

Then the warning bell rings, and we pack up our belongings and head towards the door. Bryan opens the door for me, but before we part ways in the hall, he stops walking and rubs the back of his neck with his right hand in what I pick up as apprehension.

"What's wrong?" I ask. Wondering if it's something I did.

"Um, do you think I could have your number?" Bryan asks.

At first, I'm shocked. No guy has ever wanted my number, but I quickly get over the shock and smile at him. "Sure. Give me your phone." I say, extending my hand to take his phone.

He gets into the contacts of his phone, and I enter my name and phone number. Then I text my phone from his, so I have his number too. "There, phone numbers exchanged!" I say with a smile.

"Yes, they are. Thank you. I'll text ya later," Bryan says. I nod and then walk to my next class before the bell rings.

Later that night after dinner and I'm up in my room finishing up the homework from today's classes, and my phone beeps with a new text. Thinking it's from one of the girls, I just glance at it, but when I see it's from Bryan, I try to stifle a squeal.

Bryan

Me

I chuckle at the message.

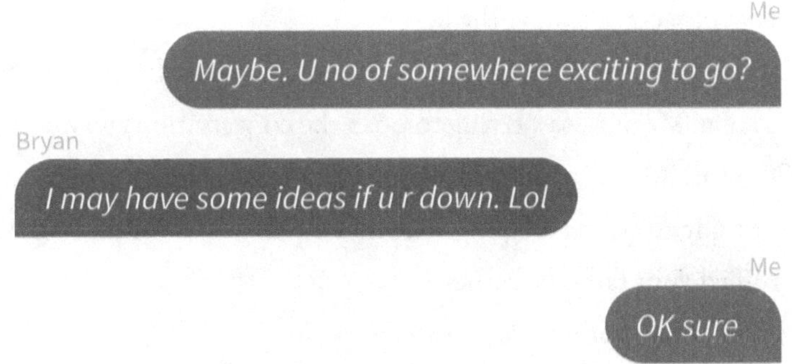

I reply with a snort, thinking his idea of fun is probably a movie where he thinks he can act all smooth and try to 'put his moves on me.'

Bryan:

I better get off here. Early to rise and all.

Me

K. It was nice talking to u :)

I say and I set my phone on my desk, but I get one more message from him.

Bryan

Good night Beautiful.

My heart skips a beat at his message, but I mentally smack myself. Maybe he thought he was messaging his girlfriend. I think about texting him back to let him know he messaged the wrong person, but then my phone rings, and I jump out of my skin.

I see it's Mom and I answer it on the third ring. "Hey, Mom." I squeak. "How's work going?"

"Hey, Sweetie. What ya doing?" Mom asks.

"Finishing up homework." I say, even though I'm far from done. I can hear my voice crack a bit at the lie.

"Okay. Who is he?" Mom asks, knowing I may have been distracted.

"No one, Mom," I say, trying to push the conversation away.

"Oh wait. Was it Bryan?" Mom asks in a teasing tone. When I don't answer right away, she laughs. "Is he that cute? Oh! Is this the same one that ruffled your father's feathers?"

"Mhm," I say, not wanting to really speak.

"Okay, he's gonna have to come over so I can meet him!" Mom says.

"Mom, no! It's nothing! We are just friends." I say, but I can tell it's starting to become more than that.

"Sure, you are," Mom says. "Well, I wanted to check in on ya before you went to bed. Love you, Sweetie, and I'll see you in the morning. Good night."

"Good night, Mom. Love you too. Have a good shift." I hang up the phone and this time I buckle down on homework and turn in for the night.

***

Bryan

Me

Good night Beautiful.

I hit send on the message and throw my phone on the bed like it's a snake about to bite me. Well, there goes nothing. Mark wants me to loosen up, fine. I don't get a message back from her, and I feel something I don't usually experience. Self-doubt. Did I push it too far? Too soon? Does she believe that it was for her? I go to pick up my phone to see if she at least read the message, and as I reach for my phone, it begins ringing. It's Mark.

I groan and I answer it on the third ring. "Yeah, Mark?"

"Hey, Bry. I found something. We need to go early tomorrow morning. Meet me at my place at five." Mark says, and I hear the clicking of his keyboard in the background.

I pinch the bridge of my nose and breathe out a sigh of annoyance.

"Okay. I'll meet you then." I hang up and I walk over to my grandparents' room, and I knock on the door before entering. "Hey Grandma, Grandpa, can I talk to you?"

I tell them that I need to meet Mark, and I can tell Grandma doesn't like it, but Grandpa just gives me a hard look as if to say he understands and to be safe. I nod, and I give them both a hug, and I make my way back to my room to pack my bag for the trip.

Chapter 5

Taylor

I am woken up by the sound of an engine starting. I open my eyes and I see it's still dark outside. I roll over to look at my clock on my bedside table, and the red font shows it's four-thirty in the morning. I groan as I get out of bed and look out my window to see what's going on. I see that Bryan's truck is still parked on the curb and is idling with the parking lights on. I watch as he walks out the front door and gets into the driver's seat and drives off. I utter a small curse under my breath at him waking me up at this time, and I crawl back in bed until it's time for me to get up for school.

When I do finally get up to go to school, I notice that Bryan and Mark are absent. I strike that as kinda weird, but it's none of my business.

"Where is the new hottie?" Casey asks as she is walking up to me with her sister and Tina on her heels.

"I was wondering the same thing. I saw Bryan leave at four-thirty this morning."

"How did you know that?!" Casey asks.

I smile at her; my friend is a little forgetful at times. "He lives across the street from me with his grandparents." I remind her.

"Oh yeah, that's right." Casey says with an embarrassing laugh.

We head to our classes, and before we know it, lunchtime rolls around, and we all gather around a table near the front door in the corner of the cafeteria.

"So, what's Lexi been up to?" Macy asks.

"You know her, always living it in the fast lane." I say.

"Is she still in California?" Tina asks.

"I talked to her the other night, and it looks like she's still there, yeah." I say, missing her all of a sudden.

"I wish she was back here with us and not in Cali doing the under cov-" Casey begins, but I cover her mouth with my hand.

"Casey! You gotta be quiet." I say a little more sternly than I intended.

"Sorry! God, me and my blabbermouth." Casey says.

"That's why Mom and Dad always tells me the secrets and not you, Casey," Macy says while flipping her blonde hair over her shoulder. ,

"I do agree with you though, Casey. I miss her too." Tina says, giving Macy a bit of a scowl.

After school is over, I decide to watch Macy and Casey practice their cheerleading routine with their squad. I make my way to the middle section of the bleachers in the third row, and I sit down, dumping my backpack onto the ground. I find myself looking at the text messages between me and Bryan from last night and smiling at them.

"You look happy." Tina says as she joins me on the bleachers with a small smile.

"Nah." I say as I try to close the message app, but Tina grabs my phone, and her smile widens.

"Oh, he likes you." Tina says while wiggling her eyebrows.

"It's just a text message, Tina." I say trying to downplay her thoughts.

I try to focus on the cheering to drown out my thoughts, but it doesn't hold my attention, and I sheepishly look at Tina.

"You think he likes me?"

"I mean, I think so. When you're in the room, he can't take his eyes off you. I think you try to block it out, but I can see it," Tina says.

"You sound like Lexi when she scans a room." I say flatly. "Okay, so tell me this. If he does like me, then why hasn't he messaged me all day?" I counter.

"No cell service, maybe?" Tina says. "And you are able to scan a room just as well, don't give me that line."

I look at her, and I want to tell her to bite me, but I know she's right. I can pick up on subtle cues from people. Just like Eric, one of the newer football players eyeing Macy right now and doing a horrible job at hiding his clumsiness, by walking right into a door jamb. Luckily, no one else saw it but me.

"Okay, point taken. So, what do I do?" I ask.

"Just play it by ear. That's all you can do." Tina says with a wink.

Later that night while lying in bed staring at the ceiling, I think back to what Tina said about the possibility of Bryan liking me. So, I take a cleansing breath, grab my phone, and open the message app.

Me

> Hey I hope u r ok I heard u leave early this morning. Thanks for waking me up btw. Lol. see u bk at school.

I message Bryan and then I turn my phone over and try to go to sleep.

***

Bryan

"Hey man, don't worry, we will find him. This was just another wild goose chase." Mark says.

"I know, man. It's just pissing me off. Every single damn time I think I'm close to pinning his bastard, he keeps slipping away."

We are finally driving back to Salt Lake after traveling to Bluff, Utah, on an apparent wasted trip. I see my phone light up on the dash, and I snatch it up to read the message from Taylor, and for the first time on this whole trip, I smile.

"Okay, who is that?" Mark asks.

"No one." I say as I lock my phone and toss it back on the dash.

"Bullshit. You don't have that goofy smile on your face for nothing." Mark says while trying to grab for my phone.

"Hey man, lay off. I don't go through your messages. Like you don't have a girl waiting on you?" I snap.

Mark looks at me like he wants to argue, but he knows I got him. He wouldn't want me to look at the messages between him and his girl, so I deserve the same respect.

I finally pull up to Mark's apartment and drop him off, but before Mark closes the truck door, he leans on the door frame and has a serious look on his boyish face.

"Listen, man, you need to keep your head in the game. We are getting close, I _know_ it," Mark says.

"Sure," I say, waving him off, and I drive back to my grandparents' house.

As I pull up, I notice that the lights in Taylor's room are off. So, I park at the curb, kill the engine, and get out. As I walk up to the door, I notice her curtain has moved, and I give a small hidden smile and walk inside the house, softly closing the door so I don't wake my grandparents.

***

Taylor

I hear a vehicle pull up outside just as I'm about to doze off. I peek out and see Bryan is home. It's dark in my room, so I don't think he sees me peeking out the window, and he walks inside without breaking his stride. Then, my phone lights up on my bedside table a minute later.

Bryan:

> Thank you for checking in with me, Taylor. And I'm fine, just tired from the long drive. C ya tomorrow. Good night beautiful

"Well, I know he was talking to me the other night for sure." I say to myself.

I put my phone back on the table without responding because I knew he'll see the 'read' notification on the message.

***

The next morning comes and, like normal, I'm off to school and I meet up with the girls in Math class. I see Bryan walk in the door, and Casey takes that cue to sit with the football players in the back and gives me a wink. Bryan walks over and takes her seat, but I notice he's abnormally quiet throughout our classes, and when free period rolls around, I try to talk to him. I find him in the library again, but this time he's on the computer, but he shuts it off before I can see what he was looking at.

"Hey, you okay? I noticed you're kind of quiet and you look annoyed." I say.

"Yeah, I'm alright." Bryan whispers.

He puts his head in his hands as if trying to stop a headache from coming and leans forward a bit on the desk. I can still hear the annoyance and frustration in his voice, so I run my hand down his back to try and calm him a bit. He looks over his shoulder at me, and I immediately remove my hand, embarrassment filling my cheeks. He smiles at me and takes my hand in his, and gives it a small squeeze.

"You're right, something is bothering me. Mark and I went yesterday to find a friend of ours, but we couldn't get ahold of him. He said he would be waiting for us to get to his place, but he bailed on us. So yeah, I've not been in the best mood today. I'm sorry." Bryan says with a sigh.

"Oh wow. That sucks. I'm sorry to hear that. I hope your friend is okay though."

We hear the warning bell that free period is about over. So, I grab my backpack, stand up, and smile at Bryan.

"I'll see ya later."

I get to the main door of the library, and I go to grab the handle to open the door when I hear Bryan run up to me. He tries to give me a lazy smile, but there is a hint of embarrassment filling his eyes.

"Hey, uh. You wanna go out sometime?" Bryan asks while running his hand nervously across the back of his neck.

For a second, I think I didn't hear him right, but when I realize he's still waiting for my answer, I give him a bright smile.

"Sure. I will say though, my parents are a little old fashioned. So, I'm sure my father would want to meet you first," I warn.

"That's fine. I honestly kind of expected that. You let me know when it's a good time to come over," Bryan says as he opens the door for me, and we both walk out into the main hall of the school.

"Sure thing." I reply.

I then see Mark come around the corner, and he throws an arm around Bryan's neck, pulling him away without a word toward the main entrance to the school. Before they walk out, I hear Bryan say in an annoyed tone, "Hey dude. Yeah, don't worry, I wasn't talking to her."

Chapter 6

Taylor

After school that evening while Mom, Dad, and I are sitting in the living room eating dinner, I gingerly bring up the topic of Bryan wanting to take me out.

"So, I have some interesting news. I was asked out on a date today." I begin.

"Oh, by who?" Mom asks.

"Don't tell me is from that dude from across the street." Dad grumbles.

"Oh, Tom. Come on, you haven't even met the boy," Mom says,coming to my defense.

"Fine," Dad says with a sigh. "But we are meeting him before he takes you anywhere."

"I expected that." I say with a nod.

"I say have him come over for dinner tomorrow evening. Say five o'clock. We will fix a nice dinner and have a *friendly* discussion." Mom says while glaring toward my father.

"Thank you, Mom. I'll tell Bryan in the morning."

And with that, we finish our meal with idle chatter, and I help Dad clean the kitchen while Mom puts Cody to bed.

***

The next day at school, I wait at the door to our morning Math class for Bryan to arrive. As soon as I see him walk past the main doors of the school, I give him a smile and watch him close the distance between us with a long, casual stride.

"Good morning, Taylor." Bryan says.

"Morning. Oh, and I told you my parents want to meet you before you take me out. They said to come over at five tonight if that works for you."

He smiles at me, and his green eyes seem to sparkle with excitement. "Sounds good. I'll be there." Bryan says with a wink.

After math class, it seems the school day ends all too quickly. Or it could have just been me giddy with anticipation. After I get home, I freshen up and put on a nice pink blouse and a pair of black leggings, and Dad is in khaki pants with a brown button-up shirt.

At five on the dot, Bryan is knocking on the door. I go to open the door and I see him in a pair of dark blue jeans and a light blue button up long sleeve shirt with the sleeves rolled up to his elbows. I try not to look at the way the muscles in his forearms move against the cloth when he puts his hands in his pockets. I finally smile at him and open the door more to let him in. Dad is just finishing up the meal for tonight, his homemade lasagna.

While we wait, we walk into the family room that's off of the kitchen and sit on the couch. I watch as Cody comes into the family room with a serious look on his face and dread what is about to come out of his mouth.

"Are you two together?" Cody asks bluntly.

Bryan laughs, and I feel my face go red.

"Cody, we are just friends." I say as coolly as I can.

"Oh. Well, you still better be nice to my sister." Cody says.

"Don't you worry, Cody. I will be very nice to her." Bryan says with a chuckle.

Right then, I kinda feel like a dog that's been dropped off at the vet or something, and the owner is telling the vet to be nice to me.

"Good." Cody says and walks away without another word.

"I'm sorry about that. He's very blunt, like his mom and, unfortunately, like me." I say in annoyance.

"Don't be, I like that kind of spunk. The right amount of it gets you places."

"Well, I have a good bit of spunk." I reply dryly.

"Good." Bryan says with a smile. We sit in silence for a few minutes before Bryan breaks it again. "You have a nice home." He says as he looks around the room.

"Thanks. This has been my home my entire life." I say.

"That's good." Bryan says with a little sadness in his eyes.

"Did you move a lot with your parents?" I ask. He looks up at me with sadness still in his eyes, and a part of me wants to know, but the other part doesn't. "Never mind, it's none of my business." I say, pushing a strand of hair behind my ear.

He smiles at me, and I decide to let him tell me when he's ready. Then I hear the door open, and a blast of cold air fills the living room before Mom can close it.

"Oh my, today was a long and tiring day. I just want food, a bath, and—" Mom begins but cuts herself short.

Mom stops mid-step and mid-sentence when she sees Bryan on the couch beside me.

"Hello," Mom says with shock filling her tone.

"Mom, this is Bryan. Bryan, this is my mother, Kathy." I say.

"Oh. Sorry about the babbling." Mom says and heads into the kitchen. "I forgot about dinner. Let me go get freshened up."

After another thirty minutes, we are finally ready to eat. I notice the table is set with four chairs at the round table with enough plates, silverware, and glasses for us. We usually never sit at the table unless it's something important and I mentally prepare for the onslaught of questions that will soon be coming from my parents as I take my seat to the right of my father at the head of the table where his back is to the door. Mom is at the opposite end of the table, and Bryan is across from me. I notice that Bryan is the furthest away from the door, whereas my father is the closest to it. A mental game of blocking him inside.

"So, Taylor how was your day?" Mom asks as she takes a bite of her lasagna.

"It was good." I say.

"So, Bryan—" Dad begins.

Oh Lord, here it comes.

But Bryan beats him to all his questions. "I'm nineteen years old. I have never been arrested for any reason. I've never had any issues with any law enforcement, and I don't drink or do drugs. I'm not a player either. I was raised to respect the girl I am interested in and to not bed her the first time I get her alone. And I also have a job with a friend of the family. Had it since I was sixteen." Bryan says.

I look from him to my parents, who are at a loss for words and just stare dumbly at him.

"Damn, he's definitely got spunk." I think to myself. *"One day your spunk is going to get you in trouble, you know that?"* I say, continuing my internal monologue.

"The food is great, by the way." Bryan says as he takes another bite of lasagna.

I can't help but laugh. But it's not at him; it's at the situation. He looks at me, giving me a coy smile, and I smile back.

"I've always said Tom is the better cook," Mom says, trying to get the conversation going.

"My granddad has tried to teach me how to cook growing up, but I never really learned much." Bryan says. "I know some now as I've gotten older, but I'm not good at it."

"Tom could show you some things, won't you, Honey?" Mom says while looking at Dad.

I try to hide my smile behind my hand while Dad stares daggers in Mom's direction.

"If you want to know more, yeah, I can show you some easy recipes." Dad says while trying to sound friendly.

"So, what do you want to do for a career after you get out of school, Bryan?" Mom asks.

"I'm not sure exactly. But I know I want to help people. I have a few ideas in my mind, but I haven't decided." Bryan replies.

"Nursing is a good career field to get into," Mom says.

"Yeah, I'm not that good with medical stuff. I'm not squeamish around blood or anything, but I just don't see myself in the medical field. I'm more of a hands-on person and living life in the fast lane." Bryan says with a small smile as if recalling a memory.

After a while of idle chatter, we finish dinner, and I watch as Dad takes Bryan into the kitchen to show him how to make chocolate pudding pies. I notice he is very calculated in what he does. Once my dad shows him how to mix the batter and what to do with one pie, Bryan is able to replicate it. Filling the pound cake crust with a dollop of chocolate pudding and topping it off with whipped cream.

Our eyes meet across the island, and he has a huge smile on his face. I just laugh at him. I watch as Dad brings in three plates all expertly laid across his forearm for Cody and Mom, and himself, and I see Bryan put a small plate down in front of me.

"Your dessert, madam." Bryan says trying to sound like a Frenchman.

"Why, thank you, kind sir." I reply with a smile.

After we all have finally had our fill for the night, I watch as Bryan puts his fork down on the plate. Then, sitting as tall as he can, he looks my father in the eye.

"Mr. Sparks. Thank you for dinner; it was delicious." He pauses and looks over at me then, back over to Dad. "I would like to talk to you about my main reason of being here tonight." Bryan says.

My father looks him up and down and then leans forward in his chair and puts his elbows on the table and rests his chin on his hands. "I'm listening." Dad says.

Bryan takes a deep breath before he opens his mouth to speak. "You have a beautiful daughter, and I would love to get to know her better." He says. "May I have your permission to date your daughter, sir?" Bryan asks.

Dad takes a moment, letting the question linger in the air before answering. "Okay, Taylor, I approve." Dad says, sounding a little shocked at the whole situation and how Bryan has presented himself this evening. Even I am surprised.

"Thank you. May we be excused?" I ask.

Mom nods and waves us off in a clear dismissal. So, Bryan and I get up and go into the living room for a bit more privacy. As soon as I walk past the couch, I spin around and give him a light smack on the shoulder.

"Damn, you got spunk! But is everything you said earlier true?" I ask.

"All of it was true." Bryan says while closing the distance between us where his Converse sneakers meet my sock-clad toes. He's not touching me, but the heat of his stare might as well be a physical thing. "I've learned the hard way that by not being clear in the beginning of a possible relationship about the expectations and boundaries have destroyed what I thought would be something good. So, I make it clear that I am not the screw 'em and leave 'em type. I messed up once, and I am never doing that again," Bryan says.

Screw what Lexi said about him. He's cute, honest, and straightforward. *I like him, and I want to get to know him.*

"Your brother is cute too; he really worries about you a lot," Bryan says with a smile.

"Yeah, he does." I say softly. *I almost died on him.*

"Hey, I better get going. Dinner was nice, and so was that family meeting." Bryan says with a sly smile on his face. We walk to the door, and he takes my hand in his and gives it a light squeeze. "I'll see you at school tomorrow."

"See ya then." I say as a blush warms my cheeks.

He opens the door and closes it behind himself. I look out the window and watch him walk across the street. Well, Cupid must work outside of the month of February, because I'm pretty sure I've been hit.

Chapter 7

Taylor

It's been a few days since my little family dinner/meeting, and Bryan has not officially asked me out yet. I try to play it cool, but I'm starting to think my parents, or mainly my father, scared him off.

I go to the library during free period to start on some research for my history homework, trying to focus on something else, so I don't keep digging myself deeper into the rabbit hole that is my unfounded worry.

I'm about halfway through my research and I see Bryan walk in, and I immediately decide to make him work for my attention.

"Hi, Taylor." Bryan says by way of greeting.

"Hi," I say, not looking up from my textbook.

"How's the homework going?"

"Good." I reply while copying down a line of text.

He's quiet for a minute and then, out of the corner of my eye, I see realization hit him. He gets up to go around the corner toward the craft section of the library. After two minutes, I see him poke his head past the shelving unit with a mini white flag in his hand, and he gives me a small smile. He walks toward the table and sits down again. I try to hide my amusement, so I cover my lips with my right hand.

"I'm sorry. I know I asked if you wanted to go out with me, then totally ghosted you. You have every right to be mad," Bryan says. "It's just I didn't expect to be traveling back to my old city so much since moving away. You forgive me?" Bryan asks while waving his flag again.

This time I can't help but laugh. "Okay. Fine. I forgive you. But this is your last chance, so you better take it, buddy."

"How about tomorrow? It's Saturday, right?" Bryan asks as he checks the date on his Galaxy Watch.

"Yeah. Are you doing anything tomorrow afternoon?" I think about it while I start to pack up my textbooks and papers.

As I toss one of my backpack straps up on my shoulder, I look at him and give a small smile."Yeah, that should work. How about we meet at the Diner just on the outskirts of town?" I ask.

"That sounds good. I'll pick you up. If my grandmother got word that I didn't drive you, she'd have my hide. She would say, that's not being a gentleman." Bryan says. "Okay. How about you pick me up at eleven-thirty?" "Great! See ya tomorrow morning then." Bryan says.

As the warning bell rings, we go to our next classes, and then just as quickly the school day ends.

Later that night, I tell my parents of my date for tomorrow over dinner, which is again held in the living room as usual.

"Oh, Taylor, that's great! And I like that his grandparents raised him that way. Don't you, Tom?" Mom asks.

"I guess that's a plus for him." Dad replies.

"Your father will come around, don't worry, Honey," Mom says.

I smiled at my parents, and then I get up to go over to my father. I stand behind him, and I put my arms around his neck and give him a kiss on the cheek.

"I will always be your little girl, Dad. And I will always love you." I say.

"It's just my little girl is growing up. I handled the make-up and the haircuts, but dating? It's hard from my standpoint, Sweetheart," Dad says.

"I know. But you raised me not to take any less than what I deserve. So, I don't plan on that happening anytime soon, Daddy." I say.

After my little talk mainly with Dad, we finish dinner and then I turn in for the night.

***

The next morning, I video chat Macy, Casey, and Tina to get their opinion on my outfit for my first date.

"Where are you two going?" Tina asks.

"To the diner down the road." I say.

"Why there? Why not an expensive restaurant?" Casey asks.

"I don't know. I want it to be just us, not some fancy menu that I can't understand." I say.

"If you're going to the diner, I would say, a nice skirt and a sweater." Macy says.

I pull out a fuchsia pink skirt that would come to my calf and I pair it with a baby pink sweater.

"What y'all think of this?" I ask as I lay the pieces against my body.

I watch as all three girls nod their agreement, and Macy is giving an 'ok' sign with her fingers.

"Thanks, girls. I gotta get ready now. I'll text ya and let ya know how it goes." I say as I click the end button on my PC.

I quickly get a shower, get dressed, put my hair up in a ponytail and do my make-up, and when eleven-thirty hits I am ready by the time Bryan knocks on the door.

"You look amazing, Honey," Mom says as she is standing in the kitchen drinking a cup of coffee.

"Taylor, sweetheart, you look beautiful." Dad says, walking over and giving me a kiss on the cheek.

We all hear the knock on the door, and Dad opens the door to let Bryan in. I see Bryan again in a pair of dark blue jeans, but today I see him in a gray three-quarter-sleeve t-shirt.

"Hello, Mr. Sparks." Bryan says and gives my father a firm handshake.

"Bryan," Dad responds. "So where are you two going again?"

"I am taking Taylor to a diner she told me about yesterday." Bryan says.

"Tom, remember, it's where Gina works at." Mom says, giving me a wink.

"Okay. You two have fun." Dad says while looking at me and giving me a kiss on the top of my head. "But not too much fun." Dad finishes, directing that statement toward Bryan.

"I will be a complete gentleman to your daughter, Mr. Sparks. I don't want to elicit the wrath of you, let alone my grandparents. Your daughter is in good hands, sir," Bryan says.

After my dad finally opens the door, Bryan walks out first, then he holds his hand out for me to follow. He walks me to his truck that he literally drove across the street and helps me in the passenger seat, shutting my door behind me.

"Okay, so where is this diner of yours?" Bryan asks as he closes the driver's side door and buckles his seat belt.

"I'll pull the directions up on my phone for you." I say.

As the GPS tells him where to go, I watch as he drives. He's cute when he's driving. He tries to look at me, but he keeps his eyes on the road. He drives with his left hand on the steering wheel, and he has his right hand on the gearshift. I can tell he is nervous as hell, which for some odd reason I get the feeling he doesn't experience this much. He is usually so confident in who he is, so this side of him is a little amusing.

"You look beautiful, by the way." Bryan says finally, breaking the silence in the cab.

"Thank you. You clean up pretty good yourself." I say.

This makes him smile, and I can see the tension melt from his shoulders.

"Relax, you seem as tense as a wind-up toy." I say.

"I'll be honest, your dad is almost as scary as my grandfather." Bryan says.

"Oh, it's not only Dad you need to worry about. It's the saying of 'don't poke the momma bear' you need to worry with."

Bryan gives a nervous laugh and follows the GPS. When we finally arrive at the diner, Bryan parks his truck in the first parking spot near the door. He gets out and then walks around the front of the truck to open my door for me and helps me down from the cab.

Just as he shuts the door, I see two boys riding their bikes down the sidewalk without a care in the world. As I start to turn my attention to Bryan, I hear a crash and I see that one of the boys is on the ground crying loudly. I instantly run towards them to see if they need help.

"Hey, are you okay?" I ask the blonde boy on the ground while kneeling next to him.

"I hit my knee." He says between sobs.

I see out of the corner of my eye that Bryan is watching me, but I focus on the boy again. I look at his knee again, the steady stream of blood running from the scraped skin. Thankfully, I have a small first aid kit in my purse.

"Can I see your knee?" I ask softly.

He nods, and I gently pull his pant leg up so I can see his whole knee better.

"What's your names?" I ask, trying to distract the boy in front of me.

"My name is Adam, and that's David," Adam says while pointing to his friend on the ground.

"Well, David. I don't think it's anything major. Does any of this hurt?" I ask while gently pressing on his knee.

He shakes his head, and I give him a smile.

"Let's get you cleaned up then." I say. "This will sting, but it will go away in a bit, okay."

I start to get the antiseptic spray and gauze out of my little bag, and I sway a little bit on my feet from stooping down for so long, so I don't get my skirt dirty from the pavement. I see Bryan sit on the curb of the sidewalk, and he pulls me sideways onto his lap. I look at him for a second, then I find myself smiling at him.

"Thank you." I say, then turning my attention to David.

I spray the antiseptic on his knee, and I see him grimace at the sting, and I cover the scrape with a piece of gauze to gently work the liquid into the scrape. After I know it's clean, I apply a bandage and pull his pant leg back down.

"There, you should be good as new in a few days." I say with a smile.

"Thanks, lady!" David says, nose still red from crying, but more tears are in his eyes.

I wave the boys off, and I look at Bryan again.

"Thanks for giving me a leg to sit on." I say with a smile at my little joke.

"No problem." Bryan says while he puts his hands on my hips to help me up.

He stands up and brushes the back of his pants off, and I have to tear my eyes away from him before I can notice how he fills out those jeans. He then takes my hand and walks back toward the diner. He opens the door and walks in first, then holds the door ajar, and I walk in under his arm. I then feel him stand behind me as we wait for the hostess to greet us.

"Hello. Table for two?"

"Yes, please." Bryan replies.

The hostess takes us to a table in the corner of the restaurant near the kitchen and I usually go for the wall because I want to be able to see around me, but Bryan pulls the chair out from the other side of the table, where my back will be to everyone.

"Sorry, but I usually like to keep eyes on the door." Bryan explains.

"Oh, okay." I say, shock filling my tone.

"It's something else that my grandfather raised me with." Bryan says.

"No, it's okay. I totally understand." I reply, waving him off like he doesn't need to explain his reason.

The hostess takes our drink order, and a few minutes later, Gina comes over with our drinks in hand, and a smile on her face, and with her gray hair up in a bun, it makes her smile all the brighter.

"Taylor, oh my, my. Your mom said you were coming in with a date, but I didn't expect him to be this cute." Gina says excitedly.

I feel my face flush with embarrassment and instantly wish I would have told Mom about a different restaurant. I look at Bryan and I see his smile is showing just as much embarrassment as I am.

"This is Gina, in case you didn't figure that out." I say. "Gina, play it cool, that's why I recommend this place."

"You know it's all in good fun, Gina says.

She takes our order and then walks back to the kitchen.

"I am so sorry. I didn't expect for Gina to be like that." I say while trying to hide my face in my hands.

"It's okay. I say get the uncomfortable things out of the way first and then it will be smooth sailing from there," Bryan says while taking one of my hands in his.

I look at him, and his confidence is back and shining bright in his green eyes, and I find myself smiling back at him. Gina brings our meals out a few minutes later, and with a wink, she leaves us on our own, and we begin to eat.

"So, have you thought of any plans for after we graduate high school?" I ask, following up on what was discussed at dinner the other night.

"Yeah, actually I have an idea finally." Bryan says. "I want to go into the police academy." He says with a sly smile.

"Oh Okay. I think you'd be a good police officer." I say.

"Why do you say that?" Bryan asks while furrowing his eyebrows.

"I've noticed that you always seem to be watching your surroundings."

"Oh, I've never noticed I did that." Bryan says. "What about you? You have any plans?"

"Yeah. My mom is a nurse and EMT at the hospital. So, she's been teaching me things, and I'm going to start picking up some classes to help for college."

"Oh, that's nice. I'm sure you'd be great at nursing," Bryan says.

"Why do you say that?" I ask, turning his own question against him.

"I don't know. You seem nice, and you want to help people. Just like with that kid just now. You didn't hesitate to go over and help him. And you seemed so comfortable." Bryan says with a smile.

I smile back at him, and I feel embarrassment creep into my cheeks. "I just acted on instinct. I saw someone that was hurt, and I knew I could help."

"I think it's a great thing you want to do." Bryan says.

After we finish eating, we just sit there and share stories. From the one time that Tina and I crashed a cheerleader party that was on the same night as the twin's birthday and bombed everyone with silly string and Reddi Whip. While the other girls were pissed that we ruined their hair, the twins were having a great time. Bryan told me of one day that he and Mark found a dead body in the woods. They were just riding 4-wheelers, and they came across this body stuffed in a hollowed-out tree. I shudder at the thought of seeing a body like that. My thoughts go to what happened to the person just before they died, and how much suffering did they feel before they passed?

We noticed it's getting later in the day, about two in the afternoon, so we decided it's time to leave and go home. Bryan pays the bill and again he opens the door of the diner, walks out first, and signals for me to follow. He then opens the passenger door to his truck and helps me in the seat. As Bryan is backing out, I notice a maroon motorcycle sitting in the parking space a little bit down the lot, and I get an uneasy feeling for some reason. I try to ignore it and focus on the road in front of me. Bryan turns on his radio, and we jam out to some rock music while on the highway.

After a few miles down the road, suddenly the truck seems to power down. The radio screen goes black, the music stops mid-song, the engine shuts off and we start coasting toward the shoulder.

" Damn it! What the hell happened?" Bryan says with a touch of annoyance.

He is able to get the truck off the road and throws the gearshift into park, hops out of the cab, and pops the hood. I follow him out to see if I can help with anything.

"Taylor, please get back in the truck where it's safe." Bryan says when he sees my door open.

"Hey, I know a little bit about engines too. Let me help." I say as I close the passenger door.

"Fine," Bryan says.

I stand up on the passenger wheel so I can look into the engine bay with him. I watch as he checks the battery connections, which they look great, no corrosion. Nothing in the air intake that would have killed the truck. Oil is fine, and so is coolant. So even I am stumped as to what happened. I look over toward the fuse box next to the battery and I notice one of the clips is not secured. I hop off the tire, and I walk around Bryan and stand on the bumper so I can get to the fuse box.

"What are you doing?" Bryan asks.

I feel him come up behind me to keep me from falling backwards, again being mindful of where his hands are holding my hips. I pop the cover off the fuse box, and right there on the main circuit is another black box. I see it's wedged into the fuse for the ECU, and I have the feeling this caused the total blackout. I pull the little box off the fuse and show it to Bryan.

"I'm pretty sure this is your culprit." I say. "Go try to start the truck."

Bryan looks from me to the box in my hand, to the fuse it was sitting on, and back to me. He then gets in the cab to try and start the truck again. As he turns it over, it easily roars to life.

"Yeah! Listen to that!" I yell over the sound of the engine.

Bryan gets out of the driver's seat and comes to the front of the vehicle to help me down. He then shuts the hood, and he wordlessly opens the passenger door to help me in. Once he closes the door while he is walking in front of the truck again, I can tell he is letting a few flavorful words roll off his tongue before he joins me in the cab.

"Thank you for finding that. Let's get you home," Bryan says tightly.

I can tell he's trying to play it off as nothing major, but the bulging vein in his neck says otherwise. I decide not to press the issue and ride with him in silence. He pulls up to my house about thirty minutes later and gets out, comes over to my side to open my door, and helps me down once again. He walks me up to the house and waits while I get my keys out of my purse to unlock the door.

"I'm sorry about my mood. I know I'm not the best company right now," Bryan says while rubbing the back of his neck.

"It's okay. I do understand a little bit. It looks like someone vandalized your truck."

He looks away from me for a moment, and I lightly touch his arm, and his gaze meets mine again. I see the anger; the fear filling them, and it breaks something in me.

"Hey, I'd be pissed if someone did that to my Focus. It's just the fact of someone being in your personal space." I say.

"God, you understand me more than most people. Thank you. And I will make it up to you somehow," Bryan says. I smile at him, and I give him a quick kiss on the cheek and then dive into the house, leaving him shocked on the porch.

***

Bryan

After a few minutes of processing what Taylor just did, I finally snap back to reality, and then the anger sets in full force again. I briskly walk back to my truck and drive to Mark's place.

As I pull up, I grab the little device from the center console, and I walk up to Mark's apartment and open the door.

"Mark? Where are you?" I yell out.

Mark comes out of the kitchenette with a plate of Chinese food. "What's up man?" Mark asks.

"That bastard found me. He put this in the F150's fuse box, and it had a remote-activated kill switch. I was with Taylor, and the whole damn truck died on me while on the interstate." I say while throwing the little black box on the island.

Mark picks up the device and gives a low whistle. "This is some techy stuff, Bryan. But I've seen better." He says with a sly smile. "Give me a bit and I'll take a scanner out and make sure there's no more hiding anywhere."

"Thanks, man. This just pisses me off so much! Every single time we look for him, he gives us the slip, but he can find me like it's nothing. I can't stand it!" I say while letting the aggravation boil over.

"We will find him, Bryan. I promise you that. It might not be the way we plan on it, but we will find him. Maybe we need to lie low for a bit. Not be so active." Mark says. "Maybe go with that Taylor girl more." He says with a wink.

"Fine. I don't like lying low, but I guess I don't have a choice." I say while looking at the box mocking me on the counter, and I imagine the face of the man that put it there.

Chapter 8

Taylor

Two months have passed, and, like usual, I wake up to go to school, spend time with the girls or Bryan, come home, eat dinner, go to bed. Wash, rinse, repeat.

When I get to school, I see the girls and Bryan waiting on me outside of our Math class. Bryan and I are now in the flirty stage in our relationship. When I told Lexi that Bryan and I were pretty much going steady, she wasn't too happy, but neither was Mark. I told Bryan that as long as we're happy, screw everyone else. We are still friends, but it's a little bit more than just plain ole friendship.

"So, are we doing anything after school today?" I ask.

The girls shake their heads no, but I see that Bryan is thinking about something.

"Okay, Bryan, what's going on in that head of yours?" I ask.

"It's not fun, or at least won't be as fun as dinner at your house, but I would like for you to meet my grandparents." Bryan says.

"I'd love to." I say with a smile.

Lunchtime finally rolls around, and as I am walking to the cafeteria, I text Mom and Dad to let them know I will be going to Bryan's grandparents after school to have dinner with them. Mom responds

"

promptly with.

I put my cell in the back pocket of my jeans, with joy filling my heart. As I turn the corner, I see Bryan and Mark talking, and I catch the last part of the conversation.

"Man, you gotta stay with it." Mark says. "Ignoring phone calls isn't helping either."

"Just stop. You were the one that kept telling me before we came here to get on with life, to get a girl. And I did. I'll still do what I'm supposed to do." Bryan says.

"Hey guys." I say, letting my presence be known.

"Hey Tay," Bryan says.

He puts his arm around my shoulder and kisses me on the top of my head. I don't say anything about it. I figured that he needed to show Mark his feelings for me and one kiss on the head wouldn't hurt. Mark gives Bryan a disgusted look and walks away.

"Is everything okay?" I ask.

"Yeah, don't worry about Mark. Sometimes he wakes up on the wrong side of the bed," Bryan says.

"Sometimes we all do."

"Anyways, I'm excited for tonight; my grandparents are just going to love you." Bryan says.

"I hope so. I'm not going to be as blunt as you were, but I will answer any questions that they have." I say.

Bryan smiles at me, and I give him a playful shove. Then I see the principal walk up to the lunch table that the girls are sitting at, so we walk over to join them.

"Hello girls, Mr. Evans." Mr. Snow greets us. "I was wondering if you would like to help us decorate the gym for the Halloween dance?"

I glance at the girls, and I know they would love it. "Mr. Snow, I will answer for the girls and myself, and we say yes, but Bryan has to answer for himself." I say.

Bryan nods a small thanks to me. "I'll be honest, I have a hectic schedule, but I will help out as much as I can," Bryan says.

"Great! You can start planning, and you can submit your ideas to me, and I will approve them. The school will provide the necessary decorations, but you will be responsible for the food and snacks." Mr. Snow says.

"Sounds good." I say. Mr. Snow walks away, and I look at Bryan. "You don't have to help us if you're too busy."

"But I want to help." Bryan says, taking my hand in his.

I smile at him. "Thanks." He bumps me on the shoulder with his, and I smile again.

"Okay, are you a couple or what?" Macy asks while swinging her fork between the two of us.

"I'm meeting his grandparents tonight." I say, ignoring the question.

"Ohhhh." They all croon in unison. "Shut up." I say with a slight smile.

"Well, I'm glad. You're eighteen and you finally have a potential boyfriend for the first time." Macy says.

"I'm nineteen, but life hasn't been easy for me. If it wasn't for Mark, I don't think I would've met Taylor. But it's better later in life than not at all." Bryan says.

"That's right." I say. "But what does Mark have to do with it?"

Bryan looks at me for a second like he said something he shouldn't have. "Oh, it's just he was insisting that I finish out my high school year with him in the same school. So, if he didn't insist on that, I never would have met you."

"Oh, okay." I say, but not fully buying it.

The bell rings, and we walk back to class hand in hand.

My final class for that day is English, the only class that I don't share with Bryan. I sit at my desk and tap my pen to the beat of the second hand. When I hear the final bell ring, I jump out of my seat, jog to my locker, and exchange things for my homework, then I shut my locker and wait for Bryan.

"You ready?" Bryan asks as he walks up to me with a smile lighting his eyes.

"Yes." I look for my keys in my backpack, but I notice they aren't there.

"Macy is going to drive your car home. My grandmother will have my hide if I let you drive yourself home, even though you need to park across the street." Bryan says. He takes my hand, and we walk out to his Ford F-150.

"This thing is so nice looking. You must take it to the car wash a lot." I say.

I look at the shiny black paint glistening in the sun, and I can almost see my reflection in the paint.

"Thanks." Bryan says. "I try to keep it nice looking."

He opens the passenger door, and I use his shoulder and the grab bar in the ceiling of the truck to get in. I could've gotten up on my own this time, but I did that to make him feel like I needed his help, plus I did have a shorter skirt on so the easier the better. He comes around to the driver's side and gets in.

"Ready?" Bryan asks.

"Yes, I am, let's roll."

We arrive at his house a tad too quickly, but I must have not been looking at the clock, because if anything we were too slow. It's crazy how your mind can fool you when you're nervous.

"Here we are." Bryan says, taking a deep breath.

"Let's go." I say, giving him an encouraging smile.

He gets out and comes around to open my door again to help me out. We both take another deep breath, and we start to walk up the steps to the door. Before we are even on the doorstep, the door opens up, and I see a woman in the doorway. She is a little hunched over, but that does nothing to stop her from walking around. Her face is showing a bit of age near her eyes, but her salt and pepper hair makes her brown eyes shine with vigor.

"Bryan, is this the girl?" She asks.

"Yes, Granny." Bryan says with a smile.

"Hello Dearie. You already seem like a nice girl. I think you did a very good job, Bryan," Granny says.

"Well, we're still just friends, Granny." Bryan says with a hint of embarrassment.

"Oh, nonsense! I can feel that you two are good for each other." Granny says in a no-nonsense tone.

"Let them go at their own pace, Gail." A gruff voice says from inside the house.

I see an older man walk into the room, and he's still fairly fit for his age. His gray hair is starting to recede from his hairline, but that makes his green eyes all the more intense.

"Sometimes she thinks she's a matchmaker." The man says.

"And when have I been wrong, John?" Gail asks with her hands on her hips.

Bryan smiles at them, and I find myself smiling too.

"You haven't been wrong, *yet*." John says.

John and Gail go to the kitchen, and I pull Bryan's ear down to my mouth. "Is she senile?" I whisper.

"No, somehow, she can actually tell if people are compatible. I've never asked her how it works." Bryan says.

"And she's never been wrong?" I ask.

"Nope," Bryan says. "Dinner's gonna be a few minutes. Come with me; I want to show you something."

I walk behind him with his fingers interlaced in mine. When we get to the stairs, he bends his arm behind his back but never lets go of my hand. When we get to the second floor, he leads me to a door; he opens it, and I get a whiff of....Bryan's cologne. He took me to his room.

We walk in and I see paintings on his walls and on the floors. They are all kinds of different things. Flowers, birds, dogs, cats, his truck, and so many other things. I look at one closer and I see the initials of B.A.E in a corner, and I look back at him. He's leaning on his desk by the window, with his arms crossed over his chest. His head hung low, and his eyes are closed. I go to him, and I separate his arms and slip in between them, putting my back to his chest, and I make his arms wrap around my waist while he rests his head on my shoulder.

"These paintings are beautiful. They should be on display somewhere." I whisper.

"That's what people tell me. I told Mark about what I do, and he laughed." Bryan says.

"Has he seen them?" I ask.

"No," Bryan says.

"Give me his number; I'll tell him that he's a freaking Jerk, with a capital J."

"Go get 'em tiger." Bryan says while chuckling.

"People would pay good money to buy these paintings."

"I don't want to sell them. This is my hobby; I don't think I could let strangers take them. I've given some to people I know, but it was a request of something they wanted." Bryan says.

"I guess I can see that." I say. I stand there for a minute, and I take a deep breath. "But since you do give one to people you know, would a....girlfriend count on that list?" I ask.

"Absolutely," Bryan whispers in my ear without a moment's thought about what I just asked.

We smile at one another at the question I just asked him. Before I could even think about kissing him, I feel his lips on mine. They are soft yet strong, this feeling between us is wild, yet controlled. When we break apart and look into each other's eyes for a moment before we hear Gail yell,

"Kids, dinner's ready!"

Chapter 9

Taylor

"**L**ooks like Grandpa John is gonna be mad," Bryan says.

"Yep. Another one for Granny."

We both walk downstairs with smiles on our faces, and we see that John is already standing by the table waiting for everyone to join him.

"Well, there's another good guess, Gail," John says, rolling his eyes.

"Really?" Gail asks as she comes out of the kitchen, drying her hands on a hand towel.

"Yes, that feeling you felt from us was right. We just made it official." I say.

"Oh, Dearie, that's great. You may have a few fights, but just don't forget that I did say that you were supposed to be together." Gail says. "And you can call me either Gail or Granny, okay, Dearie?"

"Okay, Granny. Dinner looks great, by the way." I say, taking in the chicken and roasted vegetables that fill the table.

"Thanks." John says. "I was a cook in my younger days for the Army."

"Oh, that's right. Bryan did say you were the cook of the house. Well, it looks delicious."

"It's a lot better than the Army had, I'll tell you that." John says as he takes a seat, signaling us to sit as well.

A few minutes later we hear the front door open, and I turn to look toward the sound when I hear the click of a gun cocking behind me and Bryan begins to get up out of his chair to stand in front of me, like a wall to protect me from the intruder. I turn back around to look for the gun, and I see John holding a .38 revolver.

"Whoa, John, it's me." Mark says, holding his hands up in surrender.

"Mark! You damn site know better than to open that door without knocking." John says.

"Sorry, I got word from Way....uh. Taylor, what are you doing here?" Mark asks, stopping mid-sentence at seeing me.

"Having dinner." I say simply.

"Is your phone on vibrate again?" Bryan asks, sounding annoyed.

Mark pulls his phone out and looks at it. "Sorry, man." Mark says, and he turns to leave.

"Mark, wait." I say. He stops and turns to look at me with a questioning look on his face. "Do you still think that Bryan being able to paint is stupid?" I ask.

I see Bryan smile out of the corner of my eye. *Yep, this is my spunk.*

"I just think he could use his time better." Mark says.

"Bryan, do you mind if I take him up?" I ask.

They're his paintings. If he doesn't want me to show Mark and he just wants to keep hearing his mouth, I can't change that.

"If you want to. Go show 'em tiger." Bryan says while sitting back down in his chair.

I grab Mark's hand and I drag him up to Bryan's room.

"Oh, so you've been to his room, huh?" Mark asks, and he wiggles his eyebrows.

"Shut up and look." I say as I open the door.

He does, and he shuts up about me knowing where his bedroom is and about Bryan's 'time wasting.'

"He did these?" Mark asks with shock in his voice.

"Every single one." I say, punctuating each word.

I walk away, and I join Bryan back at the table, and I smile at him. Bryan takes my hand, giving it a little squeeze, and I bump him with my shoulder. I look back at the stairs when I see Mark coming down. He's rubbing the back of his neck with one hand, with embarrassment on his face.

"Uh, keep doing them." Mark says. "They're great."

"Thanks, man." Bryan chuckles.

"Have a good night." Mark says.

When Mark leaves Bryan bumps my shoulder with his again and gives me another smile.

"Anyone that really knows you should know, if they give you a hard time about you painting then they were not raised with a taste for art." I say.

"Taylor, I want to apologize for pulling that gun out like that." John says.

"Don't be. My dad used to hunt, so he taught me how to shoot a rifle and a pistol. So did a friend of mine." I say, trailing off.

"Really?" Bryan asks, genuinely shocked.

"Yes. But you're sounding a little sexist there, buddy." I snap.

He smiles at me. Well, I hope that John and Gail like a girl with spunk because I just showed it twice.

"It just shocked me, 'cause you just don't seem like the Annie Oakley type." Bryan says.

"I am. One day I'll have to show you." I say with a sly grin on my face.

"You let me know when and I'll be there." Bryan says.

"You got it."

We help clear the table after dinner, and we wash dishes for Gail and John. Bryan and I even have friendly soapsuds fight in the kitchen. After we get rid of the suds from our clothes, we sit on the couch to watch TV, and I lean into his side to get comfortable. The way we melt into one another is amazing. It is like we were molded after one another. A perfect fit in every way. After a few minutes, I feel Bryan move, and that's when I realize that I must have dozed off.

I sit up to rub my face and out of the corner of my eye I see Bryan lie down on the couch and he pats his chest, telling me to lay down on him. At first, I second guess myself, but my parents raised me well enough to behave. So, I snuggle against him, and he wraps his arms around my shoulders, and I rest my head on his chest. I hear his heart beating at a restful pace, and I can also hear that it's strong. He must do a lot of cardio. For some reason, I don't have an issue visualizing the sound of his heart beating well into our years together.

"I...love you, Taylor." Bryan admits.

I lift my head to look into his beautiful green eyes, and they look sincere, serious, yet a little scared.

"I love you too, Bryan." I reply, my lips curving into a smile. "Promise me something."

"What?" Bryan asks while pushing a piece of hair out of my face.

"Promise me you'll never leave me."

"I promise I will never leave you for another woman. And for anything else, I promise I will fight like hell to get back to you." Bryan whispers.

He kisses me as if to seal the promise that we just made between us. And I lay back down on him, while he traces idle circles with his fingers down my back and I close my eyes with a smile on my face while I let the world fade to a blissful darkness.

Chapter 10

Taylor

"Tay, wake up." Bryan says in a sing-song voice. "We've got school." I take a deep breath, and I rub my hand over his chest. "Good morning, beautiful." Bryan says.

"Morning." I sit up, but Bryan stays where he's at on the couch. He's looking up at me, taking my morning self in.

I hope my hair isn't as bad as it usually is in the morning. I say to myself, and I touch it out of reflex.

"Your hair is fine. I'm just waiting to wake up from this dream." Bryan says.

"This is not a dream. But not having any clean clothes better be a dream."

"Go in the bathroom in the hall." Bryan chuckles. "Your mom dropped off some clothes before she left for work."

"Really?"

"Yep, Granny said she didn't say anything. And she saw us too." Bryan says with a sly smile playing at his lips.

"Well, she wouldn't say anything until she got home. That way she'll have time to ponder what she's feeling." I reply.

I get up off the couch and go to the bathroom that Bryan pointed out to me. Just like he said, I see a pair of black skinny jeans and a purple blouse waiting for me on the sink. After a few minutes, I come out and I see that Bryan is almost ready to go too. He's wearing a pair of dark blue jeans but no shirt yet. I can tell he's looking for one, though. I see a blue and white baseball-type shirt and I grab for it but I hold on to it for a few seconds as I admire the long, lean muscles in his back, and when he turns around, I see a defined six-pack and a broad chest.

"Having a good look?" Bryan asks with a smirk lifting the left side of his mouth.

"Actually, yes." I admit as I hand him his shirt.

He kisses me, and he looks me over from head to toe and back to my eyes. "Beautiful."

I feel a blush flow across my cheeks at his gaze, at his words to me. Then he's grabbing my hand, and we walk out the front door while waving our goodbyes to his grandparents. He opens his truck door for me like it's second nature now, and I climb in. When we get to school, we walk in with my arm wrapped around the crook of his elbow. I can hear Macy, Casey, and Tina scream as we walk down the hall, and I just smile like a love-struck fool.

"So, it's official, you're an item?" Macy asks.

"I guess so." I say, looking up at Bryan, and he gives me a wink.

"I'm happy for you two," Tina says with a smile.

We pass a flyer that's been haphazardly pinned to the wall next to the restrooms that already promises a spooky fun time for the Halloween Dance. Tina looks at all of us and smiles.

"We still need to work on this dance, guys. We haven't even talked about colors yet."

"You're right Tina; how about during free period we work on it?" I ask.

"Okay." The girls say in unison.

"Sure," Bryan replies. "I'll meet you all in the gym and we'll figure this out."

Later that afternoon, during free period, as promised, we all meet up in the gym and we talk about what color scheme we want to work with.

"Okay, girls, as long as you pick the colors, I can put them together." Bryan says.

"He's a fantastic painter." I say.

"Really?" Tina asks in awe.

"Yep." I say, popping the P.

"Do you think I could see your work?" Tina asks.

"As soon as you decide on colors, you all will." Bryan says with a smile.

"What about Halloween colors, like black, orange, purple, and green, but mix in the school's colors too? Blue and white." I say.

The girls all eagerly nod in agreement, and even Bryan likes my idea. He grabs the small stack of plain sketching paper and a pencil from his backpack, and he starts to put some form to the empty paper. Adding elements of the gym along with codes that corresponds to the color scheme here and there. *Blk* for black. *O* for orange and down the line, but the warning bell comes all too soon, and we are forced to put this on the back burner for now.

"I'll work on them when I get home," Bryan promises.

The girls leave, all mumbling on how fast Bryan was able to start putting our thoughts on paper, and it makes me happy that he can share this part of himself with others. Bryan takes a few more minutes to make some extra adjustments, and I stay with him to just watch him work. Then Bryan tucks the papers into his black backpack and slings it over his right shoulder and takes my hand to help me down off the bleacher.

As we are walking toward the end of the bleacher, we are stopped short as one of the school's thugs approaches us. Cutting us off from the main door of the gym. I recognized him instantly, and I always made a point to stay away. Wade Rice is nothing but bad news. His blonde hair is a mess, and his blue eyes have a tint of red in them. Most likely from whatever choice of drug he's on this week.

He doesn't say a word as he looks Bryan up and down. Assessing him. Then looks over to me, and a wicked smile plays on his lips. Bryan wordlessly steps between me and Wade as he puts his arm in front of me to try and push me further behind him. Instead of pushing me to safety, he pushed me right into the arms of another that was hiding behind another bleacher, waiting to ambush us once Wade gave the signal. When this guy wraps his arm around my neck, pinning me to his chest, I scream bloody murder.

"Shit!" Bryan growls, and I pick up a note of fear in his voice.

But I act faster than Bryan can. I quickly move my head where my chin is in the corner of his elbow, so he won't be able to crush my windpipe, and I use the creeps hold on me against him. I grab onto his forearm to help me lift my legs up and around the back of his neck, and I pull down. It's an automatic reaction to let go of whatever you're holding if you feel like you're falling forward. And that's what this dude does.

When he releases his grip on my neck, I land on my hands and I roll away from him, then I pop back up on my feet, giving the guy a good right hook to the jaw, knocking him off balance. I don't recognize this guy, so he must be a new member of Wade's crew. I look over my shoulder, where I see Bryan fighting Wade. Bryan is blocking his punches while landing some of his own.

Once Bryan sees that I am near the door, I watch him finish Wade off with a roundhouse kick to his face, and he falls to the floor with a hefty thud. Bryan starts walking toward me, but he is cut off by the newbie. He grabs Bryan's shirt so fast that Bryan can't put his hands up to block as the thug punches him square in the face. Bryan takes a few steps back and runs his thumb over his lip that had been split from the impact. I run back over to Bryan, and I crouch low on the floor, using my leg to sweep this guy's feet out from under him, and he lands hard on the ground, hitting his head on the floor, effectively knocking himself out.

As I stand up, Bryan walks over to me and wraps me in a tight hug. One hand caressing the back of my neck, the other in the middle of my back.

"I'm sorry, I'm so sorry." Bryan whispers.

"You didn't know he was there. Stop apologizing." I shoot back, adrenaline coursing in my veins.

"Let's get out of here." Bryan snatches our things, and we hightail it out of the gym, and we take one look at each other.

I know I still have a wild look in my own eyes, and seeing Bryan's still bleeding lip, we know what the other will say. Bryan takes my hand, and we jump into his truck under the wordless agreement of not caring to finish out the day.

"Let's go to my house; no one will be there for a few minutes. That way I can look you over." I say as he gets near my house.

Bryan parks at the curb in front of my house, and I jump out of the truck so fast that I don't give him the time to open the door for me. I run up and open the door to my house and tell Bryan to go and sit on the couch while I lock the door behind him then follow him into the living room. I sit on the corner of the coffee table, and I take his chin in my right hand, my medical side kicking into overdrive.

I look at his face, and my eyes instantly lock on his lip again; his arms are red, and his hands are raw from blocking Wade's punches and throwing his own.

"I'm okay, Taylor. I'm just worried about you." Bryan says. "But it looked like you knew how to get out of a situation like that." He says as more of a question.

"I had to learn to defend myself when one of my friends got hurt and my parents were paranoid. So, they made me take self-defense classes." I reply, not really thinking about what I was saying.

"Well, whoever your trainer was, taught you stuff that I didn't even know about," Bryan says.

"Some things I taught myself." I say sheepishly.

"Are you sure you're okay though? I feel so terrible pushing you right into him."

"Yes, Babe, I'm fine. And stop blaming yourself; you didn't know he was there." I say gently.

To prove to him I am okay, I move in to kiss him, but I remember his lip and I don't want to injure it more. So, I brush a light kiss over the left corner of his lip and cheek. "Better?" I ask.

He lifts the left side of his mouth in a sly smirk and nods. "Yes."

I take him by the hand and lead him into the bathroom, where he closes the toilet lid and sits down while I clean his lip off and tend to the scrapes on his arms and knuckles.

"Where did you learn this nursing stuff from again?" Bryan asks as I gently dab a gauze pad soaked with peroxide against his lip.

"My mom is a nurse, remember? I'm learning from her. And you know that I like helping people." I say with a smile on my face.

"Well, you seem to know what you are doing."

I smile at him as I continue to tend to his injuries. After everything is cleaned, I step back to inspect my work. His lip still looks red, but at least it's not bleeding anymore, and the redness on his knuckles and arms is slowly fading as well.

"Thank you." Bryan says as he stands up.

"You're welcome." I reply while washing my hands in the sink.

I try to turn around, but Bryan is right behind me, arms braced on either side of my hips, and I lock eyes with him in the mirror. He leans in, his breath a caress on the shell of my ear, and I'm thankful for his body pressing me against the vanity. That's the only thing keeping my knees from giving out.

"What happened today terrified me." Bryan says, voice low and rough.

"I know."

I keep seeing the attack playing in the back of my mind. How did we miss them?

"I know you're gonna say that I didn't, but I failed you today. I failed to see an attack before it became a threat."

From the look in his eyes, I force myself to keep my mouth shut. No matter what I say, he will still blame himself a little bit. So, I just listen to what he says.

"But I will do everything I can to keep this from happening again." He kisses my cheek as if to seal his promise, and I lean my head against his shoulder, and I stare at him in the mirror as his words fade from the air around us.

Chapter 11

Taylor

Bryan and I walk out of the bathroom, and as I lead him into the living room, we hear Dad come home from work early. As Dad walks in through the garage door, I see Bryan take a step away from my side and toward the front door, but I hold him back.

"Don't worry about him. But hey, while you're here, why don't we work on the colors for the dance?" I ask.

"Okay. Do you have colored pencils?"

"Yeah, hang on." I say.

I quickly run up to my room and grab them. When I come back down, I see Bryan pulling out the sketch he made of the gym from his backpack. He smiles at me as he takes the colored pencils from my outstretched hand, then hisses as his lip pulls from the movement. Dad notices Bryan's lip and looks at me with the silent question in his eyes.

"A few of the school bullies got into a fight with Bryan." I explain.

I leave out the fact that I was also involved in the fight, but Dad probably knows I was included in it, but he doesn't call me out on it. I sit on the one corner of the couch and tuck my legs under me, and Bryan leans his back against the arm of the couch and pulls a pillow into his lap to have a makeshift table of sorts and gets to filling in the colors. I find myself really watching him draw. His brow furrows in concentration, and his whole body seems relaxed as he works.

"You look so cute when you draw." I say.

"That's what Granny says." Bryan says without looking up at me.

"Where did you get your talent?"

His hand pauses, and I see his eyes lose their brightness for a moment before he answers, "Granny told me that I got it from my mother."

"I hate to ask this, but what happened with your parents; why aren't you with them?" I ask in a gentle tone.

"It's alright, you might as well know." He says with a sigh. He puts the orange pencil back in the box before looking up at me. "They were killed when I was five. I heard something outside one night. I remember hearing Dad cussing someone out in the front yard. Mom took me up to my room and locked me in my closet. She told me I would be safe there, and to be quiet. Then I heard the gunshots...I think I heard at least four."

I look at him while he's telling me this, and he's telling it like it was a story he made up. Like a distant emotion, but something in his voice tells me it was true, that he's recalling it from a young memory when things didn't quite seem real.

He looks back down at the sketch in front of him as he says, "I'm not sure how long it took, but I heard sirens, and I saw a man open my closet door. He told me it was okay, and I could come out. I had never met my grandparents until that day. I mean, I remember talking to them on the phone, but never in person. We moved around a lot, so I never got to meet them before that night." Bryan says. "John was the one that got me out of my closet and took me into their home."

"Does anyone know who killed your parents?" I ask.

"No." He says sharply. "Their case has been closed, but John has some buddies in law enforcement, and they're still trying to get to the bottom of it."

"Do you remember them at all?" I ask.

He takes a deep breath and looks back up at me. This time, emotion filling his eyes, small lines of silver pooling in the corners, "That is the hard part. I can't really remember them anymore. Granny and Grandpa have pictures of them, but they only help so much." Bryan whispers.

I get up from my corner of the couch and I sit on the arm of the sofa behind him. I gently rub the curve of both of his shoulders, and he leans into my touch. I take one hand, tilt his head back and I gently kiss him, still being mindful of his lip. I pull back just enough to see his glossy green eyes.

"Any time you want to talk about them or look at pictures, I'll be there.",

"Okay. I'll remember that."

We sit in silence for a few minutes, and I continue to rub Bryan's shoulders, and I feel the tension of the fight today and the talk of his parents melt from his shoulders.

"Okay, so let's talk about how we are going to mix these colors." I say as a distraction.

"Any particular way you want them?" Bryan asks while roughly wiping at his left eye.

I fight the urge to wipe at his right eye, and I let my gaze fall on the half-finished sketch, and then after a few minutes I say, "Surprise me. Let's see what you can do."

He gives me a half-grin, and he picks up the pencils again, and I watch him mix the oranges, the purples, the blacks, the greens, the blues, and the whites. After a few minutes, he finally shows me the finished product. It's a 2-D version of the gym covered in the colors we wanted. There are streamers, balloons, and even strobe lights in the same colors. And he throws in some Halloween details, like skulls, spiders, and pumpkins.

"Bryan, this is beautiful. It's Halloweenish but not scary. I love it." I say.

"Good, I'm glad to hear it."

"Hey Bryan, are you going to stay for dinner?" Dad asks while washing his hands in the kitchen sink.

"No, I need to get going. I gotta meet up with Mark later." Bryan says. "Call me later."

"I will. I love you." Bryan says as he gets up from the couch and he kisses me.

"I don't know what you are going to be doing with Mark, but please don't do anything stupid." I say as I follow him to the door.

"I won't." Bryan says with a chuckle. "I'll call you later." He pauses, and he takes my hand in his, and he takes a breath before speaking again. "But if you absolutely have to, you call me, okay?"

He kisses me again, and he opens the door and lets himself out.

I wonder where he's going and why he doesn't want me to call him unless I have to. I can tell this is going to be a sleepless night.

I go back in the family room and sit on the couch. Dad comes around the couch, wiping his hands on a hand towel.

"Is everything okay?"

"Yeah, he has to meet up with Mark for some odd reason." I say.

"He'll be back, don't worry about him. I'm sure he can take care of himself." Dad says.

You have no idea. "I know he can, I just can't help but to worry a little."

I say.

"Why don't you call one of the girls for a while and get your mind off of him?" Dad offers.

"You know, Dad, you could be a psychologist. You know how to talk to people." I say.

"No, I'm a car doctor, but I do know how to talk to my daughter." Dad replies.

I smile at him and give him a kiss on the cheek, and I go up to my room and I decide to call Lexi on my iPad.

"Hey, Lexi, can you talk?" I ask. "Sure, what's up?"

"Nothing much. Bryan left to go somewhere with Mark. But the strange thing was he told me he would call me, and I was to only call if I absolutely had to. Why would he tell me that?"

"Wait, Mark is there?" Lexi asks.

"Yeah, why?" I shoot back.

"I.... just thought that Mark was closer to me, that's all." Lexi says.

"No, he's been here for a while now." I say. "Wait, you know Mark?"

"Oh. Well, you know how guys are. They don't want you calling them while they are with their friends." Lexi says, ignoring my question.

"Bryan isn't that type. I don't know, but it wasn't like they were just hanging out somewhere. It's like they were going to do something that Bryan doesn't want me to know about." I say.

"Well, when he comes back, just ask him, and don't let him off the hook until he spills what they did."

That is exactly what I might do when he comes back.

***

Bryan

I pull up to Mark's apartment and take a deep breath before getting out of my truck. I walk up to Mark's stoop, knock once, and open the door without breaking my stride. I see Mark leaning over his island looking at a blueprint of a building, and Mark looks up as I close the door behind me.

"Nice lip, dude. What the hell happened?" Mark asks as soon as his eyes lock onto my face.

"Just some of the schools' rats jumped Taylor and me."

"Well, here, we leave in ten," Mark says.

He hands me a black duffel bag, and I take it from him, and I look at the contents. It's everything we may need for our outing tonight.

"Does *he* have any idea of what we are doing?" I ask.

Mark looks at me for a moment. The bastard likes to make me wait for answers sometimes; he knows it gets under my skin. "No. He doesn't have a clue. If he did, you know he'd be here telling us this is a fool's errand." Mark smirks.

"We'll let's hope we can prove him wrong then." I say as I zip the duffel bag and swipe the blueprint off the counter and walk out the door, tossing the bag in the bed of my truck. It's times like tonight is when I like having a black truck.

Chapter 12

Taylor

I t has been three days since Bryan left, and I haven't even gotten a text from him.

When he gets back, he is so gonna hear it.

"Taylor, I'll get off around 12:30 tonight." Mom says as she is getting her lunch ready in the kitchen for her round in the hospital tonight. "Be good, be safe until I get home. Love you."

"Okay, love you too, Mom."

Saturdays are usually filled with a day of going to the mall with the girls but instead, I had to watch Cody. Dad's out at an automotive meeting until tomorrow, so we are alone until Mom gets home around quarter-one in the morning.

The only text I do get is from Lexi.

Lexi:

How ya doing?

Me:

Not good. Bryan will be a dead man when he gets home.

Lexi

Y?

Me:

He has been gone for 3 days. No call, no txt

Lexi

Oh, he's dead when he gets back.

Me:

I'm his girl and he can't take two minutes to ask 'how r u babe'?

Lexi

Oh he'd eat grass.

Me:

Any way enough of my dramatics how have you been anything going on?

Lexi:

No, it's been quiet. I'll let you no if I need you

Me:

That's ok, I don't want mixed up in your world again.

Lexi:

I'm just picking. But it was fun while it lasted.

Me:

Yes it was. I'll let you go. TTYL

After lunch, Cody and I play a few games. I let him beat me a few times, but on some, he actually beats me. Then, I order pizza for dinner, and I have Cody take a shower then we watch *The Lion King,* the animated version. I know we've watched it a million times, but it's still a good movie that we both enjoy and sing along to the songs.

About halfway through, he falls asleep, and I carry him up to his room and tuck him into bed. I close his door but leave enough open for me to hear him, and I go back down to the family room, and I watch another movie. When the movie ends at twelve-thirty, I decide to pick up the kitchen before it gets too much later in the night.

Just when I am about to sit back on the couch and wait for Mom to come home, I hear a noise coming from our front yard. Like someone knocked a flowerpot or something over. I grab a metal baseball bat and I rip open the front door. I look around, but I don't see anything.

I let out an adrenaline-filled breath, thinking it must have been a raccoon looking for the trash can, and I turn around to go back inside but freeze mid-step when I hear something that sends a chill down my spine.

"Taylor."

I hear someone whisper my name, and I whip back around, gripping the bat tighter behind my back. "Alright, stop playing games! Come out or I'll shoot." I can't shoot them, but I can sure as hell break something.

I hear the raspy voice whisper, "I would, but it hurts to move."

Then, as I hear the voice again, I recognize the tone and then I see the trashcan move. I take a step toward the yellow and black can to get a better look.

"Ohmigod, Bryan!"

I kneel in front of him and take a good look at him. His face, his arms, his legs. Nothing is bleeding from what I can see, but his clothes are dark, so that doesn't help. But no fresh wounds on the skin that I can see on his face or neck.

He doesn't look like he got in a fight, so why can't he move?

"What happened? Where are you hurt at?" I demand.

"I think... I broke a rib or something. My side feels like it's on fire." Bryan whispers.

"Let's get you inside."

I get in front of him, and I go to his left side to help him up. I wrap my arm around his right side, but when I do, he yells out in pain, and he collapses to his knees.

"Sorry. Let's try this again. Put your right side into me and let me hold your left side."

"You can't carry me." Bryan says breathlessly.

"You let me worry about what I can and can't do, okay?"

I finally help him inside and I sit him down on the couch. I get a text message on my phone, and I pull it out of the pocket of my pajamas to look at it. "Oh, thank God," I say as I see who it's from.

Me:

Mom get here as quick as you can, Bryan just got here and I think he had several broken ribs

Mom:

Ok, I'm on my way, just don't give him any pain meds yet.

I toss my phone on the coffee table, and I look at Bryan as I run my fingers through his hair.

"Mom's on her way home. She'll be able to help you out. Right now, let's work on getting your shirt off."

I ease him up into a taller sitting position and wait for a few minutes. One for him to recover from being moved and two for me to figure out how to get his shirt off.

"Let's get your good side out first, then I can just slip it over your bad side. Sound good?" I ask.

He nods his head, and I take the end of his black shirt. I tug it up, revealing part of his rock-hard stomach, but that's where it ends. I see another piece of black material, but I don't let that stop me for now. I pull the rest of his shirt over his good arm, and then I pull it over his head. I slowly take the shirt down his right arm until it slips off completely. The other piece of fabric I see, I can now tell what it is. It's a vest. I realize it's a Kevlar vest, and my heart freezes in my chest.

Why the hell would he be wearing a Kevlar vest?

I pull the Velcro straps off from all sides, and I lift the vest off his body. The vest is what probably kept his ribs together and from getting any worse. When I finally get a good look at the vest, my hands begin to shake at what I see embedded in the material.

Why would he be wearing a Kevlar vest, and why the hell would he have a .38mm bullet embedded in it? I ask myself as I look back at Bryan sitting bare-chested on my couch, trying to breathe around the pain while holding his injured ribs.

Chapter 13

Taylor

I hear the front door open, and Mom comes rushing into the family room. She checks Bryan over and she confirms the cracked and bruised ribs. Luckily, it's only two, and they're not completely broken.

"Taylor, come with me and help me get what I need," Mom says as she walks toward the main bathroom in the hallway.

I gently touch Bryan's knee, and I follow Mom into the bathroom to get the Ace wrap and some pain medication.

"Taylor, make sure the guest room is made up," Mom says while she shakes two pain pills into a Dixie cup and closes the vanity mirror.

I look at her through the mirror, and I cock my head to the side. "Uh, have you been next to a cracked gas hose today? You do remember the guest room is attached to mine, right?"

"There's no way he can stay on that sofa. Besides, even if he wanted to try something, he wouldn't be able to handle it."

"It's ready." I sigh. "I went through it this morning."

"Are you going to help me with him?" Mom asks as she hands me the Ace wrap.

"Yes." I say as we walk back to the family room with the wrap and the pain meds.

Mom stops by the fridge to grab a bottle of water for Bryan before heading back into the living room with him.

She sits on the coffee table in front of him and offers the water and the medicine. "Bryan, take these, then I will wrap your side and then send you to bed. Okay?"

"Okay," Bryan says breathlessly, taking a swig of the water, and looks between Mom and me before leaning his head on the back of the couch.

Mom tries to wrap his side, but she can't even touch him without him hissing against the pain; he's that sensitive.

"Bryan, try to look at me. Try to focus only on me; forget about Mom," I say gently as I walk around the back of the couch.

I rub the curve of his naked shoulders. I feel the tense muscle move under my fingertips. Then I move up to rub his neck. I can tell that he's starting to feel the pressure that Mom is putting on his side again. So I try to distract him by leaning next to his ear, and his shoulders tighten for a completely different reason.

"Hey, guess where you're going to be at?" I whisper.

He opens his eyes a little and looks at me upside down, waiting for my answer.

"Across from my room." I say.

He smiles a tad. "Yeah, right," He whispers.

Mom finishes up and looks at me to go ahead and start moving him. I pick up his shirt, but I remember the hole in the fabric from the bullet. Mom takes it from me so she can sew it back up in the morning.

"Well, how about we go and look?" I ask.

I help him to his feet, and I lead him upstairs. I open my door and we walk to the left toward the guest room door.

"See? My room," I say as I wave my hand through the air, "and your room." I add, pointing to his door.

I walk him into the guest room and sit him on the edge of his bed. He looks at me with pain, sorrow, and a lingering bit of fear all mixing in his forest-green eyes. "I'm sorry I didn't call you. Things got so hectic." Bryan says while pinching the bridge of his nose.

He looks away from me, and I kneel in front of him and put my hands on his bare shoulders. "Can you tell me what happened? Why were you wearing a Kevlar vest and how did you get a thirty-eight millimeter in it?" I ask.

He looks at me when I ask him about the vest and the bullet. Like he was surprised to hear that I knew what type of vest he had on, and the type of bullet that was in it.

"Remember, my dad taught me about guns, so I know my bullets." I explain.

Bryan nods a little and looks me in the eye. "We were at an airgun range. And we always wear KV's for protection in case we want to shoot one another. We wear helmets and everything. We were supposed to get back yesterday, but we didn't get to the range until late, so we stayed the night and went the next morning, but I had crappy cell reception, so I couldn't call. When we got to the range, we shot a few rounds, and then all hell broke loose. Some crazy guy brought a real gun into the range. He started shooting, and one hit me, I guess. It's a good thing I still had my vest on."

"Don't ever do that to me again." I grind out. "If you are going somewhere, please tell me."

"I will." Bryan promises.

"Do you know if the guy was arrested?" I ask.

"Yeah. He was actually a felon that the police have been after for a while," Bryan says.

"Well, you helped catch a lunatic. Good for you." I joke.

"I don't want to catch anyone like this again." Bryan says, wincing in pain.

"I wouldn't either."

I don't realize that my hand is on my right side, where my scar is, until I notice Bryan staring at me.

"What's there?" Bryan asks as his eyes flick from my side to my face.

"I don't want to—" I begin.

"Hey, no secrets. Tell me." Bryan says, cutting me off before I can finish my sentence.

I sigh as I lift my shirt to reveal my three-inch scar. He lightly touches it and looks at me. "What did that come from?"

I sigh again. "I saved a friend from a deadly situation, but I paid the price. I put my nose where it shouldn't have been."

"What happened afterwards?" Bryan asks.

"Some guy wanted to give me a medal, but I refused. I was just helping a friend out." I say.

"Was she in some kind of trouble?" Bryan asks.

"I can't go into detail, but I've helped her twice."

Crap, I wasn't even supposed to say the gender, but wait, he said it first. So, I'm just saying what he said.

Suddenly, I hear a noise coming out of my room from my computer.

"Taylor! Taylor! Where are you?"

I hear Lexi yelling through my computer speakers. I know whatever she's going to say is a big deal when I realize that she hacked into my IP address to override the notification request.

Chapter 14

Taylor

"Lexi, chill, where's the fire?" I asked, coming out of Bryan's room and walk toward my desk.

"I heard about a shooting rampage at an air rifle range. You didn't go, did you?" Lexi asks in a rush.

"No, I'm fine. Bryan got hurt though."

"Where is he?" Lexi asks, fear lacing her voice.

"I'm right here," Bryan says, trying to lean on the doorjamb while crossing his arms over his bare chest.

"Ohmigod, he is in your room!" Lexi squeals. "And he's half-naked?"

"Lexi, calm down; it's okay." I say.

"Yeah, Lexi, calm down." Bryan says with a cocky smile on his face.

"Taylor told me that she was seeing a guy, but I never thought it was you." Lexi says with a touch of venom.

"Wait, you two know each other?" I ask in shock.

"It was after...I moved away." Lexi says.

"We went to the same summer camp program. I decided it was boring, so that's when I really picked up on drawing." Bryan says.

"You never said anything about a summer camp program, Lexi." I say, shooting a look in her direction.

"I didn't like them either, so I didn't think it was necessary to talk about them." Lexi says.

"Yeah, they were grueling. Mark couldn't even make them fun." Bryan says.

"I'm sorry for going all Donkey Kong, but the news of the shooting just really freaked me out." Lexi says, her voice tight, and I know she's holding back tears.

I notice she's looking a little too intently at Bryan. He pushes off the wall with his right hand, and as he walks over to my computer, he holds his side to keep from moving too much. I see him lean towards the screen, but he can't get too close.

I almost swear I hear him say, "He's okay," before he turns around to me after he shuts the computer down, and he seems to be a bit more relaxed than a few minutes ago.

"I guess the pain meds are doing the trick?" I ask.

"Yeah, they are." Bryan says.

I help him back to his room, and he sits on the corner of the bed again. He rests his hands on my hips and pulls me toward him where I am standing between his legs. He looks up at me, and his eyes shift back and forth, like he's looking into both of my eyes before settling to focus on one.

"Thank you, Taylor." Bryan says.

"For what?" I ask.

"For being there when I needed you. And I'll be there when you need me. And as soon as I can, I want to take you somewhere."

"Let's take it one step at a time." I say.

"I will." Bryan says with a smile.

We kiss, and a big part of me wants him to sleep beside me in my bed, but I'm pretty sure that Mom would kill me if I did that.

"You go get some rest; it's going to be a restless night for both of us," Bryan says, his voice dropping to a lower octave near the end.

I know he's thinking the same thing I am, so I take a long shower and I try to go to bed with my boyfriend across the room.

***

Bryan

A couple of hours later, I wake up to go to the bathroom. My side is still painful, but it's a manageable burn as long as I take it easy. I pass Taylor's bed, and I notice her back is turned to me. Her deep breathing tells me she's out like a light. I quietly go into the bathroom that I notice is conveniently in her room, and I close the door quietly behind me.

When I come back out, I see that she is now facing the bathroom. I pause for a moment to see if she's awake, but she lets out a little snore and I know she's still sound asleep. I see a piece of her brown hair has fallen onto her lips, and I gently take my index finger and tuck the strand behind her ear. She doesn't even stir.

I slowly back away from her and then I look up at the open doorway and my heart jumps into my throat. I have to grab at my side to keep from pulling it and force the yell back down my throat at who just scared the shit out of me. Kathy is standing in the threshold with a smile on her face and motions for me to come over. I slowly walk over to her, still holding my side.

"Don't make me regret this decision. But I'll allow you to sleep *beside* my daughter, but only if this door stays open and only if me, Tom, or both of us are home." Kathy points to a door behind her. "Our room is right there, so don't make me do anything that could be explained as an accident." Kathy warns.

"Yes ma'am. Thank you." I say with shock filling my voice.

I feel awkward getting into bed with Taylor. Both because of this stupid wrap on my side and because of Kathy watching me like a hawk, and I just have a nervous feeling period. But I get comfortable, and Taylor rolls right onto my chest, thankfully on the good side. I look back at the doorway, but it's empty. I take as deep of a breath as I can and close my eyes. I slowly take in the feeling of Taylor against me. The lingering smell of her bath soap, vanilla and mint. The feeling of her soft skin against my own. The slow and steady rhythm of her breathing while she's sleeping. The feel of her bed under my back.

I silently pray that this feeling will continue and that nothing as close as today will take me away from her. I was terrified for the first time in my entire life. I really thought I was shot and would never see Taylor again. She is right though, no matter where I'm going, *I am* going to call or text her the next time I have to leave even if that meant I would have to give the number to a second phone that I carry as a backup plan.

Chapter 15

Taylor

I wake up to a heartbeat and deep breathing, but it can't be mine because whatever my head is on is too hard to be my pillow. I open my eyes and I see a naked torso, with an Ace wrap around the ribs. Then I feel an arm around my waist.

Bryan is in my bed? Am I still dreaming?

"Good morning." Bryan says sleepily.

"You know Mom is going to kill you, right?" I ask as I sit up to look at him.

"No, she isn't. She told me I could come over here. She heard me going to the bathroom last night, and she was in the doorway. She told me that if she or your dad were home and the door stayed open, I could sleep here. She also said if I did try anything she would make it look like an accident." Bryan says.

"And she will. How do you feel?" I ask, gently touching his wrap.

"Better."

"Are you in any pain yet?" I ask.

"Some." Bryan winces as he tries to stretch out his side to see how much he can move.

"Then let's get up and get you something to keep the pain down. If you don't want a whole one, we can half it." I offer.

"Alright, you're the nurse." He says with a slight smile playing on his lips.

"Don't give me any issues and I won't have to crack the whip." I tease.

"I'll be a horrible patient then." Bryan jokes in a sultry tone.

I lightly smack him on the head and I lead him into the kitchen where Mom is making some breakfast.

"Good morning. How's the patient?" Mom asks.

"Doing pretty good." Bryan says.

I go over to Mom and give her a hug. "Thank you for what you did last night." I tilt my head, looking at Bryan.

"Just don't make me regret that decision." Mom says as she hands him his shirt from last night, with the hole sewn up.

"I won't." I promise.

"*We* won't." Bryan corrects me as he slowly puts his shirt on.

"Yes, we won't." I repeat. "So do you want that half-a-pill?" I say as I turn to look at Bryan.

"Yeah, I guess."

Mom locks eyes with Bryan, and her tone goes from pleasant to nurse mode in the blink of an eye. "Bryan, I don't want you doing anything for the next few days. I also don't want you up much. You can get up to use the bathroom or go from the couch to bed. Got it?"

"Yes, ma'am." Bryan says.

"Now, unfortunately, Tom won't be home until tomorrow, and since I'm off, I have to go to the grocery store. I'm dropping Cody off next door, so you two behave." Mom warns.

"Mom, *go.*" I say.

She gives us one last warning look and walks out the door with her keys and purse in hand. I help Bryan over to the sofa once Mom closes the door behind her.

"Hey Babe, can I have some paper?" Bryan asks.

"Sure." I say, and I give him a fairly good stack of computer paper from Dad's office. "What are you going to make?"

"I'm not sure yet," Bryan says.

I look around the house and I realize that it needs picked up. "Do you mind if I put on some music while I clean this place up?"

"Nope. Most of the time I play music while I draw anyway," Bryan says.

I put in my own mix of some of my favorite bands. *Daugherty, David Cook,* and *Taylor Swift,* to name a few. I vacuum, do dishes, dust the furniture, and do a couple of loads of laundry, so by the time Mom gets home, she will be coming home to a clean house.

I see that Bryan is tapping his foot and bobbing his head to the music as he works on his drawing. "You like this kind of music too?" I ask, yelling over the beat.

"Yeah," Bryan yells. I turn the music down a little, and I try to look over Bryan's shoulder to see what he's making.

"Nope, I don't show spur-of-the-moment art until it's done." Bryan says, pulling the paper to his chest to hide it from me.

"Brat," I say as I ruffle up his hair. He laughs at me, and I pick up a pillow but stop mid-throw when I remember his injured ribs. "You're lucky you're on bed rest right now, or I would hit you over the head big time."

"Come here." Bryan says with a smile.

I go to his outstretched hand, and I put my fingers between his. He pulls me down to his lips, and he softly kisses me. I feel like I will never get used to the feeling of them. I always get a shock when I touch his lips with mine; it always feels like a new experience.

"I love you." Bryan says as he smiles against my lips.

"I love you too."

Just like it still feels strange to say 'I love you' but that is something I will make myself get over quickly. I want to keep hearing him say that to me and I never want any of this to end.

Mom gets home later, and she can't believe that I cleaned the house up and did the laundry.

"Mom, you have to try to believe that when you come home, you won't find us doing anything." I say as I help her unload the groceries in the kitchen.

"Taylor, you have to remember this is your first boyfriend. And I'm worried about you, no matter what you tell me you're not going to do. I'm your mother; that's my job." Mom says.

"It's alright, besides Bryan's been working on something and he won't show it to me yet." I say, giving him an evil eye.

"It's almost done. Don't get your panties in a bunch."

"Bite me." I say, and I stick my tongue out at him. He balls up a piece of paper and throws it at me. I catch it and throw it back at him.

"You know, you two remind me of Tom and myself when we were young." Mom says.

"Really?" I ask.

"Yeah, we would pick on each other the way you two are." Mom says. "Don't lose that in your relationship."

I walk over to Bryan and I put my arm around his neck. "We aren't going to lose what we have, right?" I ask him.

"No way; it came too naturally." Bryan says. "Can you help me up?" I help him into a sitting position, and I sit beside him on the couch. "Here ya go, it's finished." Bryan says with a wink.

I take a small, yet somewhat thick book from him. I open it up and I see that it's a motion picture book. As I flip the pages, I see two birds in two separate cages, then they start to fly around in them until they break out of their metal confines. Over the next couple of pages, it shows the birds flying towards one another with a beautiful blue sky and wispy clouds overhead. In the last few pages, they land next to each other in a full-blooming tree with bright green leaves, and a heart hovers over their heads when their beaks touch. The last page is of the birds with their beaks still touching, but above their heads is a statement.

"The world is ours for the taking, and as long as we are together, I can't wait to see what adventures come our way."

"Bryan, I love this. Thank you." I say. I kiss him and re-read the statement. "As long as you're beside me, I won't be scared for a second."

"You know I would still worry about you." Bryan says.

Why would he be worried about me? Does he feel like something would happen if we went away together?

I lean over to his ear, and I whisper into it. "Well, if memory serves right, we make a pretty good team."

"Yes, we do." Bryan says with a smile. He kisses me again as he gets up to go to the bathroom.

"It feels good to love someone, doesn't it?" Mom asks when Bryan is out of earshot.

"Yes."

"But I will tell you if something were to happen, and you two would break up, it would feel like you lost everything you had," Mom says.

"I don't think that will ever happen." I say.

"I hope not." "Let's see how you look today, Bryan," Mom says as Bryan comes back from the bathroom and sits down a few minutes later.

She unwraps his wrap, and she looks at the bruising and the swelling. "You're looking good. Are you still sore?" Mom asks.

"Not sore, tender. I can move it's just I have to do it slowly." Bryan says.

"You only had one cracked and one bruised rib, so it's up to you if you want me to take the wrap off for a while," Mom says.

"It won't hurt me if I go without it?"

"Nope," Mom says, popping the p.

"Then at least take it off for a while," Bryan says.

"Mom would never give you an option if she thought it would hurt you." I offer.

"Let me see how well you can walk." Mom says, waving toward the floor, showing Bryan where she wants him to walk.

Bryan slowly gets up, and he extends his hand to me. I take it and I walk around the house with him. I notice how straight he's standing; he's still not quite back to normal, but he's fairly straight for just resting overnight. I can tell he's forcing himself to be that tall though, so Mom might have to put the wrap back on him.

"Let's go and sit back down. You're not quite there yet." I take him back to the family room and sit him down. I lock eyes with Mom and shake my head.

"Hey Babe, do you mind going over to my place and getting me another set of clean clothes? I'm sure the head nurse wouldn't want me leaving this house." Bryan says with a smile on his face.

"Sure."

"You'll need these." Bryan says.

I see a set of keys in his hand, but I get the feeling that they aren't his. "They're yours to keep. When I'm home, I sometimes keep the door locked, but even if I'm not home, you are welcome to go over." Bryan says with a smile.

"Thank you." I say.

I kiss him, and I take my new keys over to his house and I go up to his room and get him a change of clothes, while quickly saying hello to Granny and Grandpa and letting them know that Bryan is okay and is healing just fine before I leave.

"Thanks, Babe." Bryan says as I hand him over the black sweats and gray t-shirt, and he slowly gets up to get a shower.

"When you're almost done, let the hottest water you can take hit you in the rib that's bothering you. I think it might be mostly a cramped-up muscle now, and the hot water will loosen it up." I call over before he shuts the bathroom door.

"You're the nurse." He replies with a smile.

Chapter 16

Taylor

A few days later, Mom gives Bryan the green light to break this coop. She told us that he could still spend his nights here if he wanted to, but with the same rules as before, and we have.

On Monday morning my alarm goes off, and Bryan hits the button to turn the alarm off. "Babe, it's time to get up," Bryan says.

"Five more minutes." I say sleepily.

"No, we gotta get up," Bryan urges me again.

"Fine, I'm up." I grumble.

I sit up in bed, throwing my legs over the side, and rub my eyes as I feel Bryan moving around. He scoots in behind me and wraps his arms around my upper body, and he wraps his legs around mine.

"You awake now?" Bryan asks, leaning in close to my ear.

"Yes," I say. "You know, sometimes I hate that you're a morning person."

"You'll learn to love me for it." Bryan says as he presses a quick kiss to my cheek.

"Maybe." I tease.

We get dressed at the same time. He's in the bathroom downstairs and I'm in the bathroom in my bedroom. Like always, he's waiting on me, but I can tell he doesn't mind one bit. He drives us to school, and when we walk in, I see the principal talking to the girls.

"Hello Mr. Snow." I say with a smile.

He must be talking about the scheme for the dance that Bryan came up with a few days ago with the girls.

"I got the email from you the other day, Taylor. I love the scheme; the decorations will be waiting for you all in the gym by the end of the week." Mr. Snow says.

"I loved your drawing, Bryan." Tina beams.

"Yeah, it was pretty cool," Macy says.

"Thanks, girls."

"Guys, do you realize that we have two and a half weeks to decorate?" I say.

"Yeah, I thought that was weird that Mr. Snow already ordered them." Tina says, pushing the glasses up on her nose.

"Maybe he just didn't realize the date, or he wanted to make sure we got them in time." I reply.

I see Mark come up, and he has a shocked look on his face, and I assume he caught the last part of our conversation.

"Man, I accepted the painting deal, but helping to decorate for a dance? Really?"

"Mark, it's Bryan's choice. If he wants to help, he will. But you can't keep dogging him about this kinda stuff." I snap.

"Yeah, Mark, cool it. If you had your girl here, you'd be spending every second you could with her." Bryan says with a knowing smirk.

"Man, that's low, and you know it." Mark says with a hint of anger in his voice and briskly walks away.

"He has a girlfriend?" I whisper in Bryan's ear.

"I think he does." Bryan whispers back. "I think her name is Alexis, to be honest with you."

"Alexis, huh?" I ask. Feeling this is a strange coincidence and Bryan nods his head.

We get ready for our first class of the morning, and we sit in our seats as the final warning bell rings. Bryan then bumps my shoulder and smiles at me.

"Can we do something during free period?"

"That would depend on what it is." I say.

"I have another inspiration for a drawing."

"Okay," I say with a smile.

By the time free period rolls around, I'm giddy with excitement. It's fairly warm today, and Bryan leads me out of the building and takes me up on a small hill located behind the school. We walk through some waist-high weeds when I finally see a clearing, and in that clearing, I see an easel, with a blank canvas and some of his pencils.

"You're going to draw me, aren't you?" I ask.

"At least get an outline of you." Bryan says. "I'll fill the rest in as I have time."

He walks me past the easel and helps me down onto a blanket that he must have set on the ground before he came to get me. He gently angles my legs and head in what he said are picture-perfect angles, and he backs away toward the easel, picks up a pencil and begins his outline of me.

As I watch him draw me, I wonder what he's thinking. It must be good because he smiles the entire time. When the bell rings again, his fingers are gray from already adding shading to my picture.

"And let me guess, I'll have to wait until you're finished, right?" I ask.

"Yup. But it will be worth it."

"I know, but you should know by now, I'm not a very patient person." I say.

"Yes, you are. You just have to be willing to wait," Bryan says with a teasing smile.

He unfolds a canvas bag and slips the easel into it face down. He picks his supplies up and walks me back to the school hand in hand.

"Don't worry; I won't leave you hanging too long."

"Yes, you will, just to torture me." I whine.

"Torture, no. To pick at you, maybe." Bryan laughs.

After we get back to class, I start to think of something we can both enjoy, but I want it to be a surprise for Bryan. I find Mark before our lunch break, and I ask him where I can find a place that I'm thinking of. At first, he tries to talk me out of going there, but I insist and begrudgingly gives me the address and then walks away.

Chapter 17

Taylor

***

When we get out of school, I ask Tina to take my car home, and I meet up with Bryan at his locker.

"Hey, Babe." Bryan says when he sees me coming up to him. With a sly smile on my face.

"Hey, Bry."

"What?" Bryan asks, his brows furrowing at my devious grin.

"I thought we would do something fun today."

"What's going on in that head of yours, Babe?" Bryan asks while pushing a stray hair behind my ear.

"Will you let me drive your truck so I can take us somewhere? I want to do something that I think will be fun."

"What's going on in that beautiful head of yours?" Bryan asks again.

"Give me your keys and I'll show you." I tease.

"Alright, Babe, here you go," Bryan says. "Drive it like you stole it."

I take his keys from him, and I drive to the place that Mark told me about. After about 20 minutes, we pull up to the place, and I see a smile form on Bryan's lips when he sees that we pull up to a paintball range.

"You ready to get your butt beat by your girlfriend?" I challenge.

"Oh, Babe, I am the paintball master. I will beat you." Bryan croons with a cocky smile blooming on his handsome face.

"You ready to put your money where your mouth is?"

"Let's do this, but don't cry when I beat you." Bryan says.

"Same here."

We get out of the truck, and when we go up to the building, Bryan insists on paying for us, so I let him. We get our gear on and after a few minutes, we are ready to start.

"How about we make it easy, first one to land three hits on the other is the winner," Bryan says.

"Deal. You ready?" I ask.

"Let's do this."

He has no idea what he's up against.

We load our guns on opposite sides of the range, and then once we are ready, we turn around to face one another in the middle, then after a few beats of silence, we both rack the air guns, and the battle begins. We both immediately go behind a wall for cover.

"All I need is three hits, but I have to get close enough to get them." I say to myself.

I hear a paintball hit the wall I'm behind followed by Bryan's taunting laugh.

"Are you scared now, Babe?"

"No, you?" I shoot back.

I take a deep breath, and I poke my head out from my hiding place, and I look for Bryan. I just catch him moving to another blind, and I fire, and I'm pretty sure I hit him first.

"One for me, none for you." I yell.

"That was a lucky shot."

"Now all I need is two more." I taunt.

I look around for another blind, and I see one that would put me just on the other side of Bryan. I am about to try to get another shot off when I see something move out of the corner of my eye. I see Bryan pointing the gun at my chest, but what I don't see is any paint on his clothes. He smiles as he starts to take his first shot at me, but I use my foot and kick the gun aside and I shoot him in the chest all in one quick movement.

He just looks down at the yellow paint while I take off to another blind.

"You better try harder than that! I could have had you that time if I kept my finger on the trigger." I taunt.

All I hear is him laughing.

Come on, Babe, let me see what you've got.

I move to another blind, and I hear his gun go off, but I didn't think he hit me until I get behind my new blind. I start to feel a sting in my side, and I see red paint on my clothes.

"Tied one to one. Who can make it two to one?" Bryan says.

I smile and I begin to go to another blind, but I see a pebble on the ground. I smile again, and I kick the pebble, and I go to the other side of my blind, and just like what I wanted, Bryan moves out from his blind, and I take the shot, hitting his right shoulder. I move to another blind closer to him, and he tries to take his own shot, but he misses.

"Two to one, me."

"That was a lucky shot." Bryan says again.

"No, that was skill, babe."

"Skill?" Bryan laughs.

"This is skill, Babe."

I look out from my blind, and my heart jumps in my throat. Bryan is right in my face. He used his trash talk to mask his footsteps to get closer to me. I move just in time to miss his shot, but I don't have time to fire one of my own.

Damn, he's good.

I know we are sitting on opposite sides of the same blind. I see another pebble, and I wonder if he will fall for the same trick twice. I doubt it though, but I try it anyway, but with a twist. I kick the pebble, but I move in the same direction. And just like I planned, he came around the other side while I go the opposite direction, effectively switching places.

The score is still two to one. I hear a movement on the left side, and I try to cut the corner on my right, thinking he will be coming around from that way, but I was wrong. Bryan cuts me off on the right, and I fall on my back and see the gun pointed at my chest, but I take my own aim at him.

"So, who's going to be the quicker—" I begin, but Bryan takes his second shot at me and hits me in the right leg.

"Now, who's gonna finish it?" Bryan challenges.

We both have our fingers on the triggers, staring one another down, trying to see when the other will take the shot. At the last second, I kick my leg up and I knock his gun aside again, and I take my kill shot, hitting Bryan in the chest again.

"Gotcha," I say while blowing imaginary smoke from my gun.

"I have to admit, Babe, you're good." Bryan croons.

"Thank you." I say. "Now remember, no crying."

"Hey, you're good, but not good enough."

"What do you mean?" I ask.

"Look."

I look over my clothes and I see a speck of red on my shoe.

"It's a tie," Bryan says.

"Fine. But we will have a rematch one day." I say. "Mom will be home soon. Let's go home, and why don't you stay for dinner?"

"Sure," Bryan says.

He drives us home, and when we get there, I see a note from Mom.

I'm at the store, I'll be home soon.
Text me and let me know your home.
Love,
Mom.

I text her and let her know that Bryan and I are home, and we are going to watch TV on the couch. When she gets back, we help her fix a quick dinner, and then we all gather around the table.

"Anything exciting happen while I was gone earlier?" Mom asks.

"Bryan and I had a friendly paintball fight after school; it ended in a tie." I say, giving him a sideways glance. "What about you?"

Mom looks a little pale when I ask her that.

"What's wrong?" I ask, panic sitting in the pit of my stomach.

Mom sighs. "I ran into an old *friend* of yours." But the way she says friend isn't in a good way.

"Who?" I ask. I feel my stomach drop like a stone when she looks at me with tight lips.

"Phil," Mom says coldly.

"No. He's back in town?" I ask with a note of fear that I hope Bryan doesn't pick up.

My heart is beating so hard I can hear it in my ears. Mom running into Phil was not a good thing.

"He said he wanted to surprise you, and well, you know how that ended." Mom says flatly.

The whole time Mom and I are talking, Bryan is quietly eating.

Phil would not dare set foot on our doorstep. I don't care who he is. I will do whatever it takes to get him off this property. I think to myself.

"I thought you wouldn't want that so I told him that if he set foot on my property, he would not walk away." Mom says.

"Mom, you didn't!" I say, not realizing I was screaming.

"Yes, I did! I don't care who he is, I am not having him come near this house again!" Mom says in a controlled voice, but her tone is loud.

"Can I ask who this Phil guy is?" Bryan asks coolly.

"A scum bag that has friends in very high places, especially in the FBI," Mom says.

"What did you do to wind up under the FBI's nose, Babe?" Bryan asks with a hint of curiosity.

"Nothing." I snap. "He is trying to scare me into keeping my mouth shut."

"No, he's a nut job that should be locked up!" Mom yells.

"I know that no one could scare you into doing anything." Bryan says. "But if you see him anywhere near here, you call me. And that goes for you as well, Mrs. Sparks."

"I don't want you mixed up in this." I say with tension in my voice.

"He already said he was going to surprise you. You're my girl, so he'll have to go through me to get to you," Bryan says with determination in his green eyes. "So, I just got mixed up in this by relation."

I have never seen Bryan look like this before. He *actually* looks like he will do anything he can to keep Phil away from me. He puts his arm around my shoulders and kisses the top of my head while giving me and Mom a smile.

"It will be okay. I won't let anything happen to you or the family."

Bryan says softly.

Chapter 18

Taylor

Later that night, Bryan is sitting backward on my computer chair in my room with only a pair of black sweatpants on, his arms folded in front of him while leaning on the backrest.

"How did you meet this Phil guy?" Bryan asks.

"Just in the wrong place at the wrong time, and for some reason he has me on his radar, and he shouldn't." I say as I am sitting cross-legged on my bed.

"You would tell me if you were in trouble with anyone, right?" Bryan asks with worry in his tone.

"Yes, I would, and I'm not in trouble with anyone."

I go over to rub his naked shoulders and I realize that he's excessively tensed up. "Why are you so tense, Babe?"

"I guess I'm just worried about this guy," Bryan admits.

"Hey, don't worry about him." I say, taking his face in my hands. "He's just a scumbag, and he's not worth worrying about."

"I guess you're right." Bryan says with worry still clouding his green eyes.

We then hear a small knock at the door, and we both look toward the open doorway.

"Everything okay?" Mom asks.

"Yeah, we were just talking." I say.

"Alright, you two, night."

"Night, Mom."

"Night, Mrs. Sparks." Bryan says.

"Bryan, you can call me Kathy," Mom says with a smile.

"Okay. Night, Kathy." Bryan says. Mom smiles at us again and leaves.

"You being able to call my mom by her first name is a big thing, Babe." I say.

"I had a feeling you would say that."

"That means she's starting to like and trust you."

"Well, then maybe I'll be able to take you somewhere in the morning." Bryan says.

"Where are you going to take me?" I ask, my brows furrowing in question.

"Nowhere special. I just want to get out of the city for a while."

"I'm game." I say.

He gets up from the computer chair and we get into bed. He kisses me, and I lay my head on his chest as he wraps his arm around my waist.

"I knew you would be. But would your mom let us go?" Bryan asks.

"Well, we either just go and not tell her, or we go over and ask now. But I don't want her to separate us." I say.

Bryan takes a deep breath and looks at me for a moment.

"We can ask her now; come on." I say.

I get up and I walk over to my door, but I run right into Mom again.

"Whoa, Honey. What's up?" Mom asks with a bit of embarrassment at being caught.

"Were you going to spy on us?" I ask with a smile.

"What did you want to talk to me about?" Mom asks, ignoring my question.

"Bryan wants to take me somewhere tomorrow. Do you mind if we go?" I ask.

"Where are you going?" Mom asks while looking at Bryan.

"Mark has a cabin in the mountains, and I would like to take Taylor up there." Bryan says.

"Mom, please. I can swear on a Bible that nothing will happen." I assure her.

"No, I don't think that will be necessary. I think the fear I inflect is enough." Mom says with a slight grin.

"So, we can go?" I ask.

"I guess. Just come home in one piece. And no forest animals." Mom jokes.

"Thanks, Mom!" I exclaim as I hug her.

When she leaves to go to bed, I look at Bryan and I stick my tongue out at him before I go back to my spot beside him in the bed.

"You push your luck too much." Bryan chuckles.

"Well, if you don't, then you don't live life to the fullest. Sometimes you gotta push your luck if you want something bad enough." I counter.

"Well then, we are leaving in the morning." Bryan says.

"Can't wait."

"You won't be worried?" Bryan asks.

"Why would I be? One, you'll be there, and two, I can take care of myself." I say.

"Yes, I remember that. One day you need to teach me the fighting moves you know," Bryan says.

"Any time you're ready." I challenge.

"Alright, maybe some other time. Tomorrow will be just for us to relax and have some privacy." Bryan says.

"And maybe some hiking and taking a few pictures?" I ask.

"Whatever you want to do, Babe."

"I want to do stuff that you want to do too." I say.

"Babe, just being able to spend time with you is good enough." Bryan says.

"Can we shoot guns where we're going?" I ask.

"I don't see why not. Is that something you would like to do?"

"Sure, I say. "Plus, I can show you how good of a shot that I am. And we can have a different kind of rematch."

"Alright, that sounds good." Bryan says. "And we are going to see who gets the highest score."

"Oh, so it's another challenge, huh?" Bryan asks.

"Yep, so you better bring your A-game. Don't go easy on me either." I dare.

"Alright, I won't," Bryan says with a smile on his face while his eyes darken at the challenge between us.

Chapter 19

Taylor

I hear a man's laughter. It's mocking me. I'm lying on the ground, my right side on fire. I see him, Phil, standing over me. His evil grin sends chills down my spine.

"No one will believe you if you tell them. Everyone you love will leave you. They will think you are crazy, and I'll be in the background to make sure of that."

I wake up the next morning with a jolt from the nightmare. I turn to the right, and I see that Bryan's side of the bed is empty. I sit upright and look around for him, but I don't see him anywhere in my room.

"Bryan, are you here?" I holler.

Everyone you love will leave you.

He doesn't answer me. I get up, and I go to my doorway, and I yell again.

"Bryan, where are you?"

"Babe?!" Bryan yells back with a note of fear in his voice.

I see him at the bottom of the staircase, hands on either rail. He has on a black three-quarter sleeve shirt, a pair of blue jeans, and Converse sneakers.

"There you are." I breathe a sigh of relief.

We meet halfway up the staircase, and I hook my fingers through his belt loops. "You scared me for a minute. I didn't see you in bed, and I thought you left for some reason." I say softly.

"It's okay. I just didn't want to wake you until it was almost time to go. So, you better get dressed. I got everything in the truck." Bryan says while running his fingers through my hair. "You sure you're okay?"

"Yeah, just a bad dream. That's all." I kiss him soundly on the lips to prove to him that I'm alright but pull away before he can get into it, and I hear a low growl rumble in his chest.

I smile at him, and I go up to my room to get dressed before he can say anything. I put on a pair of jeans and a white long-sleeved shirt, pushing the sleeves up to my elbows. I go downstairs and I see Bryan waiting for me in the kitchen.

"Ready?" Bryan asks with a smile.

"Yep." I say, popping the P.

I link my hand with his, say goodbye to Mom, Dad, and Cody, and we walk out to his truck to hit the road. About two miles before the on-ramp to the interstate, I see a black Chevrolet Suburban pull behind us. I begin to ignore it, but I see two more join the first, and dread fills my chest.

"Bryan, it looks like we got company." I say with a serious tone in my voice.

"I see 'em." Bryan says in annoyance.

The three black SUVs continue to follow us as we near the on-ramp. I see a flash of black out of the corner of my eye and I see that another SUV has jumped in front of us just before we took the exit. I look at Bryan and I see anger bloom on his face.

"What are we going to do?" I ask sharply.

I look from the SUVs and back to him, and I see him gripping the steering wheel so tight that his knuckles are white. When we get on the interstate, we watch as the four vehicles box us in.

"Oh, shit!" Bryan swears.

"Do you have a gun in here and the ammo close by?" I ask, looking back to the SUVs.

"You can't—" Bryan begins.

We get slammed from the driver's side, and Bryan almost runs off the road, but he gets the truck back under control a moment later. I open his glove box to look for a gun, and I see a .42 Glock sitting next to his registration. I check the gun and I don't see a magazine in the magazine well. So, I look in his center console and I see four magazines all loaded with ammo. I take one and quickly load the gun.

Looking up, I see the sunroof above me, and I open it. I rack the chamber of his gun and look at Bryan all in a matter of a few seconds.

"Babe, no." Bryan orders.

"Try to stay as straight as you can." I say, ignoring his order.

Before I could get up through the sunroof, I hear a bullet hit the truck. I take a breath and then I pop up through the roof and I start shooting back. The SUV behind us slams into the bumper, and I take aim and shoot at the engine all in two seconds, and the vehicle immediately starts to slow down as the engine dies. When I see the SUV in the fast lane getting ready to hit us, I shoot it, but not quite fast enough. I hear another shot go off before they begin to slow down. Bryan swerves toward the passing lane, but he rights the truck quickly.

I then shoot the SUV on the other side of us making it sputter and smoke, before being forced to pull off the road. Now that only leaves the last one in front of us. The driver slams on the brakes, and Bryan swerves into the passing lane to avoid slamming into the back of the vehicle. Then he speeds up to match the SUV, and I swiftly take aim, firing low at the engine near the wheel well, and they spin out of control as we fly down the interstate to get away from them.

I slip back in the truck; close the sunroof and unload the gun to put it back in the glove box, all with expert ease thanks to Dad's lessons. I look over at Bryan and I notice he's driving with one hand, then I look over his shoulder and see that his window is cracked.

"You are a good shot, Babe," Bryan says, his voice thick and strained.

"Bryan, are you okay?" I ask. Then it hits me—the metallic smell of blood. "Oh my god, you've been shot! How far is this place out?"

"Not much farther." Bryan rasps.

"Does it have a first aid kit in there?" I ask my mind going a mile a minute.

"Yes," Bryan says tightly.

I see his hand, which is covered in blood, and I watch as he is clenching and unclenching his fist to keep the feeling in his fingers.

"Babe, pull over. I'll drive the rest of the way." I say.

"No, it's only a few more minutes. The turnoff is right here."

I see a break in the trees, and he turns off the exit. In about two minutes, we make a left turn up a steep hill that starts to bring the trees back around us. In another three painfully long minutes, we pull up in front of the cabin, and I grab Bryan's gun again from the glove box, and I put it in the small of my back. I jump out, and I go over to Bryan's side.

As I open the door, I stop in my tracks for a split second. His side is a total mess. The tan leather of the seat and parts of the door are covered in blood. Adrenaline helps you survive, but it also makes things messy. I take a breath and I help him unbuckle his seat belt.

"You'll be okay. Swing your legs out and sit in the seat sideways." I say.

He moves slowly, and I can tell he's trying to hide his pain. "You can't help me down, Babe," Bryan says roughly.

"Bryan, don't worry about it. Now use your good arm to hold on to the handle in the ceiling and put one foot out on the rail. Just take it slow and easy." I coach.

He lowers himself onto the ground, but when his feet hit the dirt, he stumbles, and I have to catch him. He almost takes me down with him, but I get him back under his own feet and we walk to the cabin. Taking the keys from his front pocket, I open the door and we walk inside. I help him sit on the couch, and I look at the damage real quick. I can still see the bullet under the skin, so it must be lodged in the bone.

"Don't worry, I'll have you fixed up in no time." I say breathless from both fear and from the exertion of helping him inside.

"I know you will," Bryan says, his face twisted in pain.

"Where's the medical kit?" I ask.

"It should be under the sink in the kitchen." Bryan says, pointing a bloody hand in that direction.

"Okay. I'll be right back." I promise.

I go into the kitchen, and I look under the sink, and I find the kit. I look in it to see if it has what I need. I see a small scalpel, forceps, stitches, antibiotic ointment, and some pain medication. I go back into the living room, and I find Bryan leaning his head back against the couch while holding his arm where the bullet went in. Blood still seeping out from around his fingers.

"Here, take these." I say, handing him two painkillers. "By the time I'm done, they should be working."

He takes them dry and lays his head on the back of the couch again.

"Let's get this shirt off. It's covered in blood." I say gently.

Even though it's a black shirt, the sheen that is left on the fabric and reflecting all the light tells me just how much blood he's lost. I gently take his uninjured side out and I slip the shirt off him completely. His chest and side are still sticky with blood, but I'll worry about that after I get the bullet out of his upper arm.

"Lay down for me Babe. It will be easier on you and me." I say gently.

I help him lay down, and I kiss his forehead before I start hurting him. "The bullet is lodged in your bone; I want you to try your best to stay still. Okay? If you have to bite down on this."

I give him a long and thick piece of gauze to bite on. He nods his head, telling me to start. I take a deep breath and I pick up the scalpel. I cut his skin to make the hole a tad bigger so I can get the forceps in. Then, I pick up the forceps and I ease them in as gently as I can. I feel Bryan tighten up under my fingertip, and I see his eyes close against the pain while flexing his good hand in an effort to stay still.

When I feel the forceps graze the bullet, I grab it and try to pull it out, but it slips, and I lose my grip on it. Bryan screams in pain, and I grab his hand, trying to comfort him. I feel so helpless watching him lie there taking deep breaths; even though I'm trying to get the bullet out, I can't make the pain go away.

"Try it... again." Bryan growls between breaths.

We lock eyes, and even though his green eyes are clouded with pain, I see confidence in them that he believes I can do this. I nod, and I try it again. This time I take my time and I make sure I have the bullet firmly in the metal tines before I start to pull back. When I get the bullet out of his arm, I see him relax almost instantly.

Bryan spits the gauze out. "How bad is it?" he asks breathlessly.

"Bad enough, but once I stitch you up, you'll be fine." I say with sweat on my brow.

I quickly sew him up, but the only thing I don't see in the kit is a clean wrap. So, I take my shirt and I cut a good size strip off the bottom half. I wrap his arm, and by the time I tie it on, Bryan has passed out. I leave him alone and clean up the mess of the medical supplies and I take another piece of my shirt and I get it wet with warm water,, and wipe off the areas of Bryan I can see. His arm, chest, and abdomen to at least be halfway clean.

After I'm done, I sit in front of the couch on the floor near Bryan's feet, and I lean my head back on the cushion. I look over at him and I watch the steady rise and fall of his chest while he's sleeping. I take a deep breath to calm the adrenaline running through my veins. It's been a while since I had to take care of a wound that severe, plus on top of those SUVs and shooting them all. It's a lot to take in for one afternoon, and it makes me think back to a year and a half ago, but I shake those thoughts from my head.

A few hours later, when the sun has almost dipped below the horizon, I see a shadow pass by the window. My first thought is to protect myself and Bryan. So, I pull Bryan's gun out from the small of my back and I crawl over to the loveseat in front of the window, and I wait for the door to open. When I see the door handle move, I ready myself, silently pulling the top rack of the Glock, but making sure my finger is not on the trigger yet, but it's just a muscle twitch away.

The door opens, and I jump up with the gun pointed at the intruder, but I also see a gun pointed at me too. Then after what seems like years pass, I recognize who's in the doorway.

"Mark!" I whisper yell.

"What are you doing here?" Mark whispers.

"Yeah, what are *you* doing here?" I counter.

"I saw that Bryan's truck was shot to hell and banged up, plus I saw some guy lurking around outside," Mark whispers.

"What did the guy look like?" I ask.

"Bald and with a face like a ferret." Mark says.

"Oh God no, he must've followed us!" I say a little too loudly.

"Who followed us, Babe?" Bryan asks groggily.

I go over to him, and I stroke his head. "I think Phil's out there somewhere. I think he was the one who sent those SUVs."

Bryan is silent for a few minutes as his brain processes what I said. "What are we gonna do?" He asks finally.

"I'm not sure yet."

"Well, I chased him away, so he won't be back for a while," Mark says.

"Mark, would you mind staying for a while?" I ask.

"Sure, if there's anything I can do, let me know." Mark says.

I see Bryan get up off the couch and start to leave the room. He's been asleep for a couple of hours, so he should be okay.

"Where are you going, Babe?" I ask.

"To get a spare gun we keep here and some more magazines." Bryan replies.

He leaves me and Mark alone for a few minutes out in the living room.

"Nice battle scar." Mark says while trying to make conversation.

I touch my side out of reflex. "Yeah." I say shortly.

"How did you get it?"

"I was helping a friend out, and the bullet missed her and hit me." I say.

"Whoa, talk about taking one for the team." Mark says with an amused chuckle.

"Yeah," I whisper. "But you know, I would do it all over again if I had to." I say with a slight smile, thinking back to a year and a half ago, and what happened just today. I look at Mark, and he smiles a little.

Bryan comes back out a few minutes later, and I notice he has clean clothes on. He throws me another magazine with his right hand, still being careful with his left arm, and I catch it and put it in my pocket all in one swift motion. He throws one to Mark, and he also tucks the magazine into his jeans. Bryan then loads the extra gun and puts a magazine in his own pocket.

"So how did you two get away?" Mark asks.

"Taylor shot them all." Bryan says with a slight smile, but I can tell he's still pissed from the whole ordeal.

"No way!" Mark exclaims and looks at me. "Bryan told me that you said you were a pretty good shot, and I'm guessing you are."

"She is Mark, she really is. She's your modern-day Annie Oakley," Bryan says with a little humor in his voice.

"I guess I am Bullet." I reply.

"Bullet?" Bryan asks.

"Yeah, it seems like you can't stay away from 'em." I say.

"Oh, gag me now." Mark says while shaking his head. "You two should come with a choking hazard warning."

Chapter 20

Taylor

Later that afternoon, I go into the small kitchenette and I find the three of us something to eat. Just because Phil is out there somewhere doesn't mean that we shouldn't eat something. For the first time this afternoon, I let myself look over the cabin.

The couch that Bryan is sitting on is a worn brown leather that's peeling in spots. There's also an armchair that doesn't match the couch at all. It's a cream and light blue embroidered cloth. It's like this cabin is filled with people's unwanted furniture, and it ends up here. Same with the small kitchen table, none of the chairs match and they are all varying colors of wood.

With all the mismatched furniture though, it still gives the cabin a lived-in feel. It's like all different walks of life have been through here and gave a bit of themselves before leaving. Bryan seems to be doing better. The bleeding has finally stopped, and so has the pain for the most part. I hear Bryan and Mark talking, so I try not to listen in on their conversation, but when I hear Mark yell, my curiosity gets the best of me.

"Dude, you let her shoot your gun!" Mark shouts while sitting on the arm of his chair.

"I didn't have a choice, man! I was kind of preoccupied with not being run off the damn road." Bryan says while running his right hand over his left shoulder like he's still trying to rub the pain away.

"He didn't give it to me; I found it, so he had no choice." I say from the kitchen to take the heat off Bryan some.

"It's just hard for me to believe that you shot four SUVs moving at eighty miles an hour." Mark glares at me.

"Well, believe it. I would go and show you, but I *really* don't feel like having ferret face shooting at me again." I snap.

"Well, we can't sit here either, Babe," Bryan says.

"I know I'm still trying to figure out how we are going to get out of here." I sigh.

"I'm parked around back under the awning. We could get out that way." Mark says. "And I'll call someone to come and pick up your truck and fix it."

"Sounds good to me; how about you, Bullet?" I ask.

"Yeah, as soon as we get back to the city, I've got a few calls to make," Bryan says, his eyes flicking to Mark.

"Let's eat something first. You need something on your stomach, Bryan." I say while bringing over three bowls of soup on a tray for all of us.

Bryan and Mark nod their heads in thanks, and Bryan scoots over on the couch so I can sit next to him, while Mark sits in his chair the right way.

After we finish our quick meal, we go out a back door that I didn't even notice was in the wall, and we pile into Mark's blue 2019 Ford Explorer.

"Stay down until I get out on the road." Mark says.

Bryan helps me settle down into the floorboards, and I keep my knees bent over the little hump in the middle of the floor. Bryan almost covers my body with his, using his good arm against the seat to prop himself up.

"So do you still want adventures with me?" Bryan asks, using his left arm to push a stray piece of hair behind my ear.

"You may think I'm crazy but, I do." I say with an embarrassed smile.

"You keep a pretty cool head on when you have to." Bryan says. "I'm usually able to think straight in situations like that, but what happened today scared the shit out of me. But it was mostly for you." Bryan admits.

"I was scared for the both of us." I whisper. "I kept thinking that your truck would blow up if they hit the gas tank."

"Let's just say that wouldn't happen." Bryan chuckles.

"Yes, it can—" I begin.

"Taylor, trust us," Mark says. "Bryan's truck and this SUV won't blow up if a bullet were to hit it."

After a few more minutes, I see that we get on the interstate, and Bryan moves where he is sitting in the backseat, and he helps me up too. Once I get buckled in, Bryan's phone starts ringing.

"Well, he calls me first." Bryan says. I see Mark look at Bryan in the rear-view mirror. "Hello?"

"Where the hell have you been, Evans!?" I hear a deep, male voice scream on the other end.

"I was at the cabin..."

Bryan stops speaking, and I assume he's listening to who's on the other end, but I can't hear what's said. But then Bryan's eyes go wide with pure fear and anger, and I feel my stomach drop in anticipation at what he may say.

"What?!" Bryan exclaims as he hangs up the phone. "Mark step on it, my grandparents' house was just on fire!" He says with a renewed fury.

When we pull up a few minutes later; the fire department and the police are still all around Gail and John's house.

"Stay here with Mark," Bryan tells me when Mark pulls his SUV up to the curb.

Bryan jumps out before Mark stops completely. I'm caught up in all the commotion in front of me that his words don't click right away.

"Who would do this?" I ask Mark as I finally open my door and get out to stand on the grass in a corner of the yard.

"I have no idea." Mark says as he joins me on the grass, his arm gently but protectively around me as we watch Bryan run up the yard to his grandparents, who are sitting in the back of an ambulance.

Then my cell phone beeps, and I look at a text message that came from an unknown number.

Unknown:

> *Next time you two do something like that it's gonna be worse.*

I hear an engine rev up behind me, and I see a maroon motorcycle idling in the middle of the road. The guy has the visor flipped down, so I can't see his face. He starts moving, and before I know what I'm doing, I walk to the middle of the street, and I stand there daring him to hit me. He swerves at the last second.

As he's passing, I yell at him. "I'm not scared of you!"

I see Mark running after me, and I meet up with him at the edge of the yard again.

"Who was that?" Mark asks as he watches the motorcycle race away.

"*The* scumbag." I reply with anger.

"Hey Annie, come here." Bryan yells for me from his place near the house.

I walk up to him, and I can smell how heavy the smoke is in the air now that I'm this close to the door.

"Did you get this message?" Bryan asks.

He shows me the same message that I got, and my stomach drops to my feet.

"It's Phil, and he just left on that motorcycle." I say with a mixture of annoyance and fear.

"You know that he's going to pick us off if we're alone, right?" Bryan says.

"Yeah, or have someone else do his dirty work like earlier today, 'cause he's too much of a damn chicken to face us himself." I say. "Anyway, how's Granny and Grandpa?"

"They'll be fine, other than smoke getting to them; they got out before the fire got bad. I'm going to see if they will stay in a hotel until the house is fixed and whoever did this is caught." Bryan says.

"What about my house?" I offer.

"Actually, your family should get out for a while too, but I know your mom would never go for that. Plus, I'm still there." Bryan says with a forced smile. "But if you want, you can keep my gun in case I'm not there for some reason." Bryan says with a serious tone I can't quite place.

"You're right; she would never go for leaving the house. But don't tell her about earlier today. She'll just worry, and right now he's just after us." I say.

"Okay. But what about the fire?" Bryan asks.

"It was arson, but by some random punk."

He pulls me in and holds me close to his chest, and I can tell by how gently his arms are wrapped around my body that he feels guilty about something, or like I'm the one who needs consoling. I don't know why he would feel that way, so I hug him back a little harder than he's holding me.

"Don't worry, we will catch that creep, and we will make him pay." I say while lifting my head to look at him in the eyes.

He'll pay for everything he has ever done. Phil will beg for mercy. He cannot keep getting by with this kind of stuff. The stunt from earlier and now this. If no one in law enforcement will help, then we will have to take him down. I think to myself.

Chapter 21

Taylor

With a weekend full of danger, I'm glad to be back in a normal routine again, like getting dressed to go to school.

"We will have to take my car until your truck gets out of the shop." I say from my bathroom as I am just putting my hair up in a ponytail and spraying the fly-aways back with hairspray.

I turn around, and I see Bryan sitting backward on my computer chair, deep in thought. Even through his burgundy shirt, I can see the muscles in his back are tight and he's bouncing his left leg with annoyance.

"Bullet, what's wrong?" I ask.

I go over and I lean against his back and put my arms around his neck while resting my head on his shoulder.

"Why would Granny open the door? They didn't break the door down to get in; she *opened* it." Bryan says.

"Didn't you ask her that the other day?"

"She was coughing too much to answer me, and I didn't want to press the issue at the time." Bryan says.

"Why don't we call in sick and go over and talk to them?"

"No," Bryan replies stiffly.

"Bryan, we have a good hunch we know who did this, if we could get proof—" I begin.

"Even if we could get proof from her, they would say that she's just an old woman; she doesn't really know what she saw." Bryan says with anger while getting up from the computer chair and goes to lean against the window to look over at the charred house across the street.

I don't understand why he's against trying to talk to his grandmother about this, and I feel he's overreacting a little bit more than he should be. It's almost like he knows someone will shove this under the proverbial rug, then I remember who we are talking about, and *I know* what this scum bag is capable of.

"I still say, go and talk to her. She has to know that someone believes her." I say simply. "And if you aren't going to go, then I will."

"You're not going to let this go, are you?" Bryan asks, looking me right in the eye.

"Nope." I say flatly. "That ferret-faced butt-wipe messed with your family, and I'm not gonna stop until he's paid for what he's done."

After a few minutes of silence, he lets out a defeated sigh. "Okay. I'll call the school."

I go downstairs and I pull out a couple of pictures of Phil and a few people that he's worked with from a fire safe lock box we have in the coat closet. Let's just say I "found" these when I first met good ole Phil. I make sure to put them in my purse before Bryan can see them.

"Okay, we're good for school." Bryan says as he's walking down the stairs.

"Good, you drive." I say, tossing him my keys and walking out the garage door to get in the passenger seat of my Focus.

I see Bryan looking at me from the doorway, with a mixture of shock and confusion at my actions. He finally gives me a small smile and shakes his head. He locks the house up and gets in the driver's seat of my car, adjusting the seat back so he can fit, and then he backs out of the driveway.

We drive out of town a bit, and he finally pulls up into a huge, twelve-story hotel.

"How much are you paying for this place?" I ask in shock.

"The agen—insurance company is paying for them." Bryan stumbles.

"Good, get the best you can, huh?"

"Yep," Bryan says with a smile. "Come on."

I follow him in, and we take the elevator to the sixth floor. He leads me to their room, and he knocks on the door.

"Granny, it's me and Taylor, can we come in?" Bryan asks through the door.

It takes a few minutes for the door to open, but it eventually does.

"Oh, Bryan!" Granny sobs as soon as she sees him.

"It's gonna be all right, Granny. We are going to catch whoever did this," Bryan says, hugging her and looking at me.

"Granny," I say gently. "I hate to, but can we talk about what happened?"

She nods her head, and she lets us walk in with her. She leads us into the living room, where I notice that John is sitting on the couch, and Granny leads us to the right, where a little kitchenette sits, and she gives John a small gesture to join us. He grunts as he gets up off the couch to follow us.

I give him and Granny a hug before he sits with us at the table. Bryan sits next to me, and he looks at me with a slight smile on his lips, and I touch him on the left arm where I know his wound is still fresh from the other day. He takes my hand off his shoulder and holds it on the table, making me realize there's more important things than his healing wound.

"What are you kids doing here? Don't you have school?" John asks, looking from me to Bryan.

"Taylor wanted to talk to you all about what happened. She's forceful when she wants to do something." Bryan says with a chuckle.

I give him a playful smack on the leg and turn my attention to Granny. "Can you start from the beginning? What happened? Why did you open the door?" I ask gently.

"I was in the kitchen, getting ready to fix John some coffee, when I saw something out of the corner of my eye, then I heard a knock at the door. I went over to the door and I heard a man say, *'I have some news on Bryan'*. Of course, I got worried, you know why, Bryan." Granny says while looking at him.

He takes her hand and gives it a soft squeeze while giving her a slight shake of his head that I would have almost missed if I weren't looking at him.

"I opened the door, and they came right in. Two guys. One held us at gunpoint and the other set the fire." Gail finishes.

"Did you get to see any faces?" I ask.

"I think so," Gail says on the verge of tears.

"Yeah, I got a look at them too." John says his eyes hard from the scene that his wife had recalled.

"Don't ask where I got these, but just look at them and tell me if you remember anyone." I say as I pull the pictures out of my purse and lay them on the table.

We leave Gail and John by themselves for a few minutes, and Bryan takes me aside into another room and shuts the door.

"How did you get those pictures?" He asks with a sharp tone in his voice.

"I got them from the last run-in with *him*." I say, feeling like I have to defend myself for some reason. "You knew this wasn't the first time I had to deal with Phil."

I can tell he wants to say something more, but his phone suddenly rings, and he leaves to take it out in the main hall of the hotel. I take a breath and return to Gail and John in the kitchen to see how they are doing and wait for Bryan to get back.

"Did you identify anything, Granny?" Bryan asks as he opens the door a few minutes later.

"Yes," Gail says with confidence she hasn't had this entire visit.

She looks at John to confirm this is who they both saw, and he nods his head in agreement.

"This is the prick that set the fire."

I take the pictures and put them back in my purse. We hug them both and then we leave their room.

As we get in my car and Bryan starts the engine, I put my hand on his right arm so he can't put the car in gear yet.

"Wait, Bryan. We need to find Phil and fast. The man that Gail and John identified was the same guy that shot at my friend and at me." I say slowly.

"What?!" Bryan shouts."

"I thought he was still in prison. But I'm assuming he was bailed out. No surprise there, I guess."

"Oh my God," Bryan says while squeezing the bridge of his nose.

My cell phone rings, making us both jump, and I see that it's Tina.

"Hey, Tina, what's up?" I ask, letting out a sigh.

"Yeah, what is up? Aren't you and Bryan supposed to be helping us?"

"Oh no, the dance; I'm so sorry, the weekend has been hell." I say with a sigh.

"Do you want to head over there and help?" Bryan asks. "It would get our minds off everything."

I pull my phone away from my ear to look at Bryan. "Yeah, there's nothing else we can do right now." I lift my phone to my ear as Bryan pulls out of the parking space and tell Tina, "We'll be over soon."

Chapter 22

Taylor

"At least we know why Gail opened the door now." I say, handing Bryan a purple streamer.

"Yeah," Bryan says. He motions for me to come closer to the ladder he's standing on. "I am so mad at the whole situation I want to beat his face in." Bryan whispers in my ear.

"I feel the same way." I whisper back.

"Could we change the subject? I'm just getting angrier talking about it." Bryan says as he climbs higher on the ladder to hang the streamer.

"Girls, what are we going to do for dresses?" Macy asks from across the gym.

"We could use new ones." I say.

"Let's go shopping!" Casey says, jumping up and down while clapping her hands next to Tina.

"Yeah, you should go and pick out a suit if you're taking me." I tease Bryan as he's stepping down from the ladder.

"Of course, I'm taking you, Annie," Bryan says while he rubs his thumb across my cheekbone and giving me a private sexy smile.

"Then you better go shopping too, Bullet." I say as I give him a playful poke in the chest.

"Annie and Bullet? What the heck?" Tina asks as she's walking over to us.

"Long story, Tina, and we would rather not talk about it right now." I say suddenly losing my playfulness.

By the end of the day, we finish the gym, and it's pretty Halloweenish, but it's tasteful too.

"It's perfect. Well done, everyone." I say.

We pick up any trash that's left, and we leave the gym a half hour later. We decided to pile into Macy and Casey's car to go to the mall and look for our dresses tonight that way we will have them before Saturday comes around in two days.

Bryan takes my car to get his own outfit for the evening. "Be careful." I say with a slight smile on my lips. "My car will explode." I whisper before he opens my car door.

"I will. You be careful too. I'll see you at home. Love you, Annie."

He gives me a quick kiss on the lips, then I hear a horn honk and I know it's the girls telling me to hurry up. I give him a smile, and I run across the parking lot, and get into Macy's and Casey's Mustang. I hop in the back seat with Tina, and I am thrown back into my seat by the force of Macy taking off down the parking lot.

I finally get situated in the seat and make sure my seat belt is tight, thanks to Macy's little stunt, and I see her look at me from the rear-view mirror and give me a small smirk. I then feel a tap on my shoulder, and I look over at Tina, and she scoots into me so she is out of earshot of the twins.

"Do you know who set Bryan's grandparents' house on fire yet?" Tina whispers.

I take a breath and look at her with a touch of anger in my eyes. "We think so, and you won't believe who it was." I pause, still not wanting to believe I am dealing with him again. "Ferret Face Phil." I whisper.

"Phil!" Tina yells in complete shock.

So much for privacy. I give her an annoyed look, and I just hope that the twins weren't paying attention.

"What about Ferret Face Phil?!" Macy exclaims.

So much for the hope that they weren't paying attention. "Bryan and I think he is the one that set his grandparents' house on fire." I say. "And another thing—his h*elper* is also out on the streets."

"What!?" The girls exclaim in unison.

"How the hell did he get out?" Macy asks with a note of fear in her voice.

"Think about it, Macy." I say with venom in my tone.

"Ohmigod."

"Phil." The girls echo each other.

"And you might as well know this too, he tried to have me, and Bryan killed the other day." I say, looking out the window.

"What?!" They all say again.

"And you're just now telling us?" Casey asks.

"Four black SUVs. They followed us onto the interstate, and I shot them all down with Bryan's gun." I say simply.

"So that's why Bryan's been calling you Annie, Annie Oakley," Tina says.

"Yeah. And he got shot in the arm so—" I begin.

"That's why you're calling him Bullet." Tina says again and I just simply nod.

"What are you going to do about Phil and his goon?" Macy asks.

"I don't know. There's not much we can do until he pops his weaselly head up again." I say with annoyance.

"What's Bryan going to do if he sees him alone?" Tina asks.

"Hopefully nothing stupid."

We finally arrive at the mall and walk right into a store with the best party dresses. Nothing pops out to me yet, but the girls find a couple of dresses to try on. Tina picks a bright orange dress, and with her black hair and her tan, she's going to look beautiful.

Macy and Casey find a dress that has ruffles and beads on it but in different colors. Macy picks a burgundy one, and Casey picks a dark hunter green. After they decide on their dresses, I finally find mine. It's a one-shoulder black and purple dress with sparkles sort of heavy on the top but they taper off as they go down the bodice. It's the last one and in my size, so it must have been meant to be. My phone beeps, and I look at it and I find myself smiling.

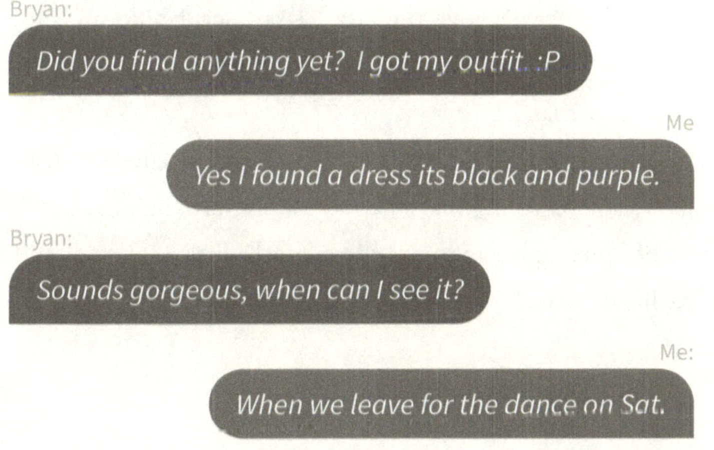

Bryan:

Grrrr, but I guess that's fair. I'm almost finished that painting.

Me:

You are such a punk you know that?

Bryan:

:P

"Is that lover boy?" Macy asks.

I nod my head, still smiling at my phone.

"Why is he a punk?" Casey asks while looking over my shoulder.

"Casey don't read my texts!"

"Why is he a punk?" Casey asks, ignoring me.

"He's working on this painting, and he won't let me see it until he's finished. So, I've been picking on him for it." I say.

"Awe." The girls croon.

"What can I say; I love the guy." I say, scrubbing my shoulder. "Sometimes." A sly smile creeps across my face.

"We can see that," Tina says.

This outing with the girls is exactly what I needed given the last few days and everything that's happened. Even though there is still the danger of Phil and his goon out there, I feel a little bit better, and I can act like life is normal even for a little while.

Chapter 23

Taylor

By the time I get home, it's late. My parents aren't home yet, but I see the Focus is parked in the driveway, so maybe Bryan's home. I let myself in and I go up to my room where I see Bryan in only sweatpants looking at the outfit he got today. I slip behind him, and I wrap my arms around his chest.

"Hey Annie. Do you like it?" Bryan asks.

I look at the gray button-up shirt and a dark purple tie with little skulls on the fabric that he already has tied around the collar. I also see a small chrome chain that I assume connects to a button on the shirt and would go into the chest pocket and with black pants to complete the look.

"Yes, I love it! I can't wait to see you in it." I say, letting my voice go sultry for a moment.

He tugs at my dress bag while taking a step closer to me, where he feels so much taller than I am and looks at me in the eye.

"Neither can I," Bryan says, letting desire drip into his voice, his green eyes going a shade darker.

I feel my heart beat harder in my chest and I forget to breathe for a moment, as I watch his smile grow more sensual. I then snap myself back to reality and I give him a mischievous smile.

"You'll live." I say kinda flatly and walk away from him to hang my dress bag up on my bathroom door.

"Yes, you will," Bryan says in a snarky tone.

"You're too good." I say, knowing he's talking about the painting.

"So are you." Bryan says, taking my chin in his hand, tilting my face so he can look deeply into my eyes. "That's what I love about you; you always keep me guessing." He says as he kisses me soundly on the lips.

I try to back away from him, but he follows me and backs me into the wall next to the bathroom. He keeps the kiss going for a few more passionate moments, taking my bottom lip between his teeth, his hand sliding into the nape of my neck to keep my head still. Then he pulls away a little, and I put my head on his bare chest. I feel him run his fingers through my hair, and with my lips still tingling from the kiss, I can't help the sigh of satisfaction that comes from my chest.

I hear him chuckle ever so slightly. The only reason I can absolutely say he did was the way his stomach jumps with the sound.

"What?" I ask, my brain finally working to form coherent thoughts.

"I just can't believe we've come as far as we have." Bryan says still playing with my hair.

"I knew once we were on the same page, we would hit it off. I was just wondering if you would ever open that same page." I say, lifting my head to look into his green eyes that are bright with admiration.

"I'm so glad I did. And I would not change anything for the world." Bryan says.

"Neither would I."

"Hey, what's your favorite flower?" He asks suddenly.

"Um. I don't know. I have several. But I'd have to say orange tiger lilies. They sometimes grow wild near the school, and I love to go and watch them sway in the wind."

"That does sound nice. You'll have to show me sometime." Bryan says as he pushes a piece of my hair behind my ear. "Oh, and guess what? I got Mark to come, and he's bringing his mystery girl."

"Really?" I ask in shock.

"Yep, but I warned him, it better not be a joke, he better not bring something stupid." Bryan says.

I smile 'cause I was thinking the same thing; he might bring a 'certain' doll or something just to tick Bryan off.

"I better get my shower. It's been a long day." I say as I reluctantly step away from him.

I shut the bathroom door and I begin to undress, but I have a feeling about something, and I pop my head out from behind the bathroom door and say, "And don't even think about looking at that dress, Bryan Alexander!"

"Damn, you know me too well." Bryan says while laughing and backing away from the bag.

I give him the evil eye while trying to hide my smile before I shut the door. After I get out of the shower and get dressed a few minutes later, I open the door and find Bryan sitting up in bed with his back on the headboard, arms folded behind his head, and his eyes closed. I gently go over and lay beside him, running my hand over his broad chest, playing with the few pieces of hair he has down the center of his pecs.

He takes a deep breath, and he opens his eyes, but he's not looking at anything in particular. I can tell he's thinking about something, but not in a good way.

"What's wrong?" I ask, still rubbing his chest.

"I hate this feeling." Bryan whispers.

"What feeling?"

"The feeling of a sitting duck. I feel like I'm in the dark waiting for the pop of a gun," Bryan says softly.

"So, do I. But you can't show it; you can't act like a sitting duck." I say. I sigh and shed some light on my past. "I was a sitting duck for a while. After I saved my friend, I felt like I had an invisible target on my back. Every time I turned around, someone was watching me. One day, I refused to look over my shoulder, and soon the people stopped following me because they couldn't toy with me anymore. I still refuse to look over my shoulder, even after what happened the other day."

Bryan wraps his arm around me, and he kisses the crown of my head. "Maybe this dance will help both of us relax."

"It will. Let's try to get some sleep."

He gets up and turns off the lights in the bedroom, then climbs back into bed, and I lay my head on his chest, listening to the steady, strong beat of his heart. I become more aware of his arm around m,e and even though everything is going crazy in our lives, I still feel safe in his arms. And I somehow know I always will.

***

After what only feels like a few minutes since I closed my eyes, we both jump up in our sleep. I get the feeling that someone is in the house. I hear Bryan's heart beating faster, and I know he's got the same feeling. But we don't hear anything. I feel Bryan get up, and he hands me a gun while he has his own.

He must really feel like a sitting duck. He's never had a gun with him the entire time that we've been together.

We make our way downstairs, but we don't turn on any lights. Bryan is in front of me, but I am following close behind.

When we get to the bottom of the stairs, I touch his back. *Do you see anyone?* I say in sign language.

He shakes his head no. I put my hand on the light switch, and he nods his head swiftly in agreement. I flip the switch, and I almost fall to the floor.

"Mom! Dad! What the hell?!" I yell.

"Sorry, Sweetie," Mom says, slurring a little.

"Are you two drunk?" Bryan asks, trying to hide his anger that's slowly morphing into amusement.

"What's with the guns?" Dad slurs.

"You two just about gave us heart attacks!" I say.

"We're sorry." Dad replies.

"Well, we are going up to bed, and I suggest you two should too." I say.

Bryan and I walk back upstairs, and we sit on the bed and just sit in silence for a few minutes.

"I almost shot your dad." Bryan says first with a tight smile playing on his lips.

"I've never seen my parents drunk before." I say in shock.

I flip the gun around in my hand where I'm holding the barrel toward the floor, and Bryan goes for the grip of the gun, but I hold firm until he looks me in the eye.

"You really are that worried, aren't you? And tell me the truth." I say, looking into his green eyes.

He sighs, "Yes."

"I should feel worse than you; Phil went after your grandparents because of what I did on the interstate." I say softly.

"It's not all you." Bryan whispers while looking up at the ceiling, then he looks back at me after a few heartbeats. "I mean, why would he go after my grandparents? If anything, he would come after me to get to you," Bryan says.

"Who knows what goes on in that crazy twisted mind of his."

"You got that right." Bryan says with a hint of disgust.

"Maybe we can stay asleep this time." I say, getting into bed.

"Maybe," Bryan says, following me into bed.

We melt back into one another and drift off to sleep, trying to forget what troubles are lurking just outside the windows.

Chapter 24

Taylor

The next day goes by normally, and I get more and more excited for the dance the following night. Little did I know I would be rudely awakened the next morning.

"Isn't this so cute?"

I open my eyes to a male voice, and when my vision comes into focus, my heart jumps up to my throat.

"Mark!" I scream, pulling the sheets up to my chest to hide my pajama top.

Bryan jumps up and turns over toward the door, snatching his gun off the nightstand and pointing it toward the doorway.

"Mark, what the hell are you doing, dude?" He asks sleepily.

"I'm returning your truck. Sorry for doing you a favor." Mark says with annoyance.

"Mark, don't walk in here like this again. Next time I won't hesitate about shooting you in the ass like I'm thinking of doing right now," Bryan warns.

"I figured you'd be up. Oh well, I'll see you tonight," Mark says as he's leaving my room.

"She better be real." I yell after him.

Mark laughs as he's going down the stairs. "Oh, you know me too well already, Tay-Tay."

Bryan gets up and goes over to the window, where he sees his truck in the driveway. "Babe, I like your car, but I'm a truck or a muscle car kind-of guy."

"I know, but can you do me a favor? Could you wreck my car so I could get a new one?" I ask.

He laughs. "Maybe later. We gotta go and pick out a cake and get some food." Bryan says.

"Okay, I'll get dressed."

Once I'm dressed, we climb into Bryan's truck, and I see that wherever Mark took it to they did a good job cleaning it up.

"You feel a little better now?" I ask.

"Yes," Bryan says with excitement.

"Well, bite me and my crappy car." I say with a smile.

"Don't tempt me." Bryan says, matching my smile. "I want to stay on the good side of your parents."

We pull into the grocery store parking lot, walk hand-in-hand inside, and go right over to the bakery.

"I would like to find a wolf; that's our mascot, and it would also work for Halloween too." I say.

"What about sandwiches?" Bryan asks.

"Um, I don't know. What do you think?"

"Roast beef, medium rare." Bryan says with a sly smile.

"Absolutely not. That's just gross!" I say in disgust.

"Fine, well done." Bryan says, hiding a smile.

"Medium rare." I say, mocking him. "If you wanted to act like a zombie, go to Mark's after the party."

I finally find the wolf cake, and it has our school colors, blue and white, on it. I walk up to the bakery counter and I see a tired-looking older woman with a hairnet on her salt and pepper hair.

"What can I do for ya?" She asks in a rough voice that came from too many cigarettes over the years.

"I would like this cake, and I need an order for two hundred well-done roast beef sandwiches." I tell the bakery lady.

"Alright, when would you like to pick this up?" She asks.

"I can pick it up at quarter after six," Bryan says.

"Okay. Pick up at quarter after six." I say to the bakery lady.

"Just bring this order slip when you pick it up." She replies.

Bryan pockets the slip, we pay at the self check out register, and we walk back out to his truck. Like a well-oiled machine, he opens the door for me, and I get in. He gets behind the driver's seat, starts the engine, and gives me a wink.

"I'll pick this stuff up, then I'll pick you up," Bryan says.

"Sounds good. You know I'm actually nervous for some reason." I say while buckling my seat belt.

"It's anticipation. It feels the same way. I feel that way when I—get ready for a game of paintball." Bryan says.

I notice the hesitation in his voice, but I don't call him on it. He has enough to worry about with Phil and what chaos he's caused. We decide to stop at Dairy Queen, and we get a bite to eat before going home. Time seems to fly on by us because when Bryan pulls up to my house, it's time to start getting ready. We go up to my room, and he takes his pant set with him, but before he walks away, he talks to my dress bag.

"I can't wait to see you on her."

"You're weird." I say, kissing him on the lips.

"I'll see the both of you at six-thirty," Bryan says with a smile on his face. He looks at me for a minute before all play fades from his face and he says, "If you need me, call me."

"I will." I say softly.

He leaves, and I start to take my dress out of the bag, but I pause and look back over my shoulder. "Bryan Alexander, leave." I warn.

"Damn. Get out of my head, woman." Bryan says with the humor back in his voice.

"Nope, either you wait like I am, or you show me what you've gotten done on the painting." I counter.

"Sometimes I can almost say I despise your ways." Bryan says. "I can say that too. Now be gone with you." I say, and I wave him away.

He sticks his tongue out at me and, for good measure, I close and lock my bedroom door. I smile and I silently laugh at him and his antics. I unzip the bag and take my dress out and hang it in my bathroom. I hear a knock at the door and I'm about to yell at Bryan, but I look out my window and I see him pull away in his truck. I open the door and I see Mom in the doorway.

"So, it's almost time for the dance, huh?" Mom asks.

"Yeah," I say with a smile.

"Sorry about last night. I guess your father and I had a little too much." Mom says sheepishly.

"If you help me get dressed, all will be forgiven."

She smiles, and she helps me with my hair and make-up. Dad comes up and watches Mom finish French braiding my hair. She even found some plastic ghosts and pumpkins to put in. I was going to do the spiders, but I was afraid I'd forget they were fake and freak out. Totally dodged that embarrassment bullet.

"Bryan is one lucky man." Dad says. "You're beautiful, Honey."

"Thank you, Dad. I will always be your little girl, though." I say as I get up to give him a hug, and he kisses me the top of my head.

"Oh, Taylor, your father and I wanted to give you something," Mom says, holding a small jewelry box.

I open it and I see a pair of dangling purple earrings set in yellow gold. "Thank you." I say.

Mom puts them in for me, and I look at myself in the mirror.

"Bryan should be at a loss for words when he sees you." Mom says.

"It looks like he'll look pretty handsome himself." I say.

"And he's got a gift for you too," Dad says.

"How do you know?" I ask in surprise.

"He showed us what he got you a little bit ago. And it's absolutely beautiful." Mom says.

I look at my clock, and it reads six-twenty-six, almost time for Bryan to pick me up.

At six-thirty on the dot, I hear a car door shut. I go over, and I see his truck parked out front, and I walk to the beginning of the stairs. I feel my heart beating rapidly with excitement as I wait for him to come into view.

Chapter 25

Taylor

Bryan walks in front of the staircase with his hands in his pant pockets, the sleeves of his gray shirt rolled up to his elbows, the chrome chain attached to the center of his tie, and disappearing into his breast pocket. His black pants make his legs seem longer than they are, and his usual black and white Converse sneakers complete the look. He looks at me, and his smile is so genuine that I feel myself blush as I slowly walk down the stairs toward him.

"You look absolutely beautiful, Taylor." Bryan says as I step down off the stairs.

"You look very handsome yourself." I say while taking his tie in my hand and running my fingers over the silk.

He takes my hand, and he walks me into the kitchen where he hands me two jewelry boxes. One is fairly large, and the other one is smaller. I open the bigger of the two and I see a necklace with pink and purple stones in it.

"Oh, Bryan, it's beautiful." I gasp.

He takes the necklace out of the box and fastens it around the nape of my neck.

He picks up the smaller box and holds it up to me. "Now, this one is going to be special. When I saw what was in the center, I couldn't leave it."

I notice something in his voice that I can't quite place. Nervousness, awkwardness maybe. He opens the smaller box, and I see a ring made of yellow gold and an oval pink stone sitting on a black cotton pillow, and in the middle of the pink stone, I see what he's talking about. I see a heart etched inside the stone. And I instantly know what he means by it being special. He slips it over my ring finger on my left hand, and he looks at me.

"This is a promise ring. I promise to love you, to be your rock when you need me to be, and to be there when you need a gentle touch. I promise to protect you with everything that I am." Bryan says, looking at me and smiling.

I smile back at him, and I kiss him as if to seal what he just said to me in stone. I know our love will sparkle as bright as this gem on my finger. Mom takes a picture of us, and then we are off.

As usual, Bryan opens my door, and I climb into his truck. "You ready?" Bryan asks before shutting the door.

"Absolutely," I say with a smile on my face, and he grins back before closing the door and hopping in himself.

While he's driving, I look at my ring again, and I love how the heart looks like it's sparkling with so many assorted colors.

"We're here." Bryan says.

I look up and I see that we are at school. I try to hide my smile at not paying attention to where we are. Bryan gets out and opens my door, the unspoken expectation between us, and helps me down. He opens the rear door of his truck, and we carry the food and the cake inside and set it up on the table inside the gym.

"We did a great job at the decorations." I say, looking around at the streamers, balloons, and strobe lights going around the gym.

"Yes, we did." Bryan says with a grin.

We walk back outside, and we decide to sit on his tailgate until everyone gets there, and Bryan pulls me into his lap, so I don't get my dress dirty.

After a few minutes, I finally see Tina, Macy, and Casey walk up. I knew the twins would have football players for dates, and I knew Tina would come alone. She'll meet up with a guy inside. As we are all talking, Bryan looks up, and I hear him laugh.

"Well, well. Mark does have a girl."

We all look at Mark's date and our jaws drop, and Bryan just looks at us like we've all gone crazy.

"Lexi!?" All four of us say at the same time.

She is wearing a solid dark purple dress with little toy spiders all over the bodice. Mark is wearing dark gray pants with a cream shirt with a dark purple tie, and he has the same spiders on him to complete the look. I jump down from Bryan's lap and I'm the first one to hug Lexi. Then the five of us are laughing and hugging like old times.

"Wait, you and Mark?" I ask.

"Yup." Lexi says, popping the P.

"How?" I ask. "When did you two hook up?"

"All in good time my friend, right now, let's dance!" Lexi says while taking Mark's hand and pulling him inside.

All of us start to walk inside when we see the principal walk by us. "Very nice job." Mr. Snow says as he looks at the finished gym.

"Thanks." We say in unison.

"Have a good night." Mr. Snow says in a spooky voice.

"Ohmigod, what is that?" Macy asks, looking at my ring.

"Bryan gave it to me along with this necklace." I say, showing off both pieces.

"Oh, so you made it official?" Lexi asks.

"Yes," Bryan says, looking at Mark and then at me.

The girls go ballistic, and all of them fawn over me and my jewelry. When the lights go down, Bryan takes my hand and leads me to the dance floor.

"Hey Bryan, Taylor, you may not believe it, but I'm happy for you. Have a good time, man." Mark says while giving Bryan's shoulder a quick pat.

"You too." Bryan says.

To my surprise, Bryan is a pretty good dancer. The music is the hits of right now, but they also throw some Halloween songs in the mix too. But I don't care. As long as I'm having fun with Bryan, it's fine by me.

After a while of dancing, we need a break. So, we sit down, and Mark and Lexi join us a moment later.

"I hear you two have a past together." Mark says.

"Mark!" Lexi exclaims while smacking him on the shoulder.

"I'm just asking." Mark says while rubbing his shoulder from Lexi's assault.

I just look at her; it's her call.

"Does Bryan know about—" Lexi asks, looking at my side.

"My scar? Yes."

"'K, Taylor is the one that saved my hide when I got into a little too much trouble." Lexi says.

"No way?!" Both guys exclaim.

"Yup." I reply with a slight blush at the truth that was just dropped on the table.

"Whoa, I *didn't* know that," Mark says.

"Way to go, Annie." Bryan says he gives me a light playful punch on the arm.

Lexi looks at me at hearing Bryan's nickname for me, but I shrug her off.

"Did you kill anyone?" Mark asks.

"What do you think?" I ask.

I want to see if Mark and or Bryan have gotten to know me any.

"I say injured, not killed." Bryan replies.

"Exactly." I say, nodding my head.

"Was that the only time?" Bryan asks.

"For what? Being shot? Yes." I say truthfully.

"Good," Bryan says with relief in his eyes.

"Who's up for cake? Better get a piece before it's gone." Lexi says while pulling me away before the guys push for too much info.

Chapter 26

Taylor

Ten o'clock rolls around way too fast, and everyone starts to leave the party. The girls and I say our goodbyes, with Lexi's being the longest. Bryan and I finally walk to his truck hand in hand. He's still in the party mood, swinging my arm as we walk and even picking me up by my waist and spinning us around. I can't contain my laughter at his antics. He then, like always, opens my door for me and helps me in the passenger seat. When he gets to the driver's side, I finally realize I forgot my purse.

"Oh crap, I forgot my purse. I'll be right back." I say as I go to grab for the door handle.

"I'll go get it for ya."

He's out of the truck before I can even say anything else. But when he closes his door, I see a manila folder slide out from under his seat.

CONFIDENTIAL

The red letters stare back at me from the floorboard, and my stomach drops at what this means. Against my better judgment, I bend over to pick it up and open the folder.

"Daryl Grove wanted for the murder of FBI agents Paul and Cindy Evans. Agent *Bryan Evans* will be undercover and is responsible for tracking down and arresting Grove. Agent Mark Stone will be his second in command."

As I read the file, my heart drops like a stone. "Oh my god, no, not again." I whisper as my hands begin to shake.

I look up and I see Bryan open the gym door and come running back to the truck with my purse in hand. I quickly put the file back under his seat and I sit up in my own like nothing's wrong. He opens his door and hands me my purse with a smile.

At first, I want to yell at him for lying to me. I knew something was off about him the more I got to know him, but I thought it came from his grandfather and being raised by an Army vet, and wanting to go into the police academy. But now I know that to be a lie. Our relationship was way too easy. And now I know why; it was a cover-up. But I will get the truth out of him.

"Ready to go home, Babe?" Bryan says with a smile.

"Yeah," I say, forcing a smile on my face.

I look out my window and I watch the shadows of the trees pass by.

I thought the FBI thing was behind me. But I guess I really love living on the edge, but tell me outright. I'm not going to be used as someone's cover without knowing it.

"I can't ever remember having this much fun," Bryan says.

"Neither can I," I say coolly.

"Is something wrong, Annie?" Bryan asks, his brow furrowing in question.

Yes, you used and still are using me.

"I just have a headache." I say tightly.

"We're almost home, Babe," Bryan says, his voice soft, and eyes filled with what some would see as concern. I look back out the window before

I can try to read into his expression more, and unshed tears burn my eyes.

Why did he have to use me? Why couldn't this love have been real? Why did the FBI have to bite me in the ass again? No, I can't break, not yet. He has to. He's the one that should feel like shit.

He pulls up to my house, and I am out of the truck before he is. "I'm going to get my shower." I say without looking back.

The more I think about it the more I want to go off. I'm certainly glad I never did anything with him that I would regret down the line. I don't want to be with a liar. Then I realize something. Lexi was warning me the whole time. But I was thinking about an immediate threat. I never would've thought that she was trying to tell me that Bryan was an agent. I finish my shower, take some Tylenol, and get into bed.

A little bit later, I feel Bryan get into bed with me. He tries to hold me, but I move from his touch. "If you had any secret at all, even if you weren't supposed to tell me, would you?" I ask, keeping my back to him and closing my eyes to keep the tears from falling into my pillow.

"If it was very important, yes," Bryan says softly. I don't know why I asked. I knew he would lie.

I hear Bryan's maniacal laugh fill the air around me. "I used you. I never loved you. You were only a piece in the puzzle. Everything I said meant nothing."

"Babe, wake up. Taylor, wake up, you're having a bad dream."

I open my eyes and I see Bryan, his green eyes full of concern.

"I'm okay now." I say, taking my eyes from him.

I get up and go to the bathroom to wash my face and to try and forget the nightmare I had.

"Alright. What's wrong? You have been distant from me since last night." Bryan says from the other side of the closed door.

I look at myself in the mirror, as if in silent question to my reflection if I want to answer him. My eyes harden, and I rush out of the bathroom, and I look right into those green eyes of his. The ones that I fell in love with the first time I met him.

"Why don't you tell me... *Agent Evans*?" I hiss.

His mouth literally drops at my comment for a heartbeat, before he finds his voice again. "How did you find out?" He asks quietly.

"I saw a file come out from under your seat last night. But what's really eating at me is that you didn't tell me yourself." I snap.

"I couldn't."

"Couldn't or wouldn't? Was everything we had just a job to you? Do you really love me, or was it just an act?" I ask.

"Annie, everything I ever told you was real. I love you—" Bryan says.

"Bullshit! You know what? Take your necklace and your stupid ring and yourself and leave!" I yell while throwing the jewelry on the bed.

"Annie, please." Bryan begs.

"No!" I yell back. "Everything I thought we had isn't real. You *used* me, Bryan! But I want you to know that at least one of us showed real love in this relationship." I say harshly.

"Mark told me not to get involved with you! But I didn't listen." Bryan raises his voice.

"I don't care what your *backup* told you. Just get out!!" I scream.

"Fine. You know I can't take anything back. I'm sorry, but this is who I am. I *am* an agent. But I still do love you, Taylor Allison Sparks. Remember that." Bryan says his voice cold as ice.

"Whatever." I snort.

I hear him pick up the ring and necklace, and I hear him walk out of my life. I pick up a pillow and I throw it at the door. I fall into my bed, and I let everything out. Mom comes in a few minutes later to see what is going on and I tell her everything.

"I'm sorry we woke you. I just—everything blew up. I can't believe he's an agent with the FBI, Mom." I sob.

"It's okay. Everything will be okay, Taylor." Mom soothes while stroking my back as we sit on my bed, and I cry into her shoulder.

***

Bryan

I leave Taylor's house and I begin to walk across the street to my Grandparents' place that's finally been rebuilt, but I know I'm not going to be able to stay right across the street from her and not try to go back over. So, I drive over to Mark's apartment. Even though it's two-thirty in the morning, I know my friend won't mind the intrusion.

I pull up to the apartment complex, and I use the spare key I have, and I let myself in. I walk over and open Mark's bedroom door to tell him I'm here, but I stop in my tracks when I see his arms around Lexi in blissful slumber. Just as I'm about to turn around, I hear Mark laugh a little in the darkness.

"Oh, so you can walk in on me and Lex, and it's okay, but you want to put a bullet in my ass when I did it to you and Taylor. Okay, sounds legit." Mark says sleepily.

I look at Mark's face, and I know he notices the sadness that I'm trying like hell to hide in my eyes, and he sits up in bed, letting the sheet fall past his bare chest.

"What's wrong, man?" Mark asks in a serious tone.

"Sorry, dude. I didn't know you had company, but I need to crash on the couch." I say while shutting the door.

I sit on the couch and begin to take my shoes off to get a little more comfortable, if it's only physical because my emotional comfort has gone to hell in a handbasket.

***

Mark

In the darkness of the bedroom, Lexi rolls over to me as I'm sitting on the corner of the bed to pick up my shirt from the floor that I discarded from our earlier romp in the sheets.

"What's his problem?" Lexi asks.

"I don't know, but something's up. Let me go talk to him." I say as I give Lexi a quick kiss. "I'll be right back." I slip into my grey sweats and walk out the door.

***

Bryan

I hear the bedroom door open, and I'm lying back on the couch with my right arm over my face, the crook of my elbow covering my eyes. I hear Mark sit in the beige wing-back chair that's in the corner of the room near the front door.

"What's going on? And don't tell me nothing. I know you too well."

Mark asks with a no-room-for-argument tone.

"She knows." I say without taking my arm away from my face.

Mark's confusion is palpable in the air as he asks, "Who knows what?" I can tell when it hits him. "Oh shit. Tay found out about you? How?" Mark asks softly.

"The damn file I have in my truck came out from under the seat last night. She found it and read it." I explain.

"Okay, but what made her kick you out?" Mark asks.

"She thought I used her."

"Okay, I can see that, I guess. I mean, we have used people before." Mark says.

"She thinks I don't love her." I say with pain filling my voice. No use in hiding it anymore.

"Now that's crazy. You love her the same way I love Lexi," Mark says with a touch of humor in his voice.

"Well, you tell her that, 'cause she's not listening to me."

Mark gets up off the wingback chair, walks over to me and puts his hand on my shoulder. "You can crash on the couch for as long as you need, bud. Don't worry, Tay will come around. She just needs time to process things." Mark says.

***

Mark

I join Lexi back in our bedroom and close the door behind me as I tug my shirt back over my head, drop my sweats down over my hips as I get back in bed beside her. She wordlessly snuggles up to my chest, and I run my hand over her long blonde hair and down her bare back, stopping just above her tailbone, knowing that will drive her crazy that I'm not caressing her bare ass.

"You are such a tease, you know that." Lexi chuckles.

"I know you love it." After a few moments of silence, I take a breath and look down at Lexi. "Is Taylor who I think she is?"

"What do you mean?" Lexi asks with a hint of apprehension in her voice.

"No one else has made the connection, but I have. Taylor is *that* mystery partner, isn't she?" I ask.

Lexi doesn't reply at first, but then her sigh tells him all he needs to know. "How did you figure it out?" She asks as she runs her fingers down the center of my chest.

"It could just be my analytical mind, but your report mentioned one thing about your partner back then. Their insanely accurate aim with a gun. Who else has freakishly good aim from what I heard?" I begin. "Taylor does." I then hand her a torn piece of paper, and her eyes widen at what I came up with. "Plus, we need to be more covert in the number scheme we use for our undercover agents." I add.

Chapter 27

Taylor

I cried most of the day yesterday, and my bed felt so cold and empty last night, and I'm full of conflicting emotions. I almost miss him, but I also hate that he lied to me, and I'm glad he's gone. I can't hold on to either emotion long before the other takes hold. I told all the girls but Lexi. I don't want to hear her say I told you so, or even take up for him. I ended up spending the weekend holed up in my room crying and silently yelling at him.

On Monday morning I don't see him at school, but I do see Mark. He tries to approach me in an effort to talk, but I brush him off. I don't see him again until that afternoon during free period while I'm walking outside, just trying to keep my mind clear of any thoughts of the past few days. I notice I'm starting to go in the direction of the clearing that Bryan took me to about two months ago when he started the outline of his drawing of me. I shake my head to clear the memory, and I force myself to turn back around, walking back toward the brick building of the school.

As I approach, I see Mark walk out of the double doors, eyes scanning the area and he sees me walking near the woods, and tries to catch up to me. I scowl, and I continue to walk away from him.

"Taylor!" Mark yells.

"I don't want to talk, Mark!" I yell back.

"Just hear me out."

"No." I snap.

He finally catches up to me and grabs my right arm with his left hand, but I jerk my arm away, breaking his hold on me. He tries again, and this time I grab his wrist and use his momentum to throw him forward, landing face-first in the grass. He rolls over on his back to stare up at me in disbelief.

"You want to try and touch me again?" I challenge. My voice steely, as I stand over him, daring him to get back up.

"All I want to do is talk." Mark says as he holds his hands up in surrender.

"What is there to talk about? He used me, end of story. I'm done." I say flatly.

"You got the nerve to talk." Mark says as he backs up enough to stand and crosses his arms over his broad chest. "Taylor, Bryan still loves you. When he told you that, he was telling the truth." Mark says.

"Mark, just leave me alone." I say, starting to get emotionally drained.

"Let me ask you, what made you think that he was using you?"

"He was undercover! Why would I think that anything that went on between us was real?" I yell.

"How did you know with Lexi?" Mark counters.

"She was a longtime friend! And I knew what she was like!" I yell, not really understanding what he was getting at.

Mark tries to touch me again and I shove his arm away so hard that it throws him off balance, and he's back on the ground again, and I start to walk away.

"I just think you're pretty low, for being the same thing." Mark says.

I stop dead in my tracks and turn back to look at him. "I was never an agent." I say my voice full of venom. "And I would never use someone the way Bryan used me."

After his words click in my mind, that he's calling me out on being the unnamed agent in Lexi's case a year and a half ago, I feel a new wave of anger toward him. "How did you find out about me?"

"If it meant flushing out your parents' killers, you would do anything to find leads." Mark says, ignoring my question. "Bryan joined the agency when he was sixteen, and you know you have to be eighteen to be recruited." Mark says. "I did my own research after Bryan said how you shot down all those SUVs on the interstate. I knew something was up with you, and something was tugging at the back of my mind to look at Lexi's file. And boom, *'remarkable aim for a non-agent. Would love to have them for real assignments.* That's what I remember Wayne putting in the file for you."

As he's telling me this, he takes slow steps toward me, and all I can do is just stand there as he approaches. He stops right in front of me, a good three inches taller than Bryan was compared to me. The toes of his Converses resting flush against my own Sketchers.

"You better think about what Bryan has *done* to you, and you better think about what *you've* done to Bryan," Mark says in a dark tone.

Mark is Bryan's friend; he will say anything to help him. But Mark didn't want us together in the first place, so why is he trying to get us back together now?

"You never really wanted us together in the first place. So just leave me alone." I say, sounding defeated, and I walk away.

Once I hit the pavement of the parking lot, I see the girls near the main door of the school. They can tell I'm worked up about something, and they all walk toward me and open their arms for me to walk into them.

"You'll get over him." Casey says gently.

"Eventually you will. You just have to work through all the emotions." Tina offers.

"Do you want us to come by your place and stay with you tonight?" Macy asks.

"That sounds good. A sleepover." I croak.

I turn around and I watch as Mark gets into his Ford Explorer. I spot Bryan in the passenger seat with his head leaning back against the headrest. Mark must say something to him because Bryan slams his fist into the dashboard. Before I can even comprehend what I'm doing, I take a step forward, and then I feel a tug at my shoulder, and I look to see Tina pull me back towards her as the Explorer drives off.

"You can't look at the guy you just broke up with, or you'll end up walking back over. If he really cares, he'll come for you." Tina says.

"Thanks, T."

She smiles, and we all get into our respective cars and drive to my house. With my girlfriends around me, I start to feel a little better than I have since our break-up.

Later that night, when we all go up to my room, Macy and Casey show us the mud masks they brought along so we could pamper ourselves tonight. So, we help each other put those on, and we paint our fingernails and our toes from my own stash of polish I keep in my bathroom. I feel pretty good, and I even find myself laughing a little when Casey, who is painting her toes a bright pink beside her sister, quickly swipes the brush over Macy's perfectly painted red toes. Macy squeals at the assault, and she tackles her sister to the floor and starts tickling her sides. We all end up joining the fray and become a pile of mud masks, wet polish, and cackling with laughter.

"So, what are you all doing for Christmas? I can't believe it's the beginning of November already." I say a few minutes later after I catch my breath.

"Nothing, just staying with the family." Macy says.

"You're not going away?" I ask.

"No," Casey whines. "Mom wants to stay home this year."

"I'm helping my mom bake and wrap again." I say as I'm touching up my right little toe with light blue polish.

"That's what I'm doing." Tina adds as she touches her mask to see if it's dry yet, but a little bit comes off on her finger, so she wipes the residue off on the washcloth.

"I enjoy baking with my mom. It's such a bonding experience over the holidays. I love it."

"Yeah. It's something that just helps the holiday seem better, more magical I guess." I say with my first real smile of the day.

After our fingers and toes dry, and we wash our masks off, we settle into bed. With the girls there, I don't feel so alone. I can sleep in my bed, and it doesn't feel as cold tonight.

Chapter 28

Taylor

I've kept myself busy these past few weeks to keep my mind off Bryan and the wave of emotions that fills my chest when I think about our break-up, by studying for mid-terms and hanging with the girls every chance we get, and before I know it, it's November 30th. I haven't seen Mark or Bryan at school, and that suits me just fine.

As I fill in the answer to the last question on my Chemistry test, the final bell rings, I rush out to my car, and I go to the diner to celebrate the end of a hectic week of tests. I don't really want to go home yet and wonder if Bryan is across the street at his grandparents today. I just don't have the energy to deal with the emotions that would cause.

After I sit down in a corner booth at the back of the restaurant near the kitchen and Gina takes my order, I hear the door to the diner open with the little bell ringing loudly in my ears. I watch in silence as Lexi drops into the seat across from me at my table, and I can see in her face that she's all business.

"What are you doing here?" I ask while taking a sip of my Coke.

"I can't stand to see Bryan sulk one more day." Lexi says, eyeing me and flipping her blonde ponytail over her shoulder.

"He *should* feel bad." I say coldly.

"For what!" Lexi snaps. "So, he didn't tell you he was an agent. But he *really* loves you, Taylor. He never once thought about using you for his cover. Wayne kept telling him to back off until this case was over, but you two actually busted this case wide open. Somehow you helped to flush Phil out." Lexi pauses a minute before she says, "You were the one that led Bryan here. For three years, he's been working non-stop to find his parents' killer. He found our file, and he saw Daryl's picture. But did you ever tell him about you—"

"I was disposable. I wasn't even named in the files. So, it doesn't matter." I say, trying to wave her off.

"Why doesn't it? Because you weren't *undercover?* Well, you were; that's why you weren't named." Lexi snaps. "It must have been hard to take knowing the man that you came to love was an agent." She says sarcastically. "But you know what? If I was Bryan and I found out about *your* little past, I wouldn't talk to you at all." Lexi says, and she walks out.

I realize with heartbreaking clarity that she's right, and so is Mark. What right did I have yelling at him and kicking him out, when I was basically the same thing? But I got it in my head that he was using me. I was mad that he didn't tell me, and that was a reason to get out of reliving my past. And Lexi is also right; when I pick up this phone and tell him that *I* was an agent, he is going to be the one that is going to be done with me. I suddenly feel like the worst person that ever lived on the face of the earth.

When Gina brings my food out, I barely eat anything, so she boxes it up for me and sends me on my way. But before I leave, I try to call Bryan, and his voicemail picks up. Exactly what I figured. I take a deep breath when I hear the beep at the end of his voicemail.

"Bryan, first I want to say I am so sorry for our fight and for something

I've been keeping from you." I say, my throat thick with emotion. "And I wouldn't blame you if you never talked to me again. The number 82772757 is me. I was a disposable agent, and I helped Lexi with one of her cases. Please don't delete this yet. I am so sorry that I yelled at you for being the same thing. I was just worried that you really didn't love me. And that everything was a lie for your cover. But I love you, Bryan Alexander Evans, and I wish you all the best in life. Goodbye, Bryan."

I hang up the phone and I let tear after tear roll off my cheek and I just sit there for a few minutes and cry. I messed up my future with the man that I really loved because of my stupidity. My insecurity. I wouldn't be mad if I was punished for the rest of my life for being the biggest hypocrite that walked the earth.

A few minutes later, I finally pull myself together enough to be able to drive home. I walk out of the diner, the bell above the door announcing my departure. I get to my car, and just as I am about to pull my keys out of my purse to unlock the door, I have a chill go up my spine and the tiny hairs on the nape of my neck stand on end. Like a sixth sense telling me something is wrong. The next thing I know, I feel an arm wrapping around my neck and a hand covering my mouth with a piece of cloth, then everything fades to black.

***

Bryan

I'm sitting on Mark's couch, staring at my phone, the shock evident on my face at what I just heard from the voicemail that Taylor left me.

"She really was a disposable agent?"

"Yes. She was my partner. I can tell you that she really feels terrible for yelling at you," Lexi says while perched on the loveseat with her legs up under her.

"She should." Mark chimes in from the kitchen while finishing up the dishes from dinner since it's his turn tonight to do them.

"Mark!" Lexi yells at him.

"I wonder if she'll talk to me now. It's been a little over a month." I ask, not really paying attention to my friends.

"She might. But now she'll think you hate her." Lexi says.

"I wouldn't talk to you if you did something like that." Mark says while joining Lexi on the loveseat and putting his arm around her shoulders.

"Shut up." Lexi says, giving Mark the side eye and shrugging out of his embrace.

I suddenly get up from the couch, walk to the front door, and let it shut loudly behind me.

Mark watches as the black F150 rolls past the window. "I wonder where he went?" Mark asks simply while Lexi gives him an eye roll.

***

I pull up to Taylor's house thirty minutes later, and I take a cleansing breath before getting out of my truck. I don't see her Focus in the driveway, but maybe she parked it in the garage. I do see Kathy's Honda CR-V in the driveway, so I go to the door and knock twice, and I wait a few beats before the door opens. When Kathy opens the door, I take one look at her tear-stained face, and I can tell something is wrong. Horribly wrong. And it makes my stomach roil in uneasiness.

"Kathy, what's going on?" I ask in a serious tone but with a hint of fear underneath that I can't shake.

"Have you seen her? Please tell me you've seen her." Kathy asks with her voice thick with unshed tears.

"Taylor? No, I was coming here to talk to her." I say, my heart pounding in my chest.

"She's been missing for about four hours." Kathy says.

"What? Where was she last?"

"She was at the diner. Gina called me to make sure she got home because she was upset. She hasn't been here." Kathy says quickly, then she looks at her phone as a message comes in. "Her Focus is still at the Diner."

"I'm on the phone with the police department now." Tom says from the living room.

"Don't bother with them. They won't do anything until it's been forty-eight hours. By that time, if it's who I think has her, she may be in serious trouble by then." I say with cool venom leaking through my tone.

"Don't tell me." Kathy says with fear tangible in her voice.

"Yeah. Phil and Daryl." I snarl. "I'm going to find her. Please call me if she makes it home or if you hear anything."

I walk off the porch and jump back in my truck and speed back to Mark's place again. I swing open the door and I find Mark making out with Lexi on the couch, but that doesn't faze me in the least with the roaring in my head at Taylor being in danger.

"What the hell, man?! You ever hear of knocking?" Mark says with frustration on being walked in on again.

"Get off your ass. Taylor's missing. I think that bastard has her." I snap.

"What?" Are you serious?" Mark asks while getting up from the couch.

"Bryan, what can I do to help?" Lexi asks.

"No, you're not getting involved." Mark says while putting his hand up to Lexi to stop her from getting up off the couch.

"Don't tell me just to leave my friend in the hands of some maniac. I need to help." Lexi says in a no-nonsense tone.

"Bring up your tracking system, Mark." I say while trying to hold a somewhat civil tone. Because right now I want to just snap at anything that just walks by. My anger is at an all-time high.

Without hesitation, Mark opens his computer and loads up the tracker system. I pull the laptop from him and enter the code that only I know of.

"You put a tracker on my friend?" Lexi says with annoyance.

"This is the only time I've used it. I wanted to be prepared for something like this." I reply.

"God, where do you have it?" Mark asks.

"Her watch. I knew that was the one thing she always had on her." I say.

After a few tense moments, I finally get a ping on the map.

"Got ya! We are bringing them down; *tonight*." I say and run out the door with the location of Taylor fresh in my mind.

Chapter 29

Taylor

I slowly wake up from a drugged-induced sleep. But all I can still see is darkness around me. I can feel that my hands are tied behind my back, but the knots are loose. I'm able to untie myself and stand up, but the dizzying rush to my head makes me fall back to my knees.

After a few minutes, I finally get my bearings and I grope the walls for a light switch. When I do find the switch, the naked bulb that I see hanging from the ceiling lights up the room. I take in the concrete walls and the dirty, blacked out windows that are way too high off the ground to me to climb out of, the one solid door to my left.

As I continue to take in the room, I have to swallow a scream. I see two skeletons in the room with me. One is on the floor and the other is still hanging by a noose in the rafters. The rope makes a creaking sound as the breeze from one of the windows makes the body sway ever so slightly. I notice they also still have their clothes on. Granted, they are heavily deteriorated, but I can tell that by the tan slacks and brown button-up shirt, and the light blue floral dress that the remains belong to a male and female.

I hate to, but I wonder if they have any form of ID on them?

I say a silent forgiving prayer for messing with the dead, and I walk up to the man that's hanging, and I feel the pockets. I find a wallet in the back pocket, and I pull out a well-worn brown leather wallet. The inside is gritty, and the antique brown colorization came from years of being untouched. I see a driver's license in the little pouch, and I pull it out so I can read the name better.

"Paul Evans. Ohmigod this... is Bryan's dad." I whisper and I drop the wallet, taking a step back, covering my mouth to keep from screaming.

I look at the female that's still sitting against the wall, and I assume that's his mother. I suddenly feel very crammed and stuffy in this room. I need to get out. Now.

I walk over to the large metal door, and I try the handle; luckily it gives and opens a crack. I slowly push the door wide open, and it only makes a slight creak at the movement. I take a moment to look around the hallways, which is made of the same concrete walls as this makeshift cell I'm in. I can tell the moon is full tonight. The light filtering in through the dirty windows, giving me just enough light to see.

The space looks so familiar to the last warehouse that I first met Phil and Daryl in that it almost makes me have flashbacks of that night, and my side flares with that ghostly burn of the bullet. I continue to look around and I see a flaw in the concrete wall, and I know deep in my bones that it came from a bullet, and somehow, I know that this is the very warehouse where this all started in.

I wait a few more precious heartbeats to take in my surroundings and I made the determination that the coast looks clear. I feel a slight breeze, which I hope will take me to a door or a window that is not as high off the ground. I take a deep breath and I venture out into the space before me. I turn a corner and I see the main door. I smile at my exit, and I take off for it. I almost make it to the door when I feel a hand wrap itself around my arm and twist it back painfully. I scream in both pain and fear.

"Oh, no you don't." A gruff but high-pitched voice says.

I am pulled around so the man can look at me. And I recognize him as Daryl Grove. The familiar middle-aged man with thick black glasses, receding hairline, and the same broad build, from a year and a half ago. His clothes consist of jeans that have a few holes in them and a white shirt that has stains on it, some that I don't even want to know the origin of.

"Well, well, well. We meet again. I see I didn't kill you the first time around. Well, I'll make sure I don't mess up this time." Daryl sneers.

I just look at him and I try to think about how I can get out of here, get out of the death grip he has on my arm. But his hold is too tight on me, and I know from the drugs that are still in my system, I am not strong enough to fight back. But the thought of finding something to beat him with, or maybe even steal his gun, enters my mind. But I don't see either option.

He drags me back to the concrete room by my arm, pulling my shoulder even more out of socket, and I have to swallow my scream of pain. I refuse to give it to him again. He throws me on the hard floor and shuts the door, this time locking it. The deadbolt clicking into place erupts through the empty, concrete room. I'm really dead now. No one knows I'm here. I lost my watch somewhere, so I can't use the remote SOS alert, and on top of that, I have no cell service. I then notice the date on my phone; December 1st. I've been here for seven hours, and my stomach drops at that thought.

At least I told Bryan I was sorry and told him about me being an agent. At least I won't die with guilt on my shoulders. But I wish that I could tell my parents and Cody that I love them one more time.

When the adrenaline wears off, my arm starts to ache from the dislocation. And I know I have to fix it. I act on autopilot as I take my arm and pop the joint back in place, gritting my teeth against the pain.

After about another two hours, I feel myself start to shake from fear, from pain, and silent tears begin rolling down my cheeks. There is no way I can get out of here. I don't have a gun, and the door is too heavy for me to break down.

I feel like a sitting duck, waiting for the pop of the gun.

When that thought hits me, the tears start to flow with heavy sobs racking my broken body. Bryan said the exact same thing to me before we broke up. I pull my knees up to my chest, and I wrap my arms around them and bury my head in my arms. I wonder if this is the punishment for me being such a hypocrite. I decide then and there to take my punishment with my eyes closed, and I wait for Daryl or Phil to come and kill me.

I make myself look at my phone for what seems like the millionth time; it's close to four-thirty in the morning. I have cried so much that now I have the dry heaves.

God, what are they waiting for?

Then, I hear footfalls. A quick pace, coming closer to the door.

Here it comes. Here comes the pop of the gun.

I hear someone turning the deadbolt, in the small room, it sounds so loud that my eardrums hurt because of it. I cover my ears and bury my head deeper in my shirt. I hear the door creak open, and even with my eyes closed, I can tell the light floods the room. And to make things worse, I smell men's cologne.

Bryan's cologne.

I draw myself up even tighter, and I somehow find more tears to shed.

Karma is really going to screw with me until the last second of my life. I take a shaky breath and I just sit there and wait. Wait for the gun to go off.

"Oh, Annie." An achingly familiar voice whispers. The timber of his voice is such a caress to my broken soul.

I open my eyes, and I turn around and look up through the dim light, shocked at what I am seeing. The familiar walk, the dark blue jeans, the way the black shirt hangs on his body in all the right places, and finally the moonlight catching those lovely green eyes.

"Bryan? Y-you came. How did you know?" I ask, still sitting there, half expecting him to be a figment of my imagination.

"Of course, I came, Annie." Bryan whispers, softly caressing my face in his hand while taking his thumb and drying my eyes. "I got your message, and I'm not mad. Actually, it explains a lot." He says with a smile.

"You forgive me?" I ask, still shocked that he's not mad and that he somehow found me.

"There's nothing to forgive, Baby Girl. Now let's get out of here." Bryan says with a smile.

He helps me up, and we quickly go to the door of the room; he pauses, looking around the corner, and he leads me out. We are almost to the main door again when Daryl steps into view. His large form blocking the main door from the outside.

"Now we have the whole party here, don't we, Daryl?" A nasally, condescending voice says.

Bryan and I turn around and we see Phil, bald-headed, eyes set to close each other, his build thin as a rail, behind us. He's wearing a beige three-piece suit, dark brown button-up shirt with a swirling cream and brown tie. With both here, they are trapping us in. Daryl is in the doorway, blocking the outside world, and Phil is keeping us from backtracking deeper into the warehouse.

"Taylor Sparks and Bryan Evans. My two *least* favorite people." Phil says as if we are the biggest inconvenience he has to deal with.

"I could say the same for the both of you." I reply with venom in my voice.

"Neither of you are surprised?" Phil asks.

"Surprised that you're a crooked agent and selling our secrets overseas? No," Bryan says simply.

"Taylor? You have anything to add to that? I know you do." Phil says, an evil smile spreading across his thin lips.

"You are a scumbag that should rot in Hell." I say.

He laughs and looks down at me. "I always liked your spunk. Even when you were a temp in the agency, you always had a mouth on you, and I knew that mouth would get you killed one day." Phil says his voice going dark.

"Is that a threat?" I ask. Stepping out from behind Bryan.

"You were always a little too cocky in my opinion. I don't like people like that. It can make them *unreliable*." Phil says.

"No, you don't like people you can't control." I spit out.

From a hidden pocket of his jacket, Phil takes his gun, and he shoots the concrete near my feet all in a matter of a few seconds. I don't move. I can't show him fear, even though I am scared to death on the inside.

"Like I said before, Phil. You don't scare me. But how about this, why did you kill Paul and Cindy? What did they do that made you have to get rid of them?" I ask.

"They got too nosy. I don't like people in my business, and Paul was getting too close. But you should know that, shouldn't you?" Phil says, eyeing me.

Bryan gets in front of me again, and I notice that Daryl has moved from the doorway to stand next to Phil, and I grab his right hand with my left.

"If you can understand this, squeeze my hand." I say to Bryan in sign language.

After a few tense seconds, he does.

"The doorway is open; do you think we can make a run for it?" I sign.

"You get ready. Call for backup to our location." Bryan signs into my hand.

I squeeze his hand to tell him I understand and that I'm ready whenever he is.

"I love you." He signs.

"Love you too." I sign back.

I see the muscles in his back and shoulders tense up to get ready for a fight, and he takes a step back, forcing me to take a step as well.

"Run!" He signs urgently in my hand.

I run out the door and fly down the stairs, using the railing to propel me faster. Once I hit the bottom, I see his black F150 in the field waiting for me. I run with everything I have to his truck. The fresh adrenaline giving me the strength I need to make the sprint. Then I hear the sound of gunfire explode behind me, and I cover my head with my arms.

I close the remaining distance, and I swing open the door to his truck, get in and I grab the CB radio. "This is Former Agent 82772757, and I need backup to the old warehouse on Lake House Lane." I say remember in my old undercover number digit for digit.

As I look out the windshield, I see Bryan is at the top of the steps wrestling for something with Daryl. Then, a few seconds later, I hear a gunshot echo in my ears, and I see Bryan's body jerk in a weird way.

My heart freezes in my chest, and it feels like time slows as I watch him fall back, then roll down the stairs and lands face down in the dirt, unmoving. My medical side kicks in instantly, and the words that I say into the CB leave a bad taste in my mouth.

"Agent Bryan Evans.... has just been... shot."

Chapter 30

Taylor

I throw the CB down, and I grab the .42 Glock that is sitting on the passenger seat and rack the slider back. I open the driver's side door, and I set the gun in the hinge, and I put my left foot on the outside rail.

I fire two shots at Daryl, one in the right shoulder, and I fire another through the railing of the stairs into his left knee. He yells out in pain and retreats into the building before I can fire off any more shots. I jump out of the truck, and I rush over to Bryan, screaming his name while I run.

"Bryan! No, oh God, please no!"

As I get closer to where he is on the ground, I fall to my knees and slide the remaining three feet to him. Not caring about my jeans ripping or my knees getting skinned from the pavement. I make a mental note to think about my knees later. I gently roll him over on his back and his left arm just flinging across his chest, coming away bloody. His eyes are open, but they don't focus on me.

I see the extent of the damage instantly. His black shirt is soaked in blood, the moonlight gleaming off the sticky, irony substance. I notice with horrifying clarity that he's been shot in the chest. And I'm sure the bullet has done extensive damage. I numbly take my jacket off, not caring about the bite of the cold air against my skin, and push it into his chest in an effort to stop the bleeding; he's aware enough to try to push it away.

"Taylor...no." Bryan whispers weakly.

"No is right!" I say as tears unknowingly slide down my cheeks. "You're not going to die on me! You are *not* going to die!"

I then feel his right hand moving around near his pocket, but he can't get his fingers in the material. His body won't listen to him. So, I help him pull a small circular object out.

A ring.

My ring that I gave back to him almost two months ago. I lift my left hand into his vision and I slip it on the ring finger of my left hand. When I look at him again, my medical side kicks in full force. He's not fighting for his breath, his pupils are not dilated, instead, his are constricted to tiny pinpricks. This is the bad side of shock; his body is too damaged to fight.

I stroke the side of his face, and his eyes eerily shift over to me. And seeing this much of his green iris is not helping.

"Bryan." I say, my throat burning with tears. "Don't give up on me. You once promised me that you would fight like hell. Please, Baby, fight for me." I whisper.

I take his right hand in mine and I kiss his knuckles softly, afraid that the slightest touch will be his last.

"That—" Bryan begins, but I see him take a shallow breath.

He takes my hand and talks to me slowly, in broken sign language. *"That promise I try... to keep. But please forgive...if.... I can't."*

"There will be nothing to forgive because you will make it." I say, stroking his head.

He smiles weakly and coughs once. Blood touching the corner of his mouth. I realize then how much blood he's lost. My jacket is soaked, and his blood is beginning to pool on the ground underneath him. I begin to hear the sirens finally in the distance and for some reason, I rest my head on his chest. That's when I hear my once strong heart beating slowly, and with every beat, I can hear what the damage is doing to him.

Every time his heart beats, I can hear the blood sloshing through the wound that must be in the main valve of his heart. Every beat is killing him more and more. I stay there, and I pull his right arm around my waist, and I hold it there.

"I love you, and I will always love you, Bryan." I whisper in his ear.

I sit up and look at him, not even bothering about the blood that is smeared across my shirt, neck, and face.

"Love.... you." Bryan crackles as I hear blood start filling his lungs, and a single tear running down his left eye, starting just over my right shoulder.

I lean in to kiss him, and I just barely get my lips to his before I see the pulse in his neck stop, his heart giving out. I notice a piece of something white land on his dark hair, and I back up to see what it is. Then I see another and another and another. It's snow.

I watch numbly as the flakes fall from the sky, one after another. Until there is a heavy, eerily quiet snowfall around us, around me. It was like the sky had opened up to cry along with me, its tears freezing in the air on the way down. I lean back down. Forehead to forehead. Not bothering about the cold air, the snow hitting my back. I'm too numb to feel anything but the slowly cooling body of the man that risked everything to save me. I'm willing to stay there, by his side until his body becomes no more, but then someone pulls me up and away from Bryan's body.

I don't even hear Mom walk up behind me and hand me over to Mark. I'm forced back to reality a little bit as he wraps his arms around me.

Warming me.

"We will do what we can, Sweetie." Mom says gently.

"It's too late. He's—" I begin, my voice cracking.

"Shhh, let's go to my place. If they can do anything to save him, they will." Mark says, looking over at Kathy and seeing his friend's limp body covered in blood.

Mark takes me away from the scene, and he puts me into the passenger side of his Explorer. I don't know how much time passes, but I know we pull up to his apartment. Mark helps me out of his SUV and walks me inside and into the bathroom. He turns on the light, and I find myself looking in the mirror. I see that I am covered in blood.

Bryan's blood, I remember.

My legs give out from under me, and Mark helps me to the floor, and I just explode.

"He's dead!" I scream. "He died in my arms because of me!"

"No, don't say that. You don't know what the doctors can do to save him." Mark says gently.

"He's dead, Mark!" I scream again. "He died as you all were pulling up." I whisper.

I look at Mark, and I can see the scene is still fresh in his mind too, and when I see the fear and the brink of tears in his dark brown eyes, I begin to cry hysterically. He tries to hold me, but I shove his arms away and I pound my fists against his chest. I just want the memories and the pain in my own heart to stop. He takes my assault without a word and waits for me to calm down. I hit him a few more times and I just settle into his chest and cry into his shirt.

"Lexi?" I hear him say softly after a few minutes.

I barely feel it when he hands me over to Lexi. I barely even know she's there. "Taylor, I'm gonna put you in the tub. Okay?" Lexi says. "Let me take your ring."

She tries to take it off, and I smack her away. "I'm just gonna clean it, and then you can have it right back. I'm gonna put it in this bowl." Lexi says, pointing to a ceramic bowl on the marble sink.

I finally relent and take it off, and I hand it to her. She takes it from me and puts it in a bowl on the sink like she promised. Lexi literally washes the blood off my body. Right now, I am just a hollow shell of who I was. I just keep seeing that scene play over and over in my mind.

When she rinses my body, and the coldness sets in I am able to come to enough to dry myself as she brings me a set of her clothes, and I dress while she cleans my ring.

"Here you go," Lexi says after a few minutes.

I put it on my left ring finger and I just stare at it. "Do you think they'll save him?" I whisper.

"I don't know, Tay; I really hope so," Lexi says with sorrow in her voice.

"Hey Lexi, can I talk to you?" Mark asks, his voice a little stronger than a few minutes ago.

Lexi follows Mark out to the living room, leaving me alone in the bathroom. I finally pull myself together enough to walk out a few minutes later, and I must interrupt the conversation because they both look at me.

"If you girls want, you can sleep in my bed; I'll sleep on the couch when I get back." Mark says, his face is still full of worry, but his eyes hold fierce determination.

"Okay," Lexi says.

"I gotta go out for a while; call if you need me." Mark says while giving

Lexi a kiss on the cheek and holding her gaze for a few moments before turning to leave.

Lexi and I are alone in his apartment, and I don't even let the strangeness of the unfamiliar place worry me. I am just existing right now.

"You gotta tell me if you need anything. Okay?" Lexi says gently.

"Okay," I whisper with tears burning my throat. I lay down on Mark's couch and I stare at the TV, but not taking a thing in.

***

The next thing I know, I see the sun shining through my closed eyelids, and I feel someone sit down on the couch beside me. I coax my eyes open, and I see Lexi first, and then I see Mark in my peripheral vision going into the kitchen. I notice that he's shirtless, and I see the silver line of a scar on his back. About three inches and just a breath away from hitting his kidney, I realize. But I don't make the same remark he did about mine when he first saw it. I'm just too exhausted.

When he comes back out of the kitchen with three coffee mugs balanced in his hands, something makes me turn to focus on him more. Past the tense muscles of his shoulders, I see bruises. All doting his chest in various areas.

That was from me last night. Last night!

Every single image, feeling, and sound comes flooding back to me, and it's all I can do to not break down and curl in on myself. I look over at Lexi again, I can tell by the way she is looking at me that it's not good. Her lips are in a tight line; her body is slumped over me. Her eyes are filled with regret.

"No! Please, no!" I sob.

After I let the tears roll down my cheeks for a few minutes, I ask the question I don't want to really know the answer to. "When?"

"They were almost finished surgery, but they couldn't get his heart to beat again. We would've told you last night, but you were already asleep." Mark says with regret.

I just stare off and I slowly take all this in. Bryan is truly dead. And I feel like a part of myself has died along with him.

Chapter 31

Taylor

The next morning, I wake up and I remember I'm in Mark's apartment. In his bed with Lexi beside me so I can keep a familiar face close, while he's on the couch, and reality hits me all over again. Bryan is dead, and the person that killed him is still out there somewhere.

"When will he have his funeral?" I ask when I finally come out of the bedroom and sit on the loveseat.

"After Daryl and Phil are caught." Mark says tightly.

He's sitting on the couch with Lexi under his arm.

"But that can take a while." I say, tears making my voice crack, but I'm able to keep them from falling.

"I know, but you know that's our procedure." Lexi says gently.

"Well, procedure sucks right now."

"I couldn't agree with you more, Tay Tay," Mark says with an annoyed and aggravated look on his face that I can't quite place. I see Mark look at Lexi, and then he looks at me, and he gives me a small smile as he walks over to sit next to me on the loveseat. "Taylor, I found this in Bryan's truck. I'm sure he was going to give it to you at some point." Mark says.

He hands me a little white paper book, and I open the cover, and I instantly recognize the handwriting,

Bryan's handwriting. 'I will always love you. 12/1'.

I start crying again at the loss of him. Then after a few minutes it hits me; I'm not the only one that lost someone. "I'm sorry. I know you lost a partner too, Mark." I say, looking at him.

"He was like a brother to me. But I know you meant a lot more to him. He went with his gut feeling, and I was wrong to try to hold him back." Mark says, standing to his full six-foot-two height and looking out the window.

I get up and I go over to him. He turns around, and I hug him. I never thought Mark be the type to cry, but I see tears fall from his dark brown eyes.

"We are going to find those sick bastards, and we are going to make them pay." Mark says, his voice thick with emotion but with determination burning in his eyes.

He smiles at me, sniffs, and wipes his tears away. I can tell that he means every word that he's saying.

"Lexi, can you take me home? I just want to be alone for a while." I say, turning to my friend.

"Sure," Lexi says with a small smile.

We walk out of Mark's apartment and we get into Lexi's 2019 white Ford Fusion. We pull up to my house a few minutes later, and I see my dad waiting for me on the front porch. When I get out, he meets me halfway down the driveway, and he holds me tight to his chest. I feel him wave goodbye to Lexi, and I hear the sound of her engine getting softer, and she drives away. Dad walks me inside, and I slowly walk up to my room and shut the door.

That night, Dad brings me my dinner, but even though I haven't eaten in forty-eight hours, I'm not hungry.

"If you're not going to eat, at least drink the milk." Dad coaxes me.

I do drink the milk but nothing else. Just as I am about to doze off, my phone lights up with a text message a little while later. My heart jumping at the thought... but I remember it can't be from him. It's from Tina instead.

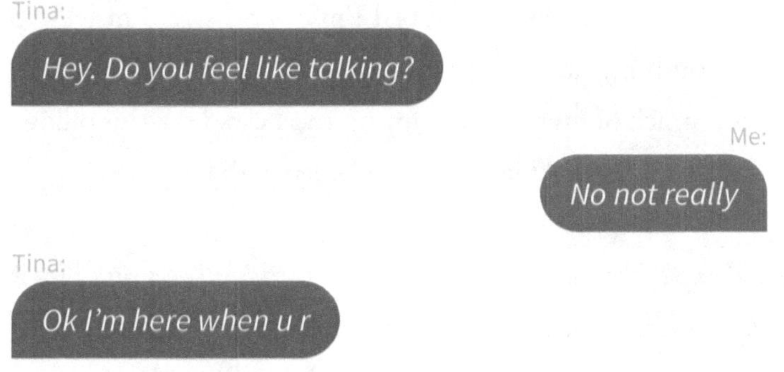

I feel the book that Mark gave me earlier in the pocket of Lexi's leggings, and I realize that I never read it yet. So, I take it out, and I look at it. And a fresh wave of anguish hits me. I see the bird drawing that Bryan made when he first started staying here. The two birds sitting in a lavish leaf-filled tree, beaks touching and a heart over their heads. But on the last page, I see a sentence in his handwriting.

We will meet again. 12/1.

He wrote this the day that he died. He must've had a feeling something was going to happen to him. I think to myself.

After a little while, I hear Mom come home from work. Part of me wants her to come up, but the other part wants her to leave me alone. She was the last one to see Bryan before they confirmed his death, and for tonight she does leave me alone. I cry silently to myself, wishing like hell that this was all a terrible dream, and I would wake up and Bryan would be beside me. But deep down I know it's not.

In the middle of the night, a smell wakes me up. The smell of Bryan's cologne. I open my eyes, but I don't see any of his cologne on my dresser. Then I realize what side of the bed I'm on, his side. I'm lying on his pillow. I push my face deeper into the soft fabric and I inhale deeply. Taking as much of his scent into my nose as I can. I take his pillow and I pull it into my chest. At least I can still sleep with his smell.

I wake up to the sound of my alarm going off. I roll over and I see Bryan.

"Hey Annie." He says, his voice soft and far away.

"Ohmygod, is this real?" I ask, reaching out for him, but I can't seem to touch him.

"I love you. Make sure you hang on to this ring." Bryan says.

He hands me a ring, then I hear a gunshot. Blood spreading across his shirt, and I'm back at the warehouse. He's wearing the same black shirt and dark blue jeans, and I watch helplessly as the blood pools around his body.

"I love you, Annie." His voice whispers.

I wake up screaming and crying. Dad swings open my door a few heartbeats later, and when he realizes that no one is in my room, he comes over and sits on my side of the bed.

"Shhh, it's okay." Dad whispers, trying to bring me into his chest for a comforting hug.

"No, it's not! My boyfriend is dead, and every time I close my eyes, he dies again!" I say with tears rolling from my eyes.

I pull away from his grip and I throw myself into my pillow. I hear him sigh in defeat, and I feel him get up and leave my room.

Chapter 32

Taylor

The next morning, I wake up, and I take in my room through sleep-clouded eyes. And while half asleep I notice that Bryan's side of the bed is empty, but it doesn't strike me as strange. He must have gotten up like he usually does and went for a run or something. So, I drag myself out of bed and walk to my bathroom to get a shower. With the towel wrapped around my body a few minutes later, I open my closet and I grab a pair of navy leggings and a bright pink sweater, and toss them on the bed.

Then, I grab a pair of Bryan's favorite jeans for him when he gets back from his shower that he should be taking by now downstairs. The hem is tattered from the jeans dragging across the many different surfaces, pavement, concrete, dirt, and grass. The right back pocket is worn at the edges from where he puts his wallet all the time. I go to throw the jeans on my bed, but I freeze with my arm outstretched and the jeans hanging loosely in my hand as reality hits me all in a rush again. I collapse to my knees, and I bring the rough material to my face, and I try to get lost in his scent again.

This never would have happened if I didn't overreact to the truth of who he was. He would still be in my arms if I wouldn't have been so afraid of my own past. I would've never been kidnapped if I wasn't distracted by my own insecurities. The thoughts rip through me as memories hit me all over again. I can't help but blame myself for his death.

I stay in bed all day, making it four days of not eating very much at all just enough to keep the growling at a minimum. I then hear Cody and my dad on the other side of the door.

"What's wrong with Taylor? Is she sick?" Cody asks.

"Sort-of. She's also very sad," Dad says.

"Why?" Cody asks. "Oh, I heard Taylor and Bryan fighting one day. That's why she's sad, right?"

"No Cody. Bryan got hurt very badly by a very bad man. And Mom couldn't help Bryan." Dad says gently.

This brings a new wave of tears to my eyes.

"Oh." Cody says, his childhood innocence not fully grasping the concept. "I'm gonna make her something that will make her happy."

I hear someone open my door, that I had locked a few days ago to keep people out. I just wanted to be left alone.

"Okay, Taylor Allison Sparks. I understand you miss Bryan, and you want to be alone but not eating much, showering, or coming out of this room for almost three weeks is inexcusable." Mom says sternly yet gently.

"I don't care." I whisper to her, feeling so broken.

I don't even fully register how long Mom told me I've been holed up in my room, breaking more and more every day.

"You know, Bryan would be very disappointed in you right now." She says, and this hits me in a way I didn't expect. I feel ashamed at her words, knowing deep down that she's right. "Have you looked at yourself in a mirror lately? You look horrible." Mom says sternly.

Then she sits on my bed and rubs my back. "Let me ask you something. How can you talk about the good times with people when you keep blocking them out? When you block people out, you're really blocking the memories of Bryan out too. And all you're left with are the bad ones." Mom says.

"I just don't know what to do." I say between sobs.

"You live life for him. Live for his memory. If you keep going the way you are, you are going to waste his memory." Mom tells me with such a softness to her voice that I know her words are filled with truthfulness.

When I try to get up, I realize how weak I really am. But when I look at myself in the mirror, I break down, but this time it's for my own personal hurt. My hair is greasy and sticking to my scalp. I have deep blue and almost purple bags under my eyes, and my eyes are so red it looks like my blood vessels have burst. And on top of all of that, I can tell I've lost weight.

"I'm sorry. I am so sorry." I say to myself, Mom, Bryan, and even God.

"It's gonna be alright now." Mom says, giving me a gentle hug.

After she helps me get a shower, I dry myself off as she gets me some clothes. I put them on, and we walk downstairs. I see my dad in the kitchen pulling a rack of cookies out of the oven while Cody is sitting at the island staring at the cookies that are cooling on the foil that Dad laid out on the counter and steals one when he isn't looking.

"Hey." I say to them, my voice wavering a little.

"I made this for you. I hope it makes you happy," Cody says with a big smile and then runs back to the island, so he doesn't miss another set of cookies.

The picture is scribbled with crayons of an orange flower with blotches of grass near the bottom and completed with a smiling sun shining down on it from the corner of the page.

"Thanks, Cody." I say and I ruffle his blonde hair, but he isn't looking away from Dad dolloping more batter on the cookie sheets.

Dad smiles at me, and after he puts the pan in the oven and sets the timer for eight minutes, then he walks over to hug me, and I return the embrace. "Welcome back to the world." Dad whispers in my ear with a touch of a smile in his voice.

"I'm glad I came back. I just have a lot of work to do." I say, taking a deep breath.

"You'll make it. And we won't let you dig another hole." Mom says with determination.

I look around, and I take a deep breath again. Christmas must be a few days away from the smell of cookies and scraps of wrapping paper I see on the kitchen table. "I can tell you now, I'm gonna need that."

"Well, right now let's get you some food." Mom says.

I head to the kitchen table after clearing off a spot in front of a chair, and I wait for her to bring me a steaming bowl of chicken pot pie. And for the first time in weeks, I eat.

Later that night, someone knocks on the door, and Mom answers it. It's the UPS man with a large package.

"Thank you." Mom says. "Merry Christmas, dive safe."

She walks into the kitchen with the shipping label, but she leaves the tall, yet somewhat thin brown box that would come up to my hips, by the tree in the living room.

"It's for you for Christmas, Taylor. I wonder who it's from?" Mom says with a smile.

"It doesn't say?" I ask.

"Nope."

I try to take the slip from her to see what it says, but she doesn't let me look at it. "Christmas is the day after tomorrow; you can wait." Mom says while shoving the folded paper in her pocket.

I look at the 'gift' and I wonder what it is.

Chapter 33

Taylor

"It's Christmas! Get up!" Cody yells excitedly a day later.

I roll over and look at my clock, the red font showing 7:03 AM. At least it's not six in the morning like last year. I get up and go downstairs and into the family room where I smell coffee brewing in the coffee pot along with hot chocolate in the crock pot with marshmallows in a glass bowl next to it.

We all open our gifts as a family once Mom, Dad, and I settle on the couch while Cody rushes over to the tree and excitedly rips open his gifts, which only takes about thirty minutes, and he runs off, his laughter filling the house while he plays with his new toys in his room.

"You have one more, Sweetie, Mom says with a smile.

She finally hands me the shipping label from the other night.

Ship to: Miss Taylor 'Annie' Sparks.

I cover my mouth and I look at the package, tears brimming at the corners of my eyes.

"Go ahead, open it." Mom says.

I get up and I go over to the package, opening the brown shipping box, and I see it's wrapped in Christmas paper as well. I rip the foil-type snowflake wrapping paper diagonally from corner to corner, and when

I see what's under the paper, I start to cry. This time, happy tears.

It's the painting I was giving Bryan a hard time about.

I see the tall pine trees of the forest that's behind the school. The shoulder-length grass around me, frozen in time, blowing gently in the wind, and with the sun behind me off to the right of my shoulder. This version of me has some stray hairs going across my eyes from the wind loosening them from my ponytail. And my smile shows nothing but happiness and love for the person who was watching me that day.

As I take in the brushstrokes of the painting, I remember that day like it was yesterday, and it warms my once cold, broken heart. I notice that Bryan did add some of my favorite flowers, orange wild tiger lilies, in the picture in different areas around me to give the painting a little more color.

"Oh my God, it's beautiful." I say, my voice thick with emotion.

"I think I see something on the back." Mom points out, with tears in her own eyes.

I look at her for a minute and then I take the rest of the wrapping paper off and look on the back of the canvas.

"Sorry it took so long. I hope you like it. –B"

I notice the number 12 in one corner and 18 in the other in a stamp font, but I brush them off as just being random numbers. I set the painting down next to the couch and I go to the garage to find Dad's hammer and I take a nail from the box he keeps in the tool chest and go up to my room, picking up the painting on the way, and I think for a minute about where I want to hang it.

I finally hang it next to my long-mirrored dresser where the morning sun can come in through the window and light up the sun in the painting. After I make sure it's straight, I touch the canvas, over the B.A.E initials in the corner, and close my eyes.

"It's beautiful, Babe. I just wish I could tell you for real, face to face." I whisper as tears burn my eyes.

"Taylor, can you come down here?" Mom yells from the family room.

I pull myself back together and take one last look at the painting and, for the first time in a while, I feel that Bryan is back with me, at least in spirit. When I come back downstairs, I see that we have last-minute visitors, and I smile at them as I join them by the door. Mom pats my shoulder and leaves us alone while she finishes up dinner with Dad.

"Hey, Mark, Lexi." I greet them with a soft smile.

"Hey," Mark says.

"Hey, you look good." Lexi observes with a small smile.

"I feel better than I have for a while. How about you guys?" I ask.

"About the same as you." Lexi says with sadness still on her face.

"No, you were better than I was. I almost wound up in the hospital." I admit.

"Why?" Mark asks in shock.

"I just shut down. I didn't eat much for two weeks." I say, hanging my head and looking at the floor.

"You seem to be doing better now." Lexi says.

"Yeah," I say, my voice stronger than before.

"You two want to stay for dinner?" Mom asks Mark and Lexi from the kitchen.

"Sure!" Lexi exclaims.

"Lexi!" Mark says. He obviously wanted to do something else, but Lexi waves him off.

"Lexi, who is this?" Cody asks as he comes over to us from the living room and looks up at Lexi.

Bending over at the waist, resting her palms on her knees, she says, "Hey Cody. This is my boyfriend, Mark."

"Hey, Cody," Mark says, kneeling down to Cody's height.

"Hi," Cody replies, taking in everything about Mark.

"You know, Cody, Mark was Bryan's best friend in the whole world." I say, my voice cracking with tears.

"Were you sad too when he got hurt and Mommy couldn't help him?" Cody asks, cocking his head to the side. Leave it to little kids to be that direct.

"Yes, I was Cody. But you know what? I'm gonna look for that man, and when I find him, I'm gonna put him where all the bad people go." Mark says, looking at me when he says the last part, and I see the fire burning in his eyes.

"You can do that?" Cody asks in awe.

"Yes, I can put bad people away for a long time." Mark chuckles.

Satisfied, Cody leaves the room, and I just smile at him.

"We will find them, Taylor." Lexi says with determination.

"It's dinnertime, everyone!" Dad exclaims from the kitchen table as he puts the ham in the center with macaroni and cheese, mashed potatoes with a boat full of gravy, and stuffing to finish out the meal. Mom had set the table beforehand with an elegant-looking tablecloth with holly leaves and berries printed on the fabric, and her best china that matches, the tablecloth. We all gather around and take our seats with mild chatter.

Dad is in his usual one near the window where he can see the door and look at Mom, whose back is toward the door. Cody is to the left of Mom and closer to her so she can help him cut his food and to keep an eye on him, so he doesn't break her china by accident. Then Lexi is to the right of Mom, followed by me and then Mark, which I notice is in the same chair Bryan sat in when he first met my family. I take a breath to push past the pain of my still, slowly healing broken heart, and in that moment, I make my decision. I just hope that it's not a fool's decision.

After we finish dinner, I can say I'm officially stuffed. While Mom and Dad finish with the dirty dishes, I take Mark and Lexi back into the living room and we all sit on the couch. I rest my elbows on my knees, and I look at them for a moment before I speak.

"Can you two do me a favor?" I ask.

"Sure, what is it?" Lexi asks.

"I don't know. It depends on what it is." Mark deadpans, but Lexi smacks him on the chest and gives him a look that says 'shut up.'

"I need you two to back me up when I talk to Wayne tomorrow."

"What are you going to talk to him about?" Mark asks.

"I'm going to ask him to reinstate my badge." I say with a new strength I didn't know I could pull out of me. "I'm not saying you two aren't doing the best you can, but I want to take those bastards down myself. Phil and Daryl have screwed with my life twice, and it ends *now*."

"And there is no negotiation in this, is there?" Lexi asks.

"Either way, I'm going to look for them. The badge only gives me permission to carry a gun legally."

"I'll take that as a no," Mark pipes in.

"So, will you two help me?" I ask.

"You lead, I'll follow." Lexi says with a sly smile. We both look at Mark. "He'll do it." Lexi says with a smile on her face.

"Alexis! I can answer for myself." Mark says with a little humor in his voice.

"Yes, Taylor, I will also help you in any way that I can. If I have to, I will even forge Wayne's name to help you." Mark says.

"No, you wouldn't." I snort.

"Yes, I would. If it meant giving Bryan and his parents justice, I would do anything short of selling my soul," Mark says sincerely.

I look at him, and I've never heard of Mark lying. And I feel that I can take what he says for face value.

Chapter 34

Taylor

"**I** know what you're going to do." Mom says as she comes into the living room right after Mark and Lexi leave.

"What?" I ask, trying not to let my face give anything away.

"You're going to go and talk to Wayne about getting your badge back."

"How did you know?" I'm shocked that she figured it out.

"Because I know my daughter, and when you took those two aside, I kinda listened in. Oh, and you don't get that mouth from me," Mom says while pointing her finger at me.

"Are you going to tell me no?" I ask, looking at her in the eye. Hoping she understands where I am coming from.

"I try to put myself in your shoes. If your father was like Bryan and I had the chance to go after those assholes, I would do the same thing. Just be careful and think wisely." Mom says while caressing the right side of my face and giving me an understanding smile.

"Thanks, Mom. And I do get my mouth from you. I get everything that makes me who I am from you." I say and I give her a small smile.

"I know. Try to sleep well so you can get those sorry excuses for men," Mom says while giving me a hug.

"I will. Night, Mom." I say with a renewed confidence in my soul.

"Night, sweetheart." Mom says.

***

I get up the next morning and I get dressed in a pair of black leggings and a red long-sleeve shirt. I see Mom and Dad sitting at the island waiting for me to come down. When Dad sees me coming down the stairs, he meets me at the bottom step.

"Your mother told me what you are going to do. While I do not like you back in that life, Taylor, I understand, Honey. Just be careful." Dad says, his voice tight with emotion.

"Thank you, Dad, and I will. I have to stop them for good this time."

I grab my keys off the hook by the garage door, get in my Focus and I drive down to the FBI Agency for the first time in almost two years. I never thought I would be walking back through these doors again, but here I am. The large brick building with albeit bulletproof glass windows looms over me as if trying to be intimidating. Trying to say that I can't handle what cases flow through these halls. I take a deep breath and I think, *'bring 'em on'*. I get out of my car and walk towards the door with determination burning in my soul as I enter the agency.

"Taylor, over here!" Lexi says as she meets me inside the building, near the main staircase.

Her hair is in a high ponytail, and she has on light-wash jeans and a pale purple top, completing her look.

"Hey. What's going on?" I ask.

"Wayne is in a meeting. It should be over soon." Mark says while walking down the stairs.

His dark blue jeans with a black and white baseball-style shirt instantly makes me think that would have been something Bryan would have worn.

"Oh." I say, shaking the image from my head and looking toward the large, black wooden door that leads to Wayne's office, which is currently closed. "By the way, Mom overheard us last night."

"She did, and you were able to come here?" Lexi asks in shock.

"She and Dad gave me their blessing and said good luck."

"Your parents are cool." Mark says. "Yeah, they are." I grin.

After a few minutes, we finally see Wayne's door open up to invite us in. We all walk up the long cream-colored marble staircase, and I knock on the doorjamb to announce my presence. I see a man sitting behind an overly large oak desk. Gray metal filing cabinets line the walls behind him. I notice there are a few newspaper clippings in black metal frames on high-profile cases that he was able to solve in his younger days in the agency.

W. Anderson and T. Huntington find missing daughter of the Vice President.

W. Anderson and L. Chamberlain bust local trafficking ring.

His office has not changed at all in almost two years since I was here last. My eyes finally land on Wayne himself. He's in a heathered gray three-piece suit, which compliments his dark skin. His short hair is still the dark brown that I remember, and he is also still muscular with a touch of plump belly that can be seen through his suit.

"Taylor! Come in, have a seat!" Wayne beams when he sees me. "Long time no see."

We go in and Lexi and I sit down in his simple black leather office chairs. The material groans a bit when we sit down, while Mark stands near the door jamb leaning against it with his hands in his pockets.

"So, what brings you in today?" Wayne asks as he folds his large hands in front of him.

"I would like to have my badge and my gun reinstated." I say just getting right into the reason for my visit.

"For what?" Wayne asks. "Is this about catching Bryan's murderer?"

"I'm not saying that whoever you have working the case isn't doing the best they can, but Daryl Grove has hurt me twice, and so has Phil. And honestly, I would like to bring them down myself." I say with determination burning over every inch of my body.

Wayne is silent for a moment as he looks me over. "And you brought Mark and Alexis to vouch for you?"

"Yes, sir." I say.

"Taylor, I'm usually 1 pretty good judge of character." Wayne says. "But I don't like to put people on the front lines that have a personal stake in a case. I would have to say no; I can't do that for you."

My stomach drops, and I get up from my chair to walk out without another word, but I stop in my tracks when I see Wayne turn around his chair and walk over to one of the large filing cabinets, the metal creaking as he pulls open the drawer.

"But I know you, and by me telling you no would put more stress on the FBI than I'm willing to take right now." He says while pulling a piece of paper out of the drawer then slams it shut. "If you could sign here, I will have your gun brought to you before you leave." Wayne says as he puts a paper in front of me and points to the area for me to sign. "Do you still shoot as well as you did?" He asks with a smile.

For the first time since Bryan's death, I give a genuine smile that lights up my whole face. "Yes, like Annie Oakley."

Chapter 35

Taylor

"Great," Wayne says with a chuckle. He hands me a badge and picks up his phone to call for my gun. "And do you want Alexis as your partner again?" Wayne asks as he takes the paper back from me to fill in my partner request.

"And also, Mark." I say.

"Alright, good luck, and stay safe." Wayne says as he grabs a stamper, and I see the APPROVED in green ink left behind.

My gun is brought up by a short-haired woman in a pencil skirt and a white top, and I take it over with pride.

"Watch out, Daryl and Phil, your time will come, and I will find you. And if it comes to it, I will kill you." I say to myself.

"Thank you, Wayne, I appreciate this more than you know." I say while walking out of his office with Lexi and Mark on my heels.

"So now that you have your badge back, where do we start?" Lexi asks as we walk down the steps.

"How many files do we have on Daryl? I know we won't have any on Phil." I ask them both.

"Just the two, ours and Bryan's," Lexi says. "Why?"

"I wanted to know if he went back to the same crime scenes." I say.

"Between our case and when he killed Bryan's parents."

"I would say yes. I mean, from the files, it was the same warehouse where his deals went down. The same one that you followed Lexi to when she figured it out too," Mark says.

"I was pretty sure that was the case too because found two skeletons in the room I was in. They were Bryan's parents."

"Wait, what?" Mark asks, stopping us as we get to the bottom step. "Bryan's parents were killed at home. Why would a set of skeletons be in there?"

"Probably to scare me then." I scoff. "I say one thing is to keep an eye on the warehouse for any activity. Agreed?"

Mark and Lexi nod their heads.

"And depending on how far the closest building is I may be able to put up cameras looking at the warehouse, and we will know when they leave and when they come back." Mark says.

"Perfect; hopefully, we will catch them soon." I say.

"I'll start looking into the buildings." Mark says.

We split our ways Mark goes to look at the buildings, and Lexi and I decide to go and do research on our dastardly duo.

After hours of doing research, I am coming up with nothing new. I suddenly remember John and Gail and I haven't been over to see them since that night. So, I drive over without much thought, but when I pull up to the curb, I realize again with perfect clarity that Bryan won't be there. I take a cleansing breath and walk up to the door and knock. John is the one that answers and lets me in with a soft smile.

"Oh, Taylor, Honey," Gail says with tears in her eyes as soon as she sees me. "How have you been, Dearie?"

"I've been better." I say with a sigh. "I am going to find Phil and Daryl and bring them in." I say with renewed determination.

"How do you plan on that?" John asks gruffly.

I smile and show them my badge. "The same way I did the first time. Undercover agent mode." I say as a small joke.

"I believe in you, Taylor. Just don't do anything too hastily." John says with a hard edge to his tone, but I know he means well. I nod and smile at them.

"I won't."

I look toward the stairs and remember the first time I walked up those very carpeted steps.

"It's still made up if you want to go up, Dearie." Gail says.

I look at her for a moment and then give her a tearful nod of appreciation. I walk up the stairs and I find myself in front of his door. I pick up on just the barest hint of his cologne lingering in the air. I open his door and I can tell Gail left it just as Bryan did. A room frozen in time.

His bed is unmade to one side, but that's the only thing out of place. His paintings are still on the walls, and I walk over to one of a purple rose suspended in a black background. I run my finger over his initials; the paint giving each letter, B.A.E. a different texture. A silent tear slides down my cheek, and I take one more look around the room, and I spot a picture of him and Mark on the desk by the window.

This must have been when they were younger, about thirteen. They each have a fishing pole in their hands and smiles brightening their face.

Live for his memory. I tell myself.

I pull myself together and meet John and Gail in the living room and say my goodbyes to them.

Chapter 36

Taylor

Saturday, February 11th.

It has been a solid two months since I got my badge back, and we have seen absolutely no sign of Phil or Daryl. Mark, Lexi, and I are all in my room with the afternoon sun shining in my window. Mark and Lexi, with various laptops open, looking at live feeds of traffic in random locations. The cameras that Mark put up are working and aren't being jammed.

I did find out that not long after that night, Phil's and Daryl's bank accounts were emptied of all funds and closed. I found Phil's car and motorcycle in an abandoned warehouse back in Fillmore, and as far as the DMV system says, Daryl never had a vehicle in his name, so no luck there.

Mark has been trying to monitor the traffic cameras to see if anything comes up on the facial recognition system, but nothing has come up. So, where the hell are they?

"Something's off. They're waiting on something. I've never seen anyone hide this long." Mark says, looking up from his computer that he has set up on my desk. "I mean, come on, no activity in bank accounts since December. Nothing on the traffic cameras at all. I've been keeping an eye on the warehouse here, but I'm only seeing this one guy coming and going. Probably just a squatter holing up there." He says, getting angrier and more annoyed as he ticks off where we have been looking.

"I've been keeping tabs back in Fillmore still too, and I haven't seen anything there either." Lexi says while closing her own laptop and lying back on my bed. "I was thinking maybe they needed more cash soon and was trying to sell some Intel to the mafia overseas again."

I pace back and forth in my room while they watch me. "What do you think they are waiting for?"

"I don't know." Lexi says in exasperation.

"Maybe they're waiting for me." I say.

"Maybe," Lexi replies.

"What about letting them kidnap me again?" I say quickly.

"I won't let that happen, no way. Out of the question." Mark says sternly.

"Well, I'm gonna ride around. Maybe I'll find something to flush them out." I say.

"Okay," Mark says with a sigh.

"Be careful." Lexi pleads.

I drive around aimlessly and I wind up in front of the warehouse. Maybe they know the cameras are out there, and they are staying inside. I pick up my phone and call Mark, who answers on the third ring.

"Yo."

"Hey Mark, have you seen the same person on the cameras around the same time? I remember you saying you saw a guy coming and going, but he didn't match Phil or Daryl's stature." I ask.

We are silent for a few minutes when Mark takes in a deep, fast breath. "Oh my god, that piece of shit has been in the warehouse this whole damn time. They have had that guy bring them food. Where are you?" Mark asks with a sharpness in his voice, angry that he didn't see it sooner.

"I'm outside of the warehouse, and the delivery man just left." I say with venom in my voice.

"Stay put. We're coming." Mark orders.

"No, I'm going in. Make sure you call this in and get emergency teams up here." I hang up before he can say anything else to try and stop me.

I get out of my car, hiding my gun in the waistband of my pants at the small of my back. My heart is beating so hard in my chest that I'm afraid that it will give me away. I start to walk up the stairs, the same stairs that Bryan fell down that night two months ago. I start to have a flashback of that night, but I pull myself together and push through. I refuse to let that happen here.

Once I'm at the door, I pull my gun out, rack the chamber back and take a cleansing breath. I try the handle, and it gives easily. I slide the door open with a slow metallic creak, and I step inside, but I don't see anyone right away. I get ready to round the same corner that led to what was once my dungeon when the hairs on the back of my neck stand on end. An apparent sixth sense telling me of trouble.

I see a pebble on the ground, and I decide to kick it with my shoe to make it seem that I am closer than I am. Just like I thought would happen, a long and spindly hand pops out to try and grab me by what would have been my throat.

"Come out and face me, you sick piece of shit." I say with every ounce of venom I can put into my voice, my gun pointed forward.

"Very strong words for....a little girl." Phil says.

"I could think of stronger words if you like." I counter.

"You know how much jail time you could get for mouthing off to an agent?" Phil asks, like he's scolding a little kid.

"If I was a citizen, I *might* worry." I scoff. "But since I'm an agent right now, I don't really think jail time will worry me. Oh, and by the way, when I hand you over to the Agency, I will tell them about the deaths of three agents and the attempted murder of two. That's five counts against you and Daryl."

I feel something move behind me, and I take a guess that it's Daryl, plus by the smirk that just spread itself across Phil's face it's a safe guess.

"If you shoot me, I shoot him. So, I suggest you get in front of me where I can see you. Plus, if you want to try and kill me, I want to face my killer, not be shot from behind." I say, my voice still tight with anger.

"You better not move!" Phil yells.

"If you don't, I'll shoot." I snap.

I win.

Daryl moves into my line of sight, and Phil gives him a dirty look, but now I have them both in front of me.

"If you're going to kill us, get it over with." Phil says, sounding bored.

"No. Killing you would be too easy. I want the both of you to suffer for as long as you can live." I growl.

"You know I'll get someone to get us out. I always do." Phil says in a low, threatening voice.

"No, you won't. Because I will spread the word that you *are* dead. And I will make sure you have absolutely no contact with the outside world."

"You can't do that. All agent sentences go through Wayne, and he won't believe you," Phil says.

"You wanna bet? How do you think I got this gun?" I ask, barking a laugh.

I hear what sounds like two car doors shutting and I take my eyes off the men for a split second to look toward the sound and Phil takes that opportunity to shove me down to the ground and knocks my gun out of my hand drawing his own to aim at the door behind me. Everything that happens next seems to happen in slow motion.

I see Lexi in the doorway, and I scramble to my feet and I run toward her. I reach out with my left arm to push her out of the line of fire when I hear Phil's gun go off. The next thing I feel is a searing hot pain in my left forearm. I grab at my arm, and I see the through-and-through wound, blood streaming down my fingers.

Out of the corner of my eye, I see my gun on the floor a few feet over, and I lunge for it, rolling with the momentum of my movement. I hear more gunfire around me, but I'm not sure where it's coming from. I finally get my gun in my right hand and turn over and aim it in front of me and I see Daryl standing there at the end of my barrel.

I feel a new fury at the memory of his gun being the one to end Bryan's life, and I squeeze my own trigger, hitting him in his left side, but I instantly know it's a graze and no real damage was done. I see Phil and Mark having a shootout, but when my shot rings through the warehouse, Phil runs out of my line of sight with Daryl following suit. I try to get up to run after them, but the world around me tilts violently, and I don't even remember dropping my gun.

The next thing I know is Lexi is wrapping her jacket around my forearm, and I see my mom walk through the warehouse door before things stop spinning around me and darkness takes my vision.

Chapter 37

Taylor

"Can you tell how bad it is?" Mom asks Lexi since her jacket is covering my injury.

Mom's voice cuts through the darkness, and I open my eyes, blinking a few times to focus on her.

"It went—all the way—through." I grind out, my voice taught with pain.

"Can you walk?" Mom asks.

I try to get up, but my head spins again from the blood loss and the pain. When I go to grab my head with my right hand, I feel a pair of arms wrap around me and pick me up off the ground.

"I'll carry her out to the ambulance." Mark says.

"Okay. Taylor, make sure you hold your arm tightly." Mom orders.

I feel Mark tighten his arms around me, and I bring my arm closer to my chest and hold Lexi's jacket against it to try and slow the bleeding. I hear the doors to the ambulance open, and I feel Mark take a step up to get in the vehicle.

"Taylor?" Mark says, laying me on the gurney and holding my right hand for a moment. "We will take care of Phil and Daryl, and then we will be at the hospital. Okay?" Mark says with a touch of fear in his dark eyes.

"Okay. Be careful." I tell him weakly.

"I will." Mark says.

Mom gets in the back once Mark leaves. He shuts the door, and I hear him hit the back twice, signaling the driver to move. I barely feel when Mom sticks an IV line in my right arm.

"You're gonna be alright, Sweetie." Mom says while trying to hold her emotions in check. I give her a weak smile, and we barely start to move before the world around me goes black.

***

I'm woken up by a faint beeping sound, but for a few minutes, I cannot figure out what the sound is coming from. I open my eyes, and I see ceiling panels with little black dots on the tiles, and then it clicks in my mind. A heart machine.

I'm in the hospital.

"Hello again, sweetheart. Welcome back." Mom says gently.

"I'm glad to be back." I whisper, my throat dry and painful.

My arm starts to hurt, and I lift it into my view.

"They did a bone graft, so the doctor put a cast on your arm to mold the graft. So, it should be taken off after a couple of days." Mom says.

"Has Lexi and Mark been here yet?" I ask, my mind clearing some, and the memories come flooding back.

"I think they went to the cafeteria. I'll call them." Mom says.

"K." I say.

"Do you want me to get you anything?" Mom asks.

I shake my head no. After she leaves, I feel myself start to doze off again, and I am woken up a few minutes later when Lexi and Mark walk in.

"Hey tiger, how ya doin'?" Mark asks with relief in his eyes at seeing me awake.

"Better."

"Nice cast." Lexi says, pointing to the pink cast on my arm.

"It's only going to be on for a week. You can sign it if you want."

"Cool." Lexi says as she picks up a marker off my bedside table.

Both Lexi and Mark sign it. And I do too. I saved lives again, so I think I deserve to sign my own cast.

"Do you know how long you'll be in here?" Lexi asks.

"No, I'm guessing about a week or two, but it really depends on if I get an infection or not." I say. "Has Wayne been here?"

"No. Not yet. What were you going to talk to Wayne about?" Mark asks.

"I was going to tell him what I think should be the sentence for Phil and Daryl." I explain.

"Tell us," Mark says.

"I was going to tell him that they should have no contact at all with the outside world. Not even with guards. And they should have a robot deliver any meals they will get. And it should be posted in every place they can think of saying they are both dead." I say.

"Wow." Lexi says.

"I definitely don't want to get on your bad side," Mark says. "But I couldn't have said it better."

"Wayne said he might come by and talk with you in a bit," Lexi says.

I nod my head, but I feel myself wanting to drift off again.

"We gotta jet; we'll see you later." Mark says.

Lexi and I hug, and I lightly shake Mark's hand. "Come back soon." I say.

"Count on it." Lexi says. And Mark smiles at me.

A few minutes later, Mom comes back in my room. "I like that sentence you told Mark and Lexi about," Mom says.

"You always listening in on my conversations?" I ask jokingly. "Thanks. At least I may be able to make good on my threat."

"And just so we are on the same page, Mark is an agent too, right?" Mom asks while pointing to the door.

"Yes. He was Bryan's partner. And in all honesty, partner in crime too. If you seen Mark doing something that was dangerous, Bryan was there too." I say, smiling while I fiddle my blanket with my right hand.

"But if Bryan was here, they would have a third wheel, wouldn't they?" Mom asks, but her look tells me she already knows the answer. She knows me too well. So, I smile at her. "I thought so," Mom says.

"But Lexi would be there too. I bet when Mark was here, she was going crazy in Cali not being here with him." I say.

"True. I guess I raised a daredevil." Mom says.

"Unfortunately, you did." I smile.

A nurse pops her head in. "Kathy, 525 is roughhousing with his visitor again."

"I gotta go. I'll see you later." Mom says with a bit of annoyance in her voice. "Hey, 525! Didn't I tell you to settle down?!" Mom yells as she walks out of my room.

I don't pay attention to the voices that are echoing in the hall as the exhaustion takes my mind again. I close my eyes and I try to take a nap.

Chapter 38

Taylor

A few days later, the doctor comes in early that morning to check on me while he pulls up the X-ray that was taken a little while ago on his tablet computer.

"You're healing nicely, Agent Sparks. I think the cast can come off a little early. We will put a splint on and clean it daily." The doctor says to me. He then turns his attention to Mom. "Kathy, could you take the cast off and put ointment on her wound and let it get some air, then splint her arm later?"

"Yes, Doctor." Mom says. "See, I told you. Let me get the saw, and I'll be right back," Mom tells me when the doctor is out of the room.

It's still weird to have the word 'agent' in front of my last name. I never would have thought that I would be back in this role, but it somehow feels right for me. It feels like home in a weird way.

Mom comes back with the cast saw and cuts off the cast, and I see my injury for the first time. It's a bright angry red color, and the black stitches make it look even redder. Mom then puts ointment on my arm and lets it air out for a little bit.

"Now, I would like for you to do me a favor. Could you look at these charts and help me out?" Mom asks while setting some patient files on my bedside table.

"I don't think I can handle work." I say, feigning passing out.

"You can manage." Mom says with a smile. She throws a pair of green scrubs at me. "I thought you would like to have a little more clothing as well."

"Kathy?" The same nurse from yesterday pops her head in sounding annoyed at a patient.

"525?" Mom asks without even looking.

She nods her head, and Mom rolls her eyes.

"Who is this 525 person?" I ask.

"Can't say. Everyone's identity is confidential." Mom says. "But you might find it pleasing." She adds with a smile and a wink.

I realize that I am on the floor for the Secret Service personnel. And I remember that I actually fit in on this floor. It seems that this 525 guy is feeling a lot better, so that's a good thing.

"Take him for a walk." Mom says as she's walking out of the room and waves a hand toward the door down the hall.

I shrug her annoyed demeanor off and I pull my covers back so I can get out of bed and change in the bathroom, which is still a little difficult because of my arm. It still hurts to close my hand, but I manage it. It feels good to be covered up all the way and not have my backside open for all to see.

I get back to my bed, sitting on the side as I pull the bedside table in front of me, and I start looking through the charts to make sure all medication labels are there and that the notes make sense. I'm in room 502, so 525 is the last room on this side of the wall.

501 is a man from the CIA who was shot in the leg. 505 is a woman from the DEA; she broke her leg while in a foot chase. 506 through 510

are from the FBI. One with another gunshot wound, one with a stab wound in the thigh, one with pneumonia, and the last one with a broken arm.

Finally, an hour later, after I make sure they are caught up on all medications, I see the file for the rambunctious 525 and I read through his file. Gunshot wound to the left side of the chest. But unlike all the other charts, I see his name and my heart both leaps with joy and constricts with sorrow and confusion.

"Bryan Evans." I whisper with a question in my tone.

I look at my doorway, my throat tight with emotion and tears. I get out of bed, open the door and I look down the hall. I see the number over the door and I blink back more tears.

No, he died that night. I know he did. It's probably another Bryan Evans with the same wound. All SS people can get the same wound. I think to myself, but I take a step out of my room before I really comprehend what I am doing. *But nothing ventured, nothing gained.*

I slowly walk toward the room, my breath catching when I stand near the doorway. I take a deep stabilizing breath, and I nudge the partially open door with my right hand. I am instantly hit with the smell that reminds me of Bryan. Not his cologne but his bath soap. Pine needles and citrus.

I walk over to the unmade bed and run my hand over the sheets. The material is just starting to get cold from the absence of a warm body.

No. It's not him. It can't be. It's someone with the same name, the same injury, the same bath soap. I know he died that night under my fingers.

I feel the hairs on the back of my neck stand up, and just as I am about to turn around, I hear the one name that warms me to the core and the only voice that I had longed to hear these past three months.

"Annie?"

Chapter 39

Taylor

I turn completely around to find Bryan standing in the threshold of the doorway. The blue scrubs hang on him, showing off the muscular body that I never thought I would feel again. He looks at me with shock evident in his green eyes.

"Bryan?" I say, my voice cracking on his name. I don't notice the tears on my cheeks until Bryan is close enough to wipe them away with the pad of his thumb.

"Shhh. It's okay, Baby," Bryan whispers as he caresses my face in his right hand.

I lean into his touch and bring my hand up to cover his against my cheek. I look into his green eyes that are bright with life, and he has a slight smile playing on his lips. That's when I notice the five o'clock shadow on his face, and it makes him look hotter and more distinguished. He takes another step toward me, and I take an instinctive step back until I run into the wall.

Bryan closes the distance between us, so close no one could get a pin between us. He places his hands on either side of my head, bracing himself against the wall, and his full smile comes across his lips. He slowly edges his mouth closer to mine, and I smile as I close my eyes.

At first, when his lips touch mine, his kiss is soft, but then it's like something breaks between us and he deepens the kiss and I meet him stroke for stroke as his hands roam my body. Down my arms, across my stomach, his right hand gripping the curve of my ass. Bryan then begins to travel kisses down my jaw, and when he gets to my neck, I bend to allow him more access, and he stops when he gets to my collarbone. He pulls back enough to look into my eyes again, and I still see he has that lazy smile he gets after he kisses me.

"I thought—you died in my arms that night. Lexi and Mark told me they lost you during surgery." I say, my voice still small and quiet. Almost afraid that if I speak too loudly, he will disappear again.

Bryan closes his eyes for a moment as if trying to work past the anger from the apparent lie that I was told and then gives me a mischievous smile. "I cheated death. I knocked on its door and said, 'not today pal'." He says, trying to sound a little funny.

He then takes a breath, his tone turning serious. "I wish I could have told you that I was okay two months ago, but I didn't have any say in it. Wayne said it was best for you and for me. To stay safe." Bryan says gently with a look of sorrow in his eyes.

He runs his hand over my face again, and I close my eyes and I lean into his touch again. I'm still scared he will disappear when I open my eyes the next time.

"What happened to your arm?" Bryan asks, his tone going darker while lightly touching just below the injury that is still getting air.

I look at my arm and I look back at him, but he speaks before I can even form a thought.

"No—" Bryan starts. "He did not."

I stop him by kissing him again, and the tension that I seen building instantly evaporates from his body as he takes in the feel of my lips against his. I can tell just how badly he has wanted to be near me by the way his body towers over mine. As if to bring me into his own world to keep the both of us safe from any prying eyes.

Our first make-out session was like an introduction; this is pure desire. The way he's still caging me in against the wall. Bryan was usually so reserved in the way he touched me; it was always polite. But now, he doesn't hesitate to show me just how much his body craves mine. And I allow it. Allow him to bend me as he wants. I part my lips for him, and he growls as his tongue slips in and claims my mouth. I can't help but arch my back against the wall at the feel of him exploring me. I want him closer.

He smiles against my lips as he rolls his hips into me, making me feel just what I do to him, and the scrubs do little to hide the hardness of him against my own scrub-clad center. A small moan escapes my lips, and he swallows the sound with a low, dark laugh rumbling in his chest.

"Now that's what I call a make-out session." I say as I pull back to catch my breath.

"I'm sorry, I should have asked first. But my time here and facing the fact that I did almost die twice, I'm not holding back when it comes to you and me anymore. I want the whole damn world to know that you *are mine*. And I am going to spend my days showing you just how much I love you. I need you by my side. But know you have the power of a simple word." Bryan declares as his eyes dart back and forth to look into mine. "Say stop and I will, and the only question will be 'What can I change to be better for you?'"

"I love you, Bryan. I missed you so much." I say with tears in my eyes.

"You're not going to get rid of me anytime soon, Annie," Bryan says as his eyes travel down my arm and going dark when he sees the wound again.

I use my right hand and I touch the side of his neck and his eyes lock with mine again, "I'm okay now. Phil and Daryl are in jail."

Bryan backs up a little and he sweeps his eyes over me and smiles. I find myself blushing under his stare, and I look over toward the window and I notice his paint supplies are in the corner of his room.

"Oh, did you get my painting?" Bryan asks as he sees the direction I am looking in.

"Yes!" I say suddenly. "I absolutely loved it!" He looks at me with an expression that says he's waiting for something else from me. "What?" I ask.

"That's all you have to say about it?" Bryan chuckles.

"What else is there?" I remember the painting, and then it hits me. "12, 18. You finished it on December eighteenth!"

"Now she gets it." Bryan says as he taps the side of my temple. "I couldn't stand knowing you had no hope. So, going against Wayne's orders, I started giving Mark little things to give you. Like the book he gave you the morning after. It was the original one I gave you before, but I dated it for December first. Then I asked him to bring me the painting, and I worked on it in this room." Bryan says with a smile. "I got your mom to stamp the date on there, and Mark had a friend of his drop it off posing as a UPS driver. I waited for your mom to come back in and tell me how it went the next morning. She told me that you saw the date, but you didn't put two and two together. But you took it right up to your room to hang it up." Bryan says.

"Yeah, and I think you'll love where I put it." I say with a smile. "When are you getting out, since those two have been captured?" I ask as I toy with the collar of his blue scrub shirt between my fingers.

"I have to have one more stress test, and depending on how that goes, I'm looking at in the morning, maybe." Bryan says with his hands still on my hips. "God, I have missed you so much." He says with tears brimming in his eyes. "I finally have my Baby Girl back in my arms."

I break down and cry into his chest. I feel his arms wrap around me tightly, his own tears falling into my hair. He tugs me over to the bed, and I follow without question.

Chapter 40

Taylor

We lay on the hospital bed in his room, and I melt right back into him like he never left me three months ago.

"So how are you doing? I hear you're giving Mom and other nurses a lot of grief." I say as I fiddle with the fingers of his right hand.

"Your mom knows I'm just picking. That's why they always yell for her. That, and I am getting restless." Bryan says. "But I will tell you I did have a nasty infection, but I got over that about a little over a month and a half ago. But what about you? What happened?" He asks while pointing to my arm. "No one even told me that you were in here."

"Once I got over my depression, which I will tell you was horrible." I say with shame evident in my voice.

"Your mom told me about it." Bryan says softly while playing with a piece of my hair.

"Well, when I got over that, I went to Wayne and asked for my badge to be reinstated." I say with confidence back in my voice.

"No way! You got your badge back?" Bryan asks in shock.

"It was still my temp but, yes. Lexi, Mark, and I looked for Phil and Daryl for a solid two months." I groan.

"Mark didn't say anything to me about this," Bryan says, sounding a little annoyed.

"He probably didn't want you to worry."

"Probably, but I am still going to call him out on it." Bryan says.

"But like I said, we were able to finally catch Phil and Daryl, but Mark and Lexi made the arrests. I was taken to E.R. soon after as I was shot."

"So, if I get my badge reinstated, would you get a real one?" Bryan asks while playing with the fingers of my left hand, being careful not to move them too much to pull my wound.

"I don't know. I think I'm done with the Agency." I say. "But if you want yours back, don't let me stop you." I add quickly.

"I'm not gonna make you do anything you don't want. I was just asking."

"Well, for right now let's just worry about getting home. Then we can talk about the future." I say.

"Sounds like a plan." Bryan says with a smile.

He wraps his right arm around my shoulders, pulling me closer to him. I grab his left hand and pull it against my chest just under my chin, and I lean my head against his chest. I swell with happiness as I hear my strong heartbeat again thumping against his rib cage. I thought I would never hear this sound again.

"I have missed you so much." I whisper.

"So have I," Bryan says just as softly in my ear.

We hear a small knock on the door, and we look toward the doorway, and I see Mom with a smile on her face at the two of us together again.

"I'm glad the two of you are back together, but I have Bryan's test here." Mom says as she's holding a syringe in her right hand and pulling in the ultrasound machine behind her.

I feel Bryan take a deep breath, and he reluctantly releases me from his embrace.

"Do you want me to come back? I know this is a difficult test." I ask Bryan while pushing his hair back from his eyes, just now noticing it's a little longer than the last time I saw him.

"No. I want you to stay," Bryan says, holding my hand. "I am never letting you out of my sight again." He says, his tone going on the sultry side.

I feel the heat of embarrassment flood my cheeks, especially since he said it that way in front of Mom, but she doesn't call him out on it. He sits up enough to take his scrub shirt off and lies back on the bed. I notice he's a little softer than he was before. Again, my medical side kicking in to notice the small things. I attribute the loss of muscle mass is due to not being able to work out like he used to, and the infection he said he had probably had a play in it as well.

I also notice the small white gauzy bandage on the left side of his chest, and I know it hides what I thought to be the killing wound from my sight. Mom pulls his left arm toward her and cleans off the IV line with an alcohol wipe before injecting a needle filled with clear liquid into his vein. That strikes me as a little weird. She usually fills the needle in front of the patient. But I brush it off. Maybe she filled it before she came in.

I feel Bryan squeeze my hand as the drug takes effect, making his heart beat faster. Mom then pulls the ultrasound machine closer to his bed. Grabbing the tube of jelly, she squeezes a dollop onto his chest and takes the wand around to look at his heart. I see the blue and red coloring light up as she switches into that mode to look at the blood flow and wait for her to finish, all the while interlacing my fingers with Bryan's and running my thumb over his knuckles to keep him calm.

"You're looking good, Bryan. You look to be all healed up. I see no leaks." Mom says with relief.

She hooks up the bag of saline that's hanging from a pole behind Bryan's bed, and she opens the IV line to full drip to flush the medicine out and gives him a Coke to drink. After a few seconds, she looks at the heart monitor, and I see her lips form a tight line.

"This usually doesn't last this long." Mom says flatly.

"What's wrong?" I ask, looking from Mom to Bryan.

He has started breathing faster to cope with his racing heart, and he's holding my hand tighter. For the first time since I've been with him, I see fear in his face, and it breaks my heart.

"It will be alright." I say. I look at Mom, and she just looks at me with a worried expression on her face. "Close your eyes and try to relax." I say gently to Bryan.

He closes his eyes as I have a silent conversation with Mom.

"What's wrong with him?" I ask.

She just looks from me to Bryan and to his heart machine, which is beeping rapidly in the room.

"Mom?" I urgently sign again.

"I think he was drugged. I was handed the syringe from his doctor. Or at least it looked like his doctor. I shouldn't have taken it; I usually fill them myself. I am so sorry, Taylor."

I look at Bryan and watch his face contort with pain, and he squeezes my hand again.

"What can we do?" I ask.

I will bring in another saline bag so we can keep flushing him out." Mom replies.

My cell rings suddenly. The sound becoming so loud in the small room and Bryan seemingly jumps out of his skin.

"Shhh, it's just my phone, Babe." I soothe. "Close your eyes again, relax" I pick up my phone and I answer it on the fourth ring. "Hello?"

"Taylor, where are you?" Mark says, his voice taut with stress.

"Still at the hospital, why?" I ask.

"Are you with Bryan?"

"Yes." *What's wrong?* I think to myself.

"Phil escaped." Mark says with a flare of anger in his voice.

"Hold on." I say. *"Mom, stay here, I gotta go and talk to Mark."* I sign. "Bryan, I'll be right back, okay, Baby?" I kiss his forehead and I walk out of his room before I speak again. "Alight Mark, we have an issue here. I think Phil is in the hospital because Bryan was just drugged."

"What!!" Mark yells. "Damn it!"

I can tell he must be in his Explorer and on his way to the hospital because I hear him hit the steering wheel with his fist several times before I hear him come back on the phone.

"Get here as fast as you can. I'm gonna lock the whole hospital down. You know he's still in here waiting for him and for me." I say. "He's not going to get out if I have any say in it."

I hang up and I walk over to the nurses' station down the hall a bit from Bryan's room, and I look at the charge nurse with cold fury in my eyes. "Lock down every floor now. We have a security breach."

Chapter 41

Taylor

The nurse locks this floor down and puts out an immediate code so all the other floors do the same.

"The FBI is on their way. No one leaves their floor; I don't care what the reason is." I say with a surprisingly calm yet authoritative tone.

I walk back to Bryan's room and I glance at the monitor to see if there's any improvement, but he's no better. His heart is beating erratically, and I can tell by the furrowed brows marring his face that it's taking a toll on him. I gently sit on the side of his bed and I take his hand in mine again. He opens his eyes, looks at me, and smiles weakly.

"Everything's gonna be okay." I tell him.

Mom touches my shoulder and says, "I have to look at my other patients. But I'll be back." She adds in sign language, *"You have to tell him. And tell him whatever Mark told you; I know the hospital is on lockdown."*

I nod my head as she leaves. I look back at Bryan, and I take a deep breath. "Babe. I need to tell you something." I lean down, and I touch my forehead to his. "Babe....you were... drugged."

He opens his eyes, and I hear the monitor beeping faster. "What?" Bryan whispers.

I close my eyes and tell him the rest. "And I think Phil is here." I say.

"Phil... drugged me?" Bryan asks.

"I think so. He posed as a doctor and handed Mom the syringe for your test. But she has your IV back in to flush your system out."

After a few minutes of sitting in silence, the swift beeping of the heart monitor is the only noise that fills the room.

"Babe, please turn that sound off." He says with annoyance and frustration.

"Sure." I get up and I turn the sound to mute, but knowing it will still go off if it needed to makes my chest tighten with worry.

"Thanks." Bryan sighs.

"You're welcome." I say as I run my fingers through his hair trying to get him to relax.

I put my hand on his chest but I quickly snap it back to my own. I can feel his heart beating violently through the wall of his chest. I close my eyes in an effort to stop myself from imagining what he's feeling right now.

"Am I.... gonna... die?" Bryan whispers with fear in his voice.

"No. If you made it through a gunshot, you should make it through this."

I place my hand on his shoulder as he closes his eyes again. I can't tell him that he might. I can't say it myself. I found him after three months, and I can't think about losing him again, this time for good. Mom comes back around and looks at the monitor and gives me a look. That look says she doesn't like the way he's not responding to the IV fluids.

"I thought you would like to have this." She says, handing me my gun.

"Thanks," I say.

Just as she's about to leave, I see Mark and Lexi walk up to the doorway. I put my finger to my mouth and look at Bryan. They nod and walk in, but I can see the fear in their eyes.

"Taylor?" Is all that Lexi says before I cut her off.

"So far, I haven't seen him."

"Is he... dead?" Mark signs.

"No, Mark, I'm... not dead yet, you asshole," Bryan says, cracking an eye open.

"Just asking, man." Mark says while putting his hands up in surrender.

I scoot up closer to Bryan's bed, and I take one arm and keep it out of his line of sight.

"I can't lose him again. He has been like this for at least an hour. I'm scared he won't last much longer." Lexi comes over and takes my hand.

"He's strong. We have to believe he'll make it." I fight back my tears, and I nod my head at her words.

"We better make another sweep. We'll drop back by in a little while," Mark says, his tone turning serious as he and Lexi walk out the door.

I stay where I am near Bryan's bed, gently stroking the little bit of stubble that's on his face. Then, I run my fingers through his hair, and I kiss him every few minutes. I don't want to stop touching him. If I keep touching him, then I know he's still with me. He's still alive. Suddenly that sixth sense of mine goes on full alert. I feel the hairs on the back of my neck rise, and I make myself look in the doorway.

"How sweet. You better get every last second, 'cause once I'm finished with him, I'm coming after you," Phil says with venom in his voice.

Bryan's eyes snap open and flick toward the door at Phil's words. I feel his body tense up under my own, preparing for a fight.

I take his head in my hands to make him look at me when I say, "Let me deal with him."

I look over my shoulder at Phil with cold fury in my eyes. I slowly stand up and take a step away from Bryan's bed as I pick up my gun off the bedside table and I aim it at him.

"You won't kill me. You don't have the guts." Phil says with unfounded victory in his voice.

"No, I won't, because killing you would be too easy. I should, for all the hell you've put us through. But I won't sink to your level." I say in a deathly calm tone.

"You mean to tell me your boyfriend is dying *again*, and you won't kill his murderer? That doesn't sound like love to me," Phil mocks.

"You wouldn't know love... if it came and... bit you in the...ass, Phil," Bryan says while fighting for his breath.

"Shut up. You're not in the position to talk." Phil snaps.

We hear a commotion outside, metal scraping against the tile floor, and then I see someone pick up a metal stool and hit Phil in the back with it. The metal ringing from the impact, and he drops to the floor with a heavy thud.

"It looked like you needed help." Mom says with triumph.

"Thanks." I say with a shaky smile.

She hands me a pair of zip ties, and I stoop down, setting my gun on the floor, and cuff Phil's arms behind his back. After I'm satisfied that Phil is secure, I hear a nurse scream from down the hall. I whip my head in that direction, and I see a group of nurses around Daryl, who is holding another nurse close to his body. His left hand holding her by the throat, while his right hand pushes a gun to her temple a few feet away.

"Where is he?!" Daryl yells, his eyes ping-ponging wildly between the four nurses around him.

The nurses just shake their head; their entire bodies vibrating with fear. I grab my gun from the floor, and I stand up in one quick motion and stride off down the hall. Not an ounce of fear in my blood, and confidence filling my body with every step. I am in my element here, just like I was when I first helped Lexi two years ago. I know I am meant to help people, but maybe not the way I thought I would through nursing.

"Hey, Daryl?!" I say, drawing his attention as I close the distance between us.

He looks at me, and I shoot him in the elbow of his left arm since that was the point that was the furthest away from the victim. He instantly lets go of the nurse with a yelp of pain at the same time I see Mark and Lexi come running up the hall. Mark runs and effortlessly tackles Daryl to the ground. He holds him there while Lexi secures the metal handcuffs on his wrists like the fluid team they are.

They both stand on either side of Daryl and pick him up easily and hand him over to Wayne, who is standing down the hall near the elevator. Satisfied that the threats are no longer a concern, I turn back and go to Bryan's room to let him know that everything is okay now, but I freeze the last few feet away from his room. I don't see Phil on the floor where I last left him unconscious, and zip-tied in front of the nurse's station.

I sprint the remaining distance toward his room, and I look toward Bryan's bed from the doorway. I see Phil on the bed, his legs straddling Bryan's stomach. Phil's back is to me, and I watch as the muscles bunch up in his shoulders as he forces his upper body deeper into the mattress, and it hits me with perfect clarity at what he's doing. He is strangling Bryan.

Without much thought, I take my gun, and I aim it at Phil. And I fire. The gunshot ringing through the small room is almost deafening. I see him instantly go ramrod straight, blood blooming against his white shirt.

I know the bullet went directly through his spine. Phil slowly slides off the bed and onto the floor, unmoving. I look at Bryan, and things click in my mind so fast it makes me dizzy with fear. His eyes are closed, his right arm is just hanging off the bed, and there is no rise and fall to his chest. My eyes then shift over his heart monitor, and my own heart plummets to my feet. The line is....straight.

Before I realize what I'm doing, I jump on top of him and start chest compressions. I must have yelled for Mom because she's there near his head, giving two quick breaths for me while I keep the compressions going.

"Come on, Bryan. Don't give up." I rasp, my voice raw with unshed tears.

We keep doing this for several minutes. I push on his chest, and Mom breathes for him. Over, and over, and over, and over. Silent tears break past my lashes, soaking my cheeks, but I can't stop. I can't give up on him. Just as Mom is in the middle of breathing for him, I see his chest rise higher than it has, and then I hear coughing come from Bryan.

I watch as Bryan's chest continues to rise and fall on its own. His shaky breaths filling the room around me. My face warms with joy, and I collapse into his chest, and I feel his arms wrap around me weakly in response.

"Thank God." I sob into the curve of his shoulder.

After a few minutes of silence, I take in the feeling of Bryan's arms around me again, the slow rise and fall of his chest against mine. I will the adrenaline to fade from my veins, but that is short-lived when I hear another gunshot ring out in the room.

Chapter 42

Taylor

I look over my shoulder, and I see my gun in Bryan's trembling right hand. Smoke still drifting off the barrel. I look in the doorway and I see Daryl clutching his stomach, blood oozing from between his fingers. Still standing, but just barely. I glance back to the gun still clutched in Bryan's shaky hand, and as he takes a steadying breath, his arm stops trembling for a heartbeat before he pulls the trigger again, hitting Daryl in the head, right between the eyes.

His body falling face forward with a sickening thud onto the linoleum floor. I slowly sit up and take the gun out of Bryan's weakening grip and lay it on the bedside table as his arm drops to the side of the bed, totally exhausted. He slowly turns his head from the doorway to look at me, and I stare back into his tired eyes. I lean in and gently rest my forehead against his, to let him know that I'm there. That I'm safe. That he's safe now.

I take his right hand in my own, lifting it up from the side of the bed, and I rest it on his bare stomach. Now that the adrenaline is finally fading from my veins, I notice his breathing is slower. I look over to his heart monitor, and the line is at last showing a normal sinus rhythm, but the stress of it along with Phil choking him has him burned out.

"Everything's okay now. Try to get some rest." I whisper as I caress his face and run my thumb over his eyes to make him close them.

"I love you." Bryan whispers.

"I love you too." I say.

I pull my hand back, and he keeps his eyes closed. He's out cold, but still alive, thankfully. When I know he's completely asleep, I get up out of his bed and I walk over to the window, resting my hands on the windowsill. I look down at my left arm, which I now feel is aching and I notice some of my stitches must have ripped at some point during all this commotion because I have dried blood going down my arm, but I don't care in the least.

I killed a man today. Yes, he deserved it, but still, I took a life. But I saved Bryan's. So why do I feel so shitty?

I feel a pair of hands on my shoulders and I spin around, fear evident in my face and ready to fight back again, but I stop myself when I see Mark and Lexi standing in front of me. I look at them for a second. The worry in Lexi's face and the hard lines in Mark's eyes and I feel hot, wet tears slide down my cheeks. Mark pulls me into his chest and holds me, pressing my face deep into his shirt.

"I heard you killed Phil," Mark says softly next to my ear. "You feel bad and don't know why, right?" I nod in his shirt, not trusting myself to speak.

"This was your first kill. But you did the right thing. You saved Bryan's life. You should be glad the right person is still alive." Mark says.

"You won't forget about killing Phil, but it may get easier." Lexi says from the other side of Mark and puts her hand on my shoulder.

"I just didn't think about it; I was worried about Bryan, and I was thinking about how I could get Phil off." I say my voice low.

"It's okay." Lexi says.

"I also heard that Bryan killed Daryl," Mark says.

"Yeah...he did." I say.

It didn't seem real at first, but now that I remember it, it's perfectly clear. After Mark and Lexi make sure I'm okay for the most part, they leave for the night. Mom comes in and notices my arm. She wordlessly cleans my wound and restitches the ones that were ripped and leaves just as wordlessly once she's finished.

After she leaves, I crawl back into the bed with Bryan and rest my head on his chest, just like I used to at home. The slow beat of his heart is comforting to hear after such a hectic and terrifying day. I close my eyes while pulling the blankets up over us and settle in as close to him as I can. I feel his arm wrap around me almost instinctively, and I immediately fall asleep beside him.

Chapter 43

Taylor

I'm brought out of my slumber the next morning when I feel a hand gently brushing my hair out of my face. I slowly open my eyes, trying to bring the room around me into focus. I then see Bryan's arm moving in and out of my vision, lovingly stroking my head, almost like he can't stop touching me now that he's awake.

"Did I wake you?" He asks.

"No," I say sleepily.

"Liar." He chuckles.

Then it hits me like a Mack truck. He's awake. I bolt upright in bed, and I look at him. His smile is back on his face, and I see his green eyes are bright and full of life. Granted, he still looks tired but a lot better than before.

"You're okay." I say with tears in my eyes.

"Yeah, thanks to you." Bryan says with a lazy grin on his face. He takes my hand, and he kisses it. "I heard from your mom about what happened. With...Phil."

"Yeah. But I was more worried about you than him." I say.

"I would have done the same thing." He pauses and looks at the doorway before speaking again. "I recall shooting Daryl, is that right?"

Bryan asks.

"Yes, you did. He must've had his gun aimed at me, and you took my gun and killed him." I explain.

"That's what I thought. I kept seeing that, but I couldn't tell if it was a dream or the real thing." Bryan says, running his hands over his face as he takes in what I just told him.

Then he looks back at me, and his eyes travel over my body, but this time there is no heat behind them. It's pure assessment of my well-being. "Are you doing okay?" He asks as he tightens his hold on my hand.

"Yeah. I just have to get my head back on straight. Killing your boyfriend's attempted murderer *and* trying to revive your boyfriend in the same instant takes a lot out of a girl." I say.

"Wait, what do you mean, *revived*?" Bryan asks with surprise in his voice.

I look at him for a second. *He doesn't know.* "You flat-lined again, but this time I was able to bring you back myself, with the help of Mom," I say.

Bryan just looks at me and then pulls me wordlessly into his chest, stroking my hair, and I hear him take a deep breath coming to terms with that bit of information.

"It's okay. You're going to be fine." I say as I trail the nail of my index finger over the skin at the base of his neck.

"You always worry about me, don't you?" Bryan asks with a bit of humor in his voice, but a touch of sadness comes through too.

"Yes. Just like you always worry about me." I counter.

He smiles and kisses my head, knowing what I said was the truth. I barely hear Bryan's low growl in his chest before I hear the light knock on the door frame, and I roll my head against his bare chest to look toward the door to see who he sees.

"Don't growl at my mother. You want her to to go the best out of three on your life?" I whisper in his ear.

Bryan chuckles, "I'm always up for a challenge, Annie." He whispers in my ear before I feel his teeth graze my ear lobe, and I feel the blush from embarrassment and desire flood my cheeks.

"Oh, good, you're both up." Mom says as she enters the room, either oblivious to our private exchange or choosing to ignore it. Which one I'll never ask her.

"I was just going to tell you two if you wanted, you could go home later. Lexi dropped off Taylor's car about an hour and a half ago. That way the two of you could be alone for a while," Mom says gently.

"Am I ready to go home?" Bryan asks with shock evident in his tone.

"Yes," Mom says confidently. "I would say rest today and then leave tonight.

Bryan looks at me, and I smile brightly at him. The anticipation of him finally coming home filling my chest to the point of pain.

"Remember, Mom wouldn't tell you something if she thought it was the wrong thing." I say.

"Okay. Let's go home." Bryan says with a smile on his face.

Chapter 44

Taylor

Later that night we walk out of the hospital in the scrubs that we are wearing, and after some insisting from me and Mom, Bryan reluctantly sits in my passenger seat, and I drive us home. The feeling of finally having Bryan back in my life and being able to lie beside him again in *our* bed again is almost overwhelming.

When I pull up to the house, I park in the garage, and I get out and go over to the passenger side as Bryan is opening the car door. I extend my hand and wait for him to take it, but he doesn't at first.

"I am helping you, mister. So, take my hand and stop being stubborn." I scold.

"Fine. I guess you're right." Bryan scoffs as he tries to hide the slight waver in his left leg when he stands up, but I don't call him out on it.

I open the garage door to the house, and we walk in. I can tell Bryan has his feet securely under him, so I let him go on ahead of me. I shut the door behind me and I lean against it as I watch Bryan slowly walk through the entryway and into the beginning of the living room. He hasn't changed much at all. His shoulders are still broad, and his walk is getting more confident with each step he takes. I push off the garage door and I walk up behind him.

He stops walking through the house when I wrap my arms around his waist. He puts his hands on my arms as I lean my head into his back, and we stay there for a few moments. Taking in one another in a familiar space. As if finally realizing that we are really back in each other's arms and that this isn't all just another dream. He pulls my arms loose and brings me around his body to face him. He holds me close to him with his hands on the small of my back, and I put my hands on his chest, and I feel the tape from the bandage crinkle under his shirt at my touch.

He grabs my hands by the wrists, stepping back just enough to separate our bodies, and he rests them on his hips, just at the top of his pants where my thumbs are already on his smooth skin. He wordlessly tugs his blue scrub shirt off by the back of the collar and tosses it to the floor. Then he curls his arms around my waist again, pulling me closer. I take in the curve of his bare shoulder, his still-defined arms, and washboard abs. My eyes finally land on the bandage on the left side of his chest. The reason that I thought he was dead for three months, hiding under the white gauze. I take my right hand and I trace the tape around the bandage, as the flashback of that night tries to drag me under.

Bryan hooks his finger under my chin to make me look at him, and he smiles. "It needs changed, anyway." With his arms still around me, I gently pull the bandage off, revealing the healing wound. It's a healthy pink color, and the stitches are almost ready to come out.

"It looks very good. You're almost back to normal." I say softly while I gently run my index finger around the wound, being careful not to touch it.

"I won't be back to normal until I've gotten a shower and I'm lying next to you." Bryan says, his voice going into that sexy timber that warms me to the core.

"Go get your shower." I say as I playfully push him toward the bathroom.

I go up to my room and I open my dresser drawer to pull out my favorite PJs, a velvety soft pink and gray checkered long-sleeve set, and put them on the sink in my bathroom. I go back to the drawer, and I pull out a pair of Bryan's favorite gray sweatpants, and I feel a bright, full smile play on my lips when I toss them on the bed for him. Taking solace that he is finally here to pick up the clothes I set out for him, unlike the jeans from three months ago.

When I get in the shower, I let the hot water beat against my back for a while. I let it wash all the events of the past three months down the drain. When I finish my shower, I feel so much lighter than I have for a while. I get dressed, and as I come out of my bathroom, I find Bryan lying in my bed, leaning against the headboard like it's the most casual thing in the world. The sight of him there again makes my chest constrict with happiness, and I feel tears prick the corner of my eyes. I quickly wipe them away as I crawl into bed and lie beside him.

"Now I feel better," Bryan says as he pulls me into his side.

"I am so glad to have you back." I whisper.

"I'm glad to be back." Bryan says, kissing the top of my head.

"Oh!" I gasp. "Did you see where I put your painting?"

Bryan's eyes scan the room, and when he finds the painting a smile spreads across his face.

"That was a good spot, Babe. The sun will come in and light it up." Bryan says.

"I put it up as soon as I unwrapped it." I say. "It is so beautiful."

"I'm glad you like it. See, if you wait, good things will come." Bryan says with humor bright in his voice.

"Yeah, like you." I say.

"Yeah, like you," Bryan says softly. "Are you sure you're doing okay, with everything that's been going on?"

"Yes. I'm fine now. I don't feel as bad as I did." I say.

I find myself looking at his scar. He takes my chin in his hand and makes me look at him. "It's just a scar now. Just a reminder of what we've been through. I'm not going anywhere, Annie," Bryan says, his green eyes searching mine as if trying to find comprehension.

"I know." I say.

I lay my head on his chest, and I run my middle finger down the center of his chest, and I listen to him breathe.

"Your mom said you were pretty bad for a few weeks. How bad were you? And please don't sugarcoat it." Bryan asks. I take a deep breath, and I let it go.

"I was pretty bad. Three weeks later, and I haven't eaten much at all, or showered, or even gotten out of this bed." I say with shame in my voice.

"You really did that, didn't you, Annie? You broke that badly," Bryan whispers with anguish in his voice.

"Yes. I know it was wrong, but at the time I didn't care. Being alone was just too much. But Mom finally pulled me out of it." I say.

"Your mom said you were having a hard time, and Wayne made the order where I couldn't even talk to you over the phone. So, she said she would snap you out of it, and I'm glad she did." Bryan says.

"I still can't believe Wayne gave me my badge back," I say, thinking back to that day in his office.

"He can tell if you are capable or not. That's how I got in so young. You know he trained me himself. The other agents were messing with me because I was the young rookie. So, I showed them what I was made of and now they look up to me," Bryan says. "I never got to tell you, but after I listened to your voicemail, I was kinda shocked, but yet I wasn't. Like I said before, it explained a lot of things about you. Like your dead-straight aim. Your confidence. You handled Phil like you have done this kind of thing for years." Bryan adds.

"I guess I am kind of good. But still, even if I don't go back, if you want your badge, don't let me stop you."

"Let's worry about that once we are fully back on our feet," Bryan says.

"Bullet, I'm serious." I say.

"Annie, so am I. We will talk about this once we have a chance to get back to normal." Bryan says. "I'm not gonna rush back into this. I wanna take my time. I might not even go back. I finished what my main goal was; to find my parents' murderers. But yes, that will be my decision."

"Okay," I say.

We hear a car door slam outside, and Bryan gets up and looks out the window and gives me a sly grin. "Your mom. So much for being left alone for a while." He chuckles.

Mom comes upstairs, taps softly on the door frame as she walks in, and sits on the bed beside Bryan.

"Now remember, you two, the rules still stand." Mom says with a tear in her eye at the two of us together again. She lays a hand on Bryan's knee and then looks at me.

"Mom, we know." I say.

"I'm just being a mother." She gives a pointed look at Bryan before she walks out.

I see Bryan trying to hide a smile and look at him with the question on the tip of my tongue. "If she sends me back to death's door, I won't be coming back. She'll make sure of that." Bryan jokes.

"I warned you in the hospital, didn't I?" I ask, pointing my finger at him. "But she won't do that. At least not without me saying otherwise first." I say with a smile, and I cup my hands on either side of his face, and I pull him in for a gentle kiss, and I feel him smile against my lips as he meets me stroke for gentle stroke.

Chapter 45

Taylor

The next morning, I wake up and find Bryan sitting shirtless on the side of the bed. Getting up on my knees, I scoot closer to him, and I wrap my arms around his torso, resting my head on his shoulder.

"Good morning. What'cha doin'?" I ask.

"Physical therapy." Bryan says as he's squeezing a metal grip strengthener in his left hand.

"Why? What's wrong?" I ask.

"The bullet messed up some nerves that go to my shoulder, and I had a hard time moving my arm the first couple of weeks." Bryan says.

I get off the bed and I stand in front of him, putting my right arm out in front of me. "Squeeze my hand."

He takes my right hand in his left and squeezes. I can tell he has strength in it when his grip almost takes me to my knees. "Well, your hand is fine. Mine, on the other hand now, may need checked," I say as I shake my hand to get the joints moving again.

He rolls his eyes, and I smile. "Now try to push my hand down." I say as I again put my hand out, palm down, and he put his hand on top. But he can't push it down.

"Try your right arm." I say.

He uses his right arm, and he pushes my hand down without an issue. "That's bad, isn't it?" Bryan asks.

"No, I don't think so. They just didn't work on your arm enough. I'm guessing they were focused on your hand to pull the trigger for shooting. And as far as the Agency goes, you'd be fine on that part. But in a hand-to-hand fight, you're dead meat." I deadpan.

"I don't plan on getting into any fights." Bryan begins. "I'm not—"

"Bryan Evans!" I exclaim, cutting him off and putting my hands on my hips. "If you really want to go back to the agency, then you need to get up off your butt and help yourself." I take a step closer to him, standing in between his legs and resting my hands on his bare shoulders. "I will help you and support you all the way. Besides you need to get back on your feet, who's going to help me out if I get into trouble?"

"Alright. What do you want me to do?" Bryan asks with a sly smile on his face, knowing he's lost this battle of will.

"We are going to build your arm back up. So, we need to start small." I say.

We go down to the kitchen, and I grab a big can of green beans as Bryan sits on the bar stool at the island.

"I thought spinach made you stronger?" Bryan says, smiling.

"Not to eat, to lift, smartass. Lift them like you're lifting a hand weight."

He takes the can and curls his arm up to his shoulder.

"Do you feel like you're struggling to lift it?" I ask.

"No, it's easy." Bryan says.

"Okay. Let's go to a five-pound weight and see how you do."

I go to the hall bathroom to get the weight out from under the sink and bring it back to the kitchen.

"Sorry about it being pink." I say apologetically.

"Gotta start somewhere, huh?" Bryan says with a shrug.

"Now take it slow. This is heavier than the green beans." I say in warning.

He slides his hand under the weight, wrapping his hand around it, and lifts it. He can lift it with minimal issues, but he can't control it when he brings it down; his hand slams into the island.

"Shit! That hurt. At least I know I have complete feeling in my arm." Bryan says as he tries to shake the pain away.

"It's okay. At least you got it up there. Now try again, but let me control the fall." I coach.

I wrap my hand around his wrist, but I make sure I don't help him lift it. I only put resistance when he brings it down. "Did you feel the difference?" I ask when his hand rests on the countertop.

"Yeah. I do."

I help him a few more times, but I start to pull back when I feel that he's starting to handle it himself until I completely take my hand away and he's lifting and lowering the weight himself.

"See, you can do it now. If you step it up, just take it easy." I say.

By the end of the day, he is up to a ten-pound weight, and I can tell he's feeling better about the therapy by the brightness in his eyes. He even plays a few rounds of tic-tac-toe with Cody while Dad is fixing dinner.

"Taylor! Come play with us!" Cody giggles as Bryan tickles him after losing a game.

"Now, boys, you need to play nice." I laugh.

Bryan turns his attention from Cody to me, grabbing me by the hand and pulling me down in between his legs, pulling my back to his chest and encircling his arms around my waist. I turn to look over my shoulder, and he has his famous lazy smile playing on his lips.

"Show me how you beat this kid. I swear he's cheating." Bryan chuckles.

"No, I'm not! You are just bad at this game!" Cody giggles again.

"It's okay Cody, Bryan is just a sore loser, is all." I laugh.

We play another few rounds and, like always, I let Cody win some, but then I do set him in his place and beat him too. Gotta teach the kid how to be a humble loser at times too.

When Bryan and I are lying in bed that night, I can tell something is on his mind.

"What's wrong?" I ask.

He takes a deep breath before he asks, "How was it so easy for you to believe I was dead?"

I take a deep breath of my own and I look at him as I trace my finger around the scar on his chest.

"Because of the way your body wasn't fighting." I say as I think back to that night. "You were on the bad side of shock. Your pupils should've been the size of your irises, but they weren't. They were tiny pinpricks, and your breathing wasn't erratic. But I think what really told me was when I put my head on your chest, and I could hear the blood gushing out of your valve with every beat of your heart." I say my throat dry.

I feel him wrap his arms tightly around me, bringing me deeper into his side, and I feel him kiss my head. "Your mom told me that they had to shock me a few times in the ambulance to bring me back." Bryan says. "And do you know what I said when I came to?"

"What?" I say, lifting my head from his chest to look him in the eye.

"'Where's Taylor?'" Bryan whispers softly.

"Tell me what happened after you were in the ambulance." I ask.

"Well, I gotta backtrack a little bit and tell you how I found you first." Bryan says in a tone that shows his cockiness, but then he takes a deep breath and tells me all of what happened when I was thinking the worst.

Chapter 46

Bryan

I put the GPS coordinates from Mark's tracking system in the navigation system on my truck, and I speed away from the apartment with Mark and Lexi close behind me. The GPS takes me to a forest about fifteen minutes from the diner. I pin the location on my phone before I hop out of my truck, not even bothering to kill the engine. Mark and Lexi meet me once I enter the tree line, and we walk toward the red dot on my phone.

"Why the hell would they take her here?" Mark asks.

"I don't ask questions with this bastard. He just better pray that she's not hurt." I growl.

We finally close in on the location on my phone, and a mixture of relief and fury builds in my chest as I pick up her watch.

"Oh shit. That's not good." Mark deadpans.

"No shit, Sherlock." I snap.

I run my hands through my hair and turn to walk back to my truck. "I'm sorry for snapping at ya, man." I tell Mark as he is again on my heels with his hand interlaced with Lexi, holding her close to him.

"I understand your thoughts right now, man. I do." Mark says as he and Lexi exchange a look, that I don't have time to unravel.

"Where else would he be?" I ask in a gentler, but still focused tone.

"He could be back at the warehouse, where he would have his meetings for intel drops." Lexi offers.

"You two go back to the apartment and see if you can run facial recognition from the traffic cameras, and I'll check out the warehouse." I say.

We go our separate ways, and I do my best to keep it together to find Taylor.

Come on, Baby Girl, please be there. Please don't let me be too late.

I pull up to the warehouse, and I silently walk up the concrete steps, and I sneak into the eerily quiet building. It's so quiet I can hear a pin drop if I listen hard enough. But I do hear what sounds like crying. I pause as I cut the first corner, willing my erratic heartbeat to slow in my chest, and I listen again to make sure I'm not hearing things. I hear the muffled sobbing again, and my heart breaks at the same time as it soars in my chest.

Taylor.

I run the last few feet down the hall I find the solid metal door, and I hear her sobs float from under the cracks. I unlock the sliding lock with a resounding metallic noise, and I shove open the door as the sight of her hits me. Sitting in the middle of the floor, her legs pulled tight to her chest, arms wrapped around her knees, deep heaving sobs wracking her slender form. She looks at me, and it takes everything in my power not to fall to my knees before her.

"Oh, Annie." I whisper, afraid my voice will break her further.

She looks back at me like she's seeing a ghost, and I smile as I kneel down to her.

"Bryan? Y-you came; how did you know?"

"Of course, I came, Annie." I say as I gently caress her face in my hand, wiping away her tears with the pad of my thumb. "I got your message, and I'm not mad. Actually, it explains a lot." I smile.

"You forgive me?" She asks in shock.

"There's nothing to forgive, Baby Girl. Now let's get out of here." I say as I pull her to her feet and we try to sneak out the door, but we are cut off by Phil and Daryl.

I'm terrified when Taylor steps in front of me to challenge Phil, but I know how this asshole works too. From my dad's notes on him, I know he talks shit and wants to play mind games. But for people that don't have the wool pulled over their eyes, he's easy to read. The beady eyes, the sweat on his brow, he knows that if we make it out of here, he's done for. I step back in front of Taylor, and she grabs my hand. I feel her sign something into my palm.

"If you can understand this, squeeze my hand." I do, and she tells me that the doorway is open, but I don't dare take my eyes off the duo in front of me.

"You get ready. Call for backup to our location."

She squeezes my hand again, and I sign one more thing to her. *"I love you."*

As Taylor takes a step away from me to run outside, I force Daryl's and Phil's eyes on me. I lunge at Daryl with my right arm pulled back ready to punch his face in, but I miss him by just a fraction of an inch. As I prepare to follow up with a left hook, he kicks me in the chest, throwing me backward through the doorway. My back slams into the metal railing that runs up the concrete steps, knocking the breath out of my lungs, and I fall to my left knee.

When I look up, Daryl takes a step in front of me, with a gun in his left hand, and I instantly know with horror filling my veins that in a single heartbeat, he will aim it at Taylor to try to shoot her in the back. I jump up, and I wrap my right hand around the barrel. Every instinct in my mind screaming at me to keep it away from my chest, but I know if I let up for an instant, he will aim for Taylor again.

I try to desperately push the barrel away, but as my adrenaline kicks into an all-time high, I feel my palm become clammy from sweat, and the barrel slips. A gunshot rings in my ears, and then a fire so hot blooms in my chest, and I instantly feel my body freeze and lock up. I feel myself falling down the concrete stairs and land face down in the dirt, but I can't move.

I don't know how much time passes before I feel hands grab at the back of my shirt to turn me over. My left arm is just dead weight as it slides uselessly across my chest and flops onto the ground.

I see Taylor take her jacket off and push it into my chest, but I don't know why. I try to push it off, but just my right arm will listen, and it's only responding halfway.

"Taylor.... no." I whisper.

She says something about going to die, but I can't make out all her words. I then remember the ring in my pocket, and I try to grab for it, but again my right hand won't listen to me. The next thing I know is I can just barely make out the blurry image of her slipping the ring on her finger.

As I hear her tell me to fight like hell, I slowly start to notice some things about my body that are not right. It takes everything in me to draw a breath, and my vision is starting to go dark on the edges. Something is wrong, but my brain can't understand what it is.

"That..." I try to say, but I can't get the air I need to talk, and my right hand will only function with broken sign language.

"That, promise, I try... to keep. But forgive...if.... I can't".

I feel Taylor stroke my hair and say something I can't quite understand, but somehow, I know it's her telling me it will be okay. I cough, and I taste the coppery tang of blood fill my mouth. Taylor disappears from my vision, and I'm forced to look up at the night sky. The dark star-flecked sky starts to fade further and further away as the darkness at the corner of my vision creeps in more and more.

"I will always love you, Bryan." I hear Taylor say.

I hear the fear and sorrow in her voice, and I finally understand what happened and what is happening to me. I can't make my eyes move from their fixed point in the sky, but I force myself to say what I can tell are my last words to her before the life fades from my body.

As a single tear falls from my left eye, I say, "Love...you" I just barely feel her lips graze my own before the darkness takes over.

Chapter 47

Bryan

I hear some kind of high-pitched noise. Almost electrical in nature, like something being discharged. I feel static prickling the skin on my bare chest, the black shirt I'm wearing cut in half and hanging on either side of my torso.

I open my eyes to a blurry, bright white light above me. I'm in a small box-like room, no... a vehicle. I hear the roar of an engine above my head. I see the small metal and plastic shelves lined with medical equipment. I slowly understand I must be in the back of an ambulance. My body is on fire, but yet numb all the same. The metallic stench of blood fills my nose along with the taste in my mouth.

I see a shadow out of the corner of my eye, and I hope that someone real is here with me as I ask weakly, feeling blood trickle out of the corner of my mouth.

"Where's Taylor?" I try to roll my head to the right, but I can't move much at all.

While my vision is still blurry, I try to focus on what looks like Kathy holding my hand.

"Taylor is safe, and she is with Mark."

She keeps telling me, but her voice is far away and sounds like it's underwater before darkness takes me once again with the perfectly clear image of Taylor in my mind.

The next thing I remember is, being rolled into the O.R. and Kathy telling me again that everything was going to be okay, while someone was putting the anesthesia mask on my face, then I'm unconscious again.

***

Mark

I pull up to the hospital and I rush inside, not bothering about the nurses that are yelling at me and asking what I'm doing there. I know where the O.R. should be, so I make my way toward that dreaded room looking for only one nurse, Kathy. I spot her just as I round the corner, the OR door swinging shut behind her as she takes off her blue paper mask.

"Kathy! How is he?" I ask as panic fills my still aching chest from Taylor's sorrow-filled punches.

"I don't know. The doctor just started." She lets out a pained sigh.

I look past her shoulder toward the solid metal doors, wishing there was a small window so I could see inside.

"I'm waiting here." I say with determination in my voice.

"No, you're not, Stone. Get out of here. Go home." A booming voice says from behind me.

I look over my shoulder and I see Wayne walk up in a black three-piece suit with a white shirt and a red tie to complete the look.

"Like hell I will." I snap.

"Agent Stone, that's not a request." Wayne warns.

"I am *not* leaving this hospital." I say, my voice cold and calm despite my racing heart. "My brother is fighting for his life, and you want me to turn my back on him? Fuck that."

"It really doesn't matter what happens to him, because no one other than the staff in this hospital will know." Wayne says.

"What the hell do you mean by that?" I ask slowly.

"Just what I said, Stone. No one, including Taylor, will know if he makes it out of surgery."

I stare at him. I always thought that Wayne was a smart guy, but right now, he's the dumbest man on the face of the earth. "That is not fair in the least, Wayne. I hope you know that." I growl.

"If I ran my agency by fairness, I would have lost a lot more good agents sooner than I have, Stone."

"This is going to kill Taylor!" I yell as I run my hands through my hair in frustration. "She's already a shell of herself."

"You two need to shut up." Kathy snaps, cutting me off. "This is not the place for arguments."

"You're right, Mrs. Sparks, my apologies. But Agent Stone." Wayne looks at me with stone-cold eyes. "Watch your tone with me."

He walks off without another word, and I slump into one of the chairs in the waiting room with my head hanging off the back, just staring up at the tiled ceiling, willing the racing thoughts in my head to slow down.

Kathy walks over to me and gently touches my shoulder. "I'm sure you'll figure something out, Mark. But first, let's get Bryan out of surgery."

***

Bryan

After what only feels like a moment in time, I begin to wake up again. This time it's like trying to wade through thick mud just to open my eyes. The smell of antiseptic, and cool clean air tickling my nose from something plastic resting on my lips. Then it all comes flooding back to me in fragments.

Taylor being kidnapped.

The warehouse.

Phil and Daryl.

Fighting with Daryl while Taylor runs to my truck.

Then the fire that exploded in my chest and seeing Taylor crying over my broken body.

I don't know how long it was after I got out of surgery, but I look over to find Kathy sitting on the right side in a chair. She has her head buried in her hands, and she's doing that little leg bob thing she does when she's stressed out. I try to get her attention, but my throat was so unbelievably dry and raw, and I barely had any strength to move my arm. She finally looks up at me, and her face brightens immediately when we lock eyes. She stands up and gently takes my hand in her own.

"Hey Bryan, it's okay, you're in the recovery room. How are you feeling?" Kathy asks gently.

"I'm alive....... that's about it," I croak out.

"You are extremely lucky to be alive." Kathy says, "Mark is in the waiting room. I'll be right back, okay?"

I nod my head and watch her walk away through the clear glass door of what I assume is the ICU floor. I must have dozed back off because when Mark knocks on the door, I jump at the sound and my chest explodes with pain. I groan, clutching my chest as he rushes to my side.

"Bryan, are you okay? You need Kathy?" Mark asks with a note of fear in his voice.

"No." I croak out. "Just you knocking on the door made me jump." I take a few breaths and will the pain to fade.

I hate Mark seeing me this way. I don't like to show weakness around anyone, but at the same time, I'm glad to have a familiar face.

"How's Taylor?" I ask after I get my breath back.

"I'm not gonna lie, man, she's a wreck. She was covered in your blood. I took her to my place so Lexi could clean her up." Mark's face drops into sadness as he says, "She broke down, dude. She was crying, and she hit me. But I didn't stop her. I figured she was in a lot more pain than her fists caused me." Mark says as he rubs at his chest.

I try to lift my right hand up to squeeze the bridge of my nose, and I realize again just how weak I truly am. "Does she know that I'm okay?" I ask.

"No, and she won't." Wayne says near the door.

I flick my eyes toward his massive form in the doorway at the sound of his voice.

"No, Wayne. I told you, you have no idea what this is doing to Taylor." Mark says before I can even think of a response.

"This is the best thing right now for the both of them. You know as well as I do that Phil and Daryl will be looking for them. Bryan can't fight back right now, and Taylor will be safer with her family and with you and Alexis being around her." Wayne says.

"Awe come on, Wayne, that is bullshit, and you know it," Mark yells.

I have never seen Mark blow his top as much as he is now, let alone argue with Wayne.

"You're lucky I'm allowing you to stay here. So again, don't push your luck with me, Agent Stone," Way says with a deathly serious tone that means business.

"I'll keep you up to date on things, but my decision is final." Wayne says. "Again, it's bad enough you know, but you wouldn't leave the damn waiting room." He says and walks out.

After a few minutes, and I know Wayne is out of earshot, I ask Mark for a favor as an idea pops in my head. "Hey, where is my truck?"

"Uh, probably at the agency in-pound. Why?" Mark asks.

I give him a sly, albeit weak, smirk. "We are going to tell Taylor subtle clues that I am alive. There is a little book in my center console with some birds on it. Bring it to me."

Mark's face turns from anger to a shit-eating grin at my defiance toward Wayne. He comes back a few hours later with the little booklet that I drew for Taylor when we first started going steady.

"Give me that pen from the bedside table," I say as I write, *We will meet again. 12/1*

"Okay. Please give this to her. Just say that you found it in my truck as they were cleaning it out."

"Sure thing, man. Do you want me to tell her anything else?" Mark asks before he leaves the room.

"No. This will have to be enough for now. But while you're out, go to my grandparents' house and get the canvass bag next to my desk. If you need help, Granny knows what I've been working on and what all paints I need."

"Okay. I'll be back tomorrow. And Bryan?"

"Yeah?"

"I am so glad that my brother is okay." Mark says his eyes bright and lined with emotion.

I can tell he's holding back tears, and the worry that has been sitting on his shoulders slowly fades. "I'm not out of the woods yet. I know that, but I'm going to get there." I say with exhaustion filling my words.

Mark smiles and leaves with a gentle whoosh of the door sliding behind him.

Kathy comes in a bit later and checks on me throughout the night. She gives me the pain medicine I need, but it only takes a little bit of the edge off. I want nothing more than to have Taylor in my arms right now, but deep down I know that Wayne is right, and this may be the best way to keep her safe. I can only hope that with little clues I can give her, she and figure out that I'm okay.

Chapter 48

Bryan

The next morning, I wake up to find Mark in my room trying to set up the paint supplies that I asked him to get the night before and failing miserably to set the easel up.

"Watching you set that up is more painful than I feel right now." I say, my voice rough from not using it and still sore from, I'm assuming, having tubes shoved down my throat from surgery.

"Hey man, give me a break. Your grandma had to help me take it down." Mark says while still messing with the easel.

"Just lean it over there in the corner. I'll set it up when I can get out of bed." I say.

"How do you feel anyway?" Mark asks with a bit of seriousness in his tone.

"Still hurting. But I try to think that the pain reminds me I'm still alive. How did Taylor react to the booklet?" I ask, trying to take my mind off of said pain.

"She looked at it but thought you finished it that day before you got shot." Mark says. "We are gonna need something more."

"And that's why I had you bring that painting. I have been working on that since October." I say with a smile.

"Oh, gotcha. You need to like stamp the back or something on when you actually finish it." Mark says.

"That's what I was thinking." I say.

I suddenly get tired, and Mark seems to notice. "I'll go and let you rest. "Mark says. "I will keep an eye on Taylor and keep her safe. I know this will go in one ear and out the other, but try to relax and don't worry too much about Taylor."

"You're right, all I heard is that you will keep an eye on her. I know I need to focus on healing, but I can't help but to worry about her. You'd be the same way if our roles were switched." I say.

"You're right. But seriously, I will keep her safe. I will take a bullet and or die to protect her for you." Mark says with determination in his eyes.

I have not seen Mark look this determined in a long time. He is usually a carefree person and jokes at everything he can, but once he gets into this, I call his 'agent mode' he's a force to be reckoned with.

That evening, Kathy comes in and does her routine checks on me and notes that I am starting to run a slight fever, of one hundred and one degrees·

"I'm sure it's nothing to worry about. But I'm going to keep a close eye on it." Kathy says. "Just try to get some rest."

"Kathy. Don't sugarcoat it." I deadpan. "Infection is trying to set it, isn't it? Is that why the pain medicine isn't working as well as it should?" I ask, pleading with her not to make things sound better than they are.

"It's a possibility. I'm going to talk to the doctor about putting you on stronger antibiotics and better pain meds." Kathy says, and she walks out the door to meet up with the doctor.

I look over to my left, where Kathy had set up my easel and painting for me, and I stare at the sketch that I have of Taylor.

I have to fight for her. I've made it this far. I need to get back to her. I say to myself over and over until I fall asleep to my internal mantra.

I start to wake up a few hours later, and I instantly notice I feel worse than before. I feel like I have a dull fire in my chest, and I'm cold even though I have two layers of blankets on.

Dammit. The infection has gotten worse. I think to myself.

I look to my right, and Kathy is working on my IV tubing in my right arm. "I'm sorry, did I wake you?" Kathy asks when she notices me looking at her.

I shake my head no and look at the bag she's hanging up. "This is your new antibiotic. Hopefully, this will make you feel better in the next two hours. If not, we are going to take you and put you in a sterile room. The less germs you are exposed to, the better right now," Kathy says.

"Okay. Thank you, Kathy." I whisper.

"But if that doesn't help in another two hours, we are going to take you back in surgery and put a drain tube in." Kathy explains.

I nod as a silent thank you for not beating around the bush and telling me like it is. Once she opens the valve on the medicine bag and I feel the cold bite of the liquid enter my arm, I doze off again.

The next time I wake up, I am in another room. I start to panic at first, thinking that maybe Phil or Daryl has found me and kidnapped me, but I make myself take in the room. The crisp smell of cleaner and everything is white, and I remember Kathy's words from earlier, that I may need to be moved to the ICU.

A few moments later, I hear the door slide open quickly as Kathy rushes into the room, the look of fear washing over her face. "I saw your heart monitor going faster, and I thought something was happening to you," Kathy says while taking a breath after realizing that I am alright.

"Sorry. I woke up and freaked a little because of the different room." I admit. "I thought that maybe Phil or Daryl got to me."

"It's okay. I should have woken you up, but you were sleeping so soundly." Kathy apologizes.

"It's okay. Don't apologize. I'm just paranoid, I guess." I realize a feel a tad better, but not very much.

"I don't blame you one bit," Kathy says, understanding where I am coming from.

She comes over and does her normal checks while she's there, and I notice her lips form a tight line. Something that I have come to know over the last few days is not a good sign. "What's wrong?" I ask.

"Your fever still is not coming down like I want it to." Kathy says.

"I do feel a tad better if that's any consolation." I say, trying to give her a smile, but I know it's only a weak, half smile.

"Okay. Just keep resting and I'll check back on you in a bit," Kathy says.

I watch as she walks out, her shoes squeaking on the floor, and just as she closes my door with a gentle whoosh, I let my eyelids fall once more.

I don't know how long I was asleep for this time, but I *know* something is drastically different. I can't open my eyes, and I can tell my breathing is labored. I feel myself sweating bullets, and my chest is on *fire*. No matter how hard I try, I cannot get my eyes to open. I hear muffled voices that I assume are coming through the door, but I can't make them out.

***

Mark

"This is ridiculous. Taylor should be here with him. He should not have to go through this alone." I say with anger in my voice.

I am looking at Bryan through the glass door and just watch him try to fight off the infection that's coursing through his body.

"He's not alone Mark; I am trying to be with him every chance I get," Kathy says, with a note of warning in her voice.

I look at Kathy and shake my head at her. "That's not what I meant. I'm sorry; I know you're trying to help him. But still, his girlfriend should be here. I usually don't go against what Wayne says, but this time he's just being fucking stupid." I say as I look back at my best friend and just feel helpless again.

"The OR is being prepped again. The surgeon is going to put a drain tube in and make sure there's nothing else going on," Kathy says.

"Okay. I'll be in the gym downstairs to blow off some steam. Please come and get me once he's out of surgery." I plead, with Kathy.

Kathy walks over and puts a hand on my shoulder. "Believe me when I say we are doing all we can to get Bryan through this. And believe me on this too, if I knew that bringing Taylor here wouldn't put them both in danger, I'd bring her in. This is not something that anyone should have to go through alone. But I think that her *not* being here is more helpful than you think. Yesterday, I caught him staring at that painting he's trying to finish for her, and he fell asleep looking at it. So, I honestly think he is fighting harder than if she was here holding his hand." Kathy says.

"I never would have thought of it that way." I reply with

understanding.

"Go and blow some steam off. I'll come get you once he's in recovery." Kathy says. As I am leaving, I watch the OR nurses go in to take Bryan, and Kathy walks in right behind them.

***

Bryan

"Bryan?"

All I can do is moan in response as I barely hear Kathy's soft voice through the pain-filled fog of my mind.

"Bryan, we are going to take you back into surgery. It's going to be okay, sweetheart." Kathy says.

I moan again and listen to the wheels turn on the hard, squeaky flooring of the hospital. After what feels like a lifetime, I feel the bed stop, and I feel hands grab at my arms and legs and pull me from my bed onto what I think is the surgery table.

Just with that motion, a fiery, hot pain rips through my chest again, and my own scream fills my ears. I barely make out a rough male voice saying, "Quickly put him under." Then everything is a black abyss.

Chapter 49

Mark

I put both of my earphones in as I tug my shirt off by the collar, pulling it over my head and tossing it to the side on the floor next to me. I quickly wrap my hands in boxers' tape and I go to town on the red punching bag hanging from a set of chains in front of me.

I imagine the faces of the people that have pissed me off over the last few hours. Phil. Daryl, and even Wayne, as my fists collide with the bag. I refuse to entertain the idea of really having to live up to my lie that I told Taylor, of him truly being dead.

As the thought starts to creep in, I throw a hard right hook into the bag to stop that dreaded thought from forming. Just as I am about to go in for a high kick, I see Kathy come up to me out of the corner of my eye, and it instantly reminds me of why I usually leave one ear-bud out, so I can hear things around me, but for once, I just wanted to be lost in the music and the feel of the bag against my knuckles.

"He made it through surgery."

With those words, I sink to my knees and interlace my fingers behind my head for a moment, and I let the tears fall. Not giving a single shit about who would see me.

"The doctor said it was a good thing that we did put that tube in because while they already had him open, the surgeon checked on Bryan's heart and there was a small stitch missing and he was seeping blood from his valve again." Kathy says. "So, that was even more of a lifesaving surgery."

"Thank God. How is he?" I ask while looking at Kathy from the floor.

"I think he'll be okay now." Kathy says. "You want to go up and sit with him for a while?"

"Yes," I say as I get to my feet and grab my shirt off the floor. "Let me get a quick shower first, then I'll be up."

"Good idea. He's still going to be in the ICU for a few days." Kathy says. "So, we need to keep things as clean as possible."

***

Bryan

As I begin to wake up from my anesthesia-induced slumber, I notice a few things about my body before I can force my eyes to open. First, the fire in my chest is gone. I don't even feel a dull ache like I did before. Then my ears pick up on the slow beep of a heart machine on my left and the soft feel of the bed under my back. The antiseptic smell of the hospital hits my nose, but another smell does, too. Almost like cologne.

I finally coax my eyes open, and I look to my right, and I see someone in a yellow paper gown asleep in the chair. After I blink a few times to help my eyes focus more, I see that it's Mark. I hear my door slide open before I can say anything to wake Mark, and Kathy walks into the room. At first, she doesn't notice that I am awake, but when I roll my head to the left to greet her, she lets out a little squeak of surprise.

"Bryan, you scared me for a second." Kathy says with a hand to her chest as if to slow her racing heart.

I smile a little and try to speak, but my throat is so dry. "Here, take a little sip of water." Kathy offers.

I take a small sip, and it feels like life water to my mending body. "That's....better." I say hoarsely.

"Hey look who's finally awake. You lazy ass, making all these nurses take care of you." Mark says with a note of mocking joy in his voice.

"Screw you....asshole." I say, trying to hide my smile.

"But seriously, you were out for a day and a half, dude." Mark says, all humor fading from his tone.

I look at him in shock and then over to Kathy, the silent question in my eyes. She goes to explain what all happened over the last twenty-eight hours, and I just stare between them as the truth sinks in.

"Talk about a lucky break." Mark says.

"No, thank God. Because without, Him, I don't think I'd have made it this far." I say.

"I absolutely agree." Kathy replies.

After another day in the ICU, I'm able to go back to my room, and I finally feel like I'm on the road to recovery. Kathy comes in for what I have come to realize are her normal morning rounds to check on her patients. She has a smile on her face at seeing me already awake.

"Hey, Bryan. You are looking so much better already." Kathy says while checking all my vitals. "Your fever has finally broken, and everything else looks good."

"Yeah, I can tell. I feel better already, and the pain is basically gone. I feel a little sting here and there." I say.

"That's good to hear," Kathy says with a smile on her face.

I look over to the art supplies in the corner of the room and I decide to rest for another day before I try to finish the painting for Taylor.

Later that night, Kathy comes in and does her usual vital checks, and she changes the bandage on my chest with a fresh one. I still have the drain tube in, and it's definitely doing its job. It's gross to look at, but I hate to think of that gunk being stuck in my body again. So, I'm glad it's on the bandage and not wreaking havoc inside.

Kathy holds up a small mirror so I can see myself better, and my eyes are immediately drawn to my wound. This is the first time I can truly see what damage was done to me that night. The wound itself is still red, and the black stitches make it a lot look worse than it feels. But then I look at my eyes; they look older and ragged, and the scruff on my face is starting to show.

For an instant, I wonder if I am the same person. I mean, someone having a near-death experience can't be the same, can they? I stare at my reflection again, and I realize I am the same person. I'm just battle-worn and scarred. I look over to the painting on the easel, and I'm still madly in love with the girl it represents, and I want to go back in the field and help society stay safe from evil people like Phil and Daryl.

"Are you okay, Bryan?" Kathy asks, noticing my silence.

"Yeah. I'm great." I say with a smile.

I find myself rubbing at the scruff on my jaw, and Kathy smiles as she walks into the bathroom and brings me a pan of water and shaving supplies. She wraps a towel around my neck to keep the cream and hair out of my wound. I don't need another infection just over shaving.

After I finish forty-five minutes later, Kathy helps me wash my hair because I still can't lift my left arm over my head without feeling like I'm pulling the stitches. Once I finally feel clean, Kathy brings me a set of blue scrubs instead of the normal hospital gown.

"Thank you. This feels so much better." I say.

"I'm sure it does. Do you want to try to get up and walk over to the chair?" Kathy asks, pointing to the one in the corner in front of the easel.

I nod as she takes my right arm and helps me to my feet. I still feel a little weaker than I like, but that should go away soon now that I'm on the mend. After being satisfied that I'm under my own feet well enough, Kathy walks me over to the easel, and I notice my fingers twitch as if itching to get into the paints and pencils again. Kathy smiles as she helps me sit down on the high-backed chair, then she wordlessly walks out of my room to leave me alone with the only version of Taylor I can have right now.

Time goes by without a second thought, and when Kathy comes back in to do her final vital check, I have been working on the painting for over three hours.

"That is beautiful, Bryan," Kathy says as she takes in the painting of Taylor.

The gentle sway of the tall weeds around her from that day. The light of the sun caressing her face and the few pieces of hair that wanted to dance over her eyes from the breeze that was in the air. All frozen in time.

"Thank you." I look at the progress I have made, and I should be able to finish it in time for Christmas, which is two weeks away and my heart swells with happiness that I can at least be with Taylor if only in spirit during what would have been our first holiday together.

Chapter 50

Bryan

My door swooshes open the next morning, and Kathy walks in and I notice a syringe and a vial in her hands.

"What is that for?" I ask.

"The doctor wants to keep an eye on how your valve is healing and make sure it will hold up under pressure. So, this is a chemical stress test." She says as she shakes the vial in her right hand. "It will make your body think it's running on a treadmill."

I look from the vile to Kathy's eyes, and for a split second, I see a hint of fear fill them. I close my eyes for a second and take a breath. I look at her in the eye and I notice for the first time they look so much like Taylor's that it hurts to look into them. I don't know where I get the courage, but I hold out my right arm with the IV and give a small smile.

"Let's do it."

Kathy takes a deep breath and gives a small smile herself. "Take your shirt off and lie down in bed while I'll get everything ready." Kathy instructs.

I do as she says, and I wait for her to start the test. She places more heart monitor pads and leads on my chest and sides, and she has what I think is an ultrasound machine near the bed as well.

"You ready?" Kathy asks.

"Not really. But I know you need to." I say.

Kathy gives a sorrowful smile and injects me with the medicine. At first, I don't feel anything, but after about a minute I feel the surge of adrenaline hit my veins and my heart begins to beat faster in response. Then, an instant headache hits me from the rush, and with that, my breathing becomes faster to keep up with my heart rate.

I feel Kathy squeeze some kind of cold jelly on my chest, which sends chills down my spine. She then places the ultrasound wand on my chest and begins to look for any leakage. I try to stay still and let her do what she needs to do, trying to let the *lub, lub, lub* of the ultrasound machine calm me down.

After what feels like forever, I feel Kathy take the wand off and wipe the jelly from my chest, and she then gives me a Coke to drink.

"This will stop the medicine." She says.

I grab the Coke and take a drink as Kathy opens the IV line all the way for saline to also flush the medicine out of my system, and after a few minutes, I already feel better.

"Glad that's over." I say with a tired sigh.

I'm still a little breathless, and the headache is still there some, but it's a lot better.

"Yeah, I'm sorry, but until we know that you are healing well, the doctor doesn't want you to actually exert yourself." Kathy explains.

"I can understand that. So, what did it show?" I ask.

"Let me show this to the doctor, and I'll tell you." Kathy says.

She leaves and takes the ultrasound machine with her. As the door slides shut, I try to relax and let the rest of the medicine wear off. Just as I am about to doze off ten minutes later, I hear Kathy come back in with the doctor to go over my results.

"Agent Evans, how are you today?" The doctor asks.

"I feel like I am doing better. I do still get a little more fatigued than what I'm used to, but I figured that's part of the healing process." I say.

"Oh, absolutely." The Doctor croons as he looks at his tablet, with what I assume holds my test results. "Well, your stress test came back normal. I see no abnormalities or any leakage in the ultrasound. I will probably do one more before we are able to release you; whenever that will be."

"That sounds great. Thank you, doctor." I say.

The doctor walks out with a curt nod, and Kathy leaves on his heels to do her normal rounds, and I am finally able to fall asleep for a while to recover from the test.

Chapter 51

Bryan

Over the next week and a half, I feel better and better. While I still do need more rest than what I'm used to, I'm slowly getting up earlier and earlier. On Monday I wake up and I decide that I will try to finish up the painting for Taylor in time for Christmas on Saturday.

I glance at the wall clock that hangs over the door, and it reads six AM, my normal wake-up time. I remember that Taylor always hated that I was a morning person, and I smile at the memory.

After I go in the attached bathroom and I wipe myself off and change into a fresh set of scrubs, it's six-thirty and I realize that Kathy has not been in to do her normal morning routine yet, but I brush that off as maybe she's taking care of someone worse than me and go over to the easel and get to work.

At seven AM, Kathy finally comes in, and I can tell by her stiff movements and silent demeanor that something is wrong. She is usually, or at least with me, happy to see that I am up and moving around, but today she just walked in and began changing my bed sheets without a word.

"Kathy, what's wrong?" I ask while picking up the rag to wipe the wet paint from my fingers.

Kathy stops dead in her tracks and slowly turns around to face me, and the look in her eye makes my stomach drop.

"Is Taylor okay?" I make myself ask, but I'm afraid of the answer.

Kathy comes over and sits on the chair next to me, and she lets out a sigh as she's sitting down. "Not really. She hasn't been eating much at all, not taking a shower much, and not really coming out of her room, since you 'died'." Kathy says and making air quotations on died. "I'm terrified that she's going to end up in here too." She puts her face in her hands.

I stand up and go over and gently put my hand on her shoulder. She looks up at me, and I can tell she's holding back tears.

"I just don't know what to do for her." She says, her voice cracking with emotion.

After a few minutes, I think back on how I felt when my parents died and what my grandfather told me. "Hey, tell her this. Tell her that she's wasting my memory by staying in her room and not taking care of herself. Tell her that she has to live for me, to keep her memories of me alive. And that the more you block people out, all you're left with are the bad memories."

Kathy looks at me, and I give her a small smile.

"I don't remember much about my parents, but I still do remember the day they died and even as young as I was. I was depressed, and that is what my granddad told me. To live for my parents' memory, and that helped me." I say softly.

"Okay. I'll try that. I'll try almost anything at this point." Kathy says, sniffling.

She takes a deep cleansing breath, and then she does her usual checks on me. After she's satisfied with the results, she leaves me with my painting again.

A few hours later, I finally finish the painting, and I sit back and admire my work. But I can't savor the feeling when I think back to what Kathy told me earlier about Taylor's condition, and I wish now more than ever that I could see her. I do understand Wayne's point to some extent. But now that I am doing better, I should be able to at least call on a secure line.

I shake that desire to call Taylor out of my mind and go to the bathroom and wash the paint off my hands. Then, I turn the TV on and see what's happening on the news, and after a few minutes, I am already tired of the drivel and turn it off. As I turn around to head back to the bed, I see Kathy in the doorway, and she's looking at the finished painting with her eyes bright with unshed tears.

"That is beautiful, Bryan. Taylor will love that."

"Thank you. Now I need to figure out how to put a date on it, so hopefully she'll put two and two together and know that I'm okay finally." I say.

"Hold that thought." Kathy says.

She walks out of the room, and she comes back a few minutes later with an ink stamp in her hand, and I feel my lips form a big smile.

"That's perfect." I take the stamp and I dial the numbers to 12 and then to 18 and stamp them in the diagonal corners.

A few minutes later, Mark comes in, and he sees us around the painting, and he has that cocky smile on his face that usually tries to hold a snarky comment back.

"What, you think it's not good?" I ask daring him to say otherwise.

"If you do, I will knock the shit out of you." Kathy warns.

"No, no, no, no," Mark says, holding his hands up in surrender. "It's amazing, dude. I was going to say something else, but I decided not to." Mark says. I can tell from his tone, he is scared of Kathy.

"Uh huh," I say, rolling my eyes.

I don't think about what I am doing as I walk over and put Mark in a headlock right next to my left side, and I hear Kathy freak out.

"Bryan, what are you doing?!"

"I'm sorry! I didn't think! I just reacted!" I apologize as I let go of Mark and put my hands up in surrender.

Kathy motions for me to take my shirt off, and I do as she asks, and I go over to sit on the bed. I look sheepishly at Mark, who has backed up toward the doorway, then direct my eyes to the floor as Kathy takes the bandage off to make sure I didn't rip any stitches out. After everything looks good, she gives me a light smack on the back of my head.

"Don't you do that again!" She scolds.

"Yes, ma'am."

"You shocked me, and once I realized what you did, I didn't want to move." Mark says as he comes over to my bed. "But I have to say, it was nice to be head-locked by my best bud again." Mark says with a sly smile on his face and gives me a light smack on the back.

I push him away and get up off the bed and go to sit in the recliner. "Hey, do you think you could set up for an agent to take this to Taylor?" I ask, trying to change the subject.

"Sure. I'll take it to my place and have them pick it up there when you're ready to give it," Mark says.

"Okay great. Kathy, do you think you could get some wrapping paper for me?" I ask while looking over at her as she is making notes in my chart.

"Sure. I'll get it tonight and leave it in the car for tomorrow." Kathy says.

That night I don't sleep well because I'm worried about Taylor. I hope that Kathy can pull her out of the hole she dug because of all this. I get out of bed and sit in the recliner by the window and just look out at the nighttime sky. I watch as the stars seem to brighten and dim with the passing clouds. I look at the doorway and I see Mark leaning on the frame, a dark guardian almost, just watching me silently.

"Can't sleep either?" Mark asks.

"No. Why can't you sleep?" I ask, leaning my head back against the leather of the recliner.

"Lexi went out on some recon for Wayne for another case." Mark says. "What about you?"

"Kathy told me that Taylor isn't doing so well, and that she's just wasting away in her room because she thinks I'm dead." I close my eyes and take a deep breath, "Sometimes I wonder if it would have been better if I had listened to you and just kept to myself because I didn't want to hurt her like this." I say, guilt filling my voice.

"Bryan, dude, just stop. I was wrong to tell you to stay away. Taylor is an amazing woman, and you both are stronger because you have one another." Mark says. "You didn't know this would happen, or at least to the extent that it did. This is going to sound sappy coming from me, but I think you survived all this because of your connection to her." Mark says, his tone getting serious.

At first, I don't understand why he would say that, but then I think back to my first few hours, days, and even weeks after I was shot, and he's right. Even in my fever hazy mind, I remember thinking about Taylor, and saying her name over and over in my mind, and thinking of her face and the loving way she would touch me and look at me. So yes, she was my earthly saving grace. The rock that kept me grounded, that one thing to focus on and to fight for.

"You know what Mark; you need to be a therapist. You can talk deep when you want to." I say, letting a slight smile play on my lips.

"No, I just know my brother from another mother and what makes him tick." Mark says while tapping my forehead. I try to smack his hand away. "But even Mrs. Sparks said the same thing. You fought harder because Taylor wasn't here." Mark adds in a soft voice.

Deep down, I know what he is saying is true, and I am even more determined to get back to Taylor. "You're right. So, you have to do me a favor and catch those bastards that put me in here so I can get out of this place." I say with determination in my voice.

"Oh, believe me, I am looking in every dark, dank corner I can think of," Mark says. "I won't stop until they are found." Mark leaves a little while later, around two AM, and I try to settle down for the night.

Chapter 52

Bryan

The next morning, I wake up and I see Kathy sitting in the chair next to my bed just making notes in a chart. I notice the time on her watch, and it reads 9:30 am.

"Good morning, sleepyhead," Kathy says with a smile and a lightness to her voice.

I immediately pick up on the energetic tone in her voice, and I quickly sit up in bed.

"Whoa, don't sit up fast like that!" Kathy scolds me.

I ignore her and I ask, "How did it go with Taylor yesterday?"

"She'll be fine. You were right; telling her that she was wasting your memory is what snapped her back into reality." Kathy says. I can tell that lifted a huge burden from her shoulders.

"I'm glad I can still be of help and comfort for her, even from here." I say.

"Yes, thank you for bringing my daughter back from the brink." Kathy says.

She gives me a hug and kisses my forehead in such a motherly way that I never want to let her go. She looks away, but I still notice the tears she's trying to hide.

"Oh, did you bring me the wrapping paper?" I ask, trying to lighten the emotional mood.

"Oh, right. Yes, I did," Kathy says brightly.

She brings me the paper, scissors, and tape and helps me wrap the painting. "Taylor is going to love that." Kathy says with a smile.

"I know she will." I say with sadness filling my voice. "I just wish I could give it to her myself. This would be our first Christmas, and we can't spend it together."

"I know." Kathy says while rubbing my back.

Some of Kathy's motions remind me so much of Taylor that I almost let myself believe that she is right here with me.

"I gotta do some of my rounds. I'll shoot Mark a text and let him know to come by," Kathy says.

"Thank you." I say.

After a while, Mark comes by and picks up the painting for me, but little did I know that was the last time I would see him for two months. Then in February, he shows up, and I try to act like nothing is bothering me. But deep down I'm just thinking what made him disappear with no explanation. He is just standing in my room, and suddenly he puts me in a headlock without warning, instantly driving all thoughts from my mind.

"What the Hell dude?" I ask as I begin to kick his leg out from under him.

He lets go for an instant, and I put him in my own headlock. I see a nurse walk by the door and I hear her yell for Kathy.

"Kathy, 525 is roughhousing with his guest!"

I let go of Mark, and Kathy pops her head in, gives us both a warning look, and walks away.

"Oh, we almost got busted." Mark laughs.

"Yeah, we did." I chuckled. "But hey, where have you been these past two months.?" My tone turning serious.

"Let's just say we got a hot lead." Mark says in a bit of a cocky tone.

"Okay. And?" I ask, pressing for answers.

Mark doesn't answer me at first, and when I think he's about to, we hear his phone beep. "Sorry dude. I gotta go," Mark says.

I can tell by his body language he is all agent mode now, and that makes my stomach drop.

"Dude, what about Taylor?" I ask.

He ignores me and walks out. I try to go after him, but Kathy stops me. "Mark, don't leave me hanging like this!" I plead.

But he walks down the hall to the elevator and walks inside. I look to Kathy, who still has her hand on my chest, to stop me from going after Mark.

"Kathy, what's going on?" I ask, looking her directly in the eye, pleading for her to tell me what she knows.

"I don't know." Kathy says simply, her face not giving away anything.

I walk back into my room and sit in the chair, and put my elbows on my knees, but after a few minutes I start to think about Mark's mood and I get antsy. I stand up and walk over to the window to look outside, but nothing can hold my attention. I then I start pacing from the window to the end of the bed and back, thinking about what could be going on out there and wondering if Taylor's safe.

Kathy comes in and sees what I'm doing and comes in to try to talk me down. "Bryan, you need to sit. I don't want you up walking like this yet," Kathy pleads.

"Kathy, I know something is going on. Please tell me what it is. Is Taylor okay?" I ask.

I try to look into her eyes to see if I can get any signs, but she's got her poker face on and I can't read a damn thing. Then I realize that my heart is beating kind of fast from the adrenaline, and I sit in the recliner to try to relax.

"I can tel. I just feel it. Something is going on." I whisper.

"Bryan. You have to trust me, okay? I understand you are worried about Taylor, but I can't have you fall back down. Hey, look at me." Kathy says as she puts a hand on my right shoulder. I look at her, at the same eyes as Taylor, and I hold on to her every word. "Taylor is okay; everything will be okay. But I need you to keep it together for me." Kathy says.

I take a deep, calming breath, and I nod. "Okay. Thank you. I'm okay now."

"Good," Kathy says.

Mark comes back a few days later, and I have to almost literally bite my tongue to keep myself from asking him what happened the other day. Just as he's getting ready to leave, he tries to pull me into another headlock, but I see it coming and I put him into the wall and twist his arm behind his back.

Once again, I hear the nurse yell for Kathy, "Kathy, it's 525 again."

I roll my eyes, and I let Mark go, and he walks out with a smile on his face. And a few minutes later, Kathy comes in. "Hey Bryan, can you try to do something for me?" Kathy asks.

"Sure?" I ask, wondering what she would want me to do.

"Can you walk around the hall? I think it is time to see if you can handle a little exercise." Kathy says, trying to hide her smile.

"Uh, okay. Sure?" I say with a bit of a question in my tone.

I am so confused why she would all of a sudden ask me to do that when she yelled at me the other day for pacing in my room. But I make sure I have my shoes on and I take a walk. Then, after I complete my walk around the hall and as I hit the doorway of my door, I stop in my tracks. Because in the three long months I have been here, I see the most wonderful and beautiful woman of my dreams.

Present day

"Of course, you know what happens from there." I say as I am playing with Taylor's hair and still holding her close to my side.

"Yeah, I can't forget that. I found you, and I thought I lost you again, all within a few hours," Taylor says softly.

"I'm so sorry. I never meant to hurt you, and every day I wish you could be there with me, or at least know I was okay. The only reason Mark knew is because he wouldn't leave the hospital. Then Wayne came in and said that no one else aside from Mark and your mother was to know, and Mark actually wanted to argue with him." I say, recalling the argument again.

"I never would have thought that of Mark," Taylor says, remembering that part of my story.

"Me either. But he was different when I was in there. I usually don't see him in his 'agent' mode much outside of an active mission between us." I say using air quotations on the word agent.

"Yeah, I could tell that his thought process was different with me and Lexi too," Taylor says.

"He was probably scared out of his mind. This was the first major injury either of us had that was life-threatening." I say softly.

We both settle down deeper into the bed, and I hold Taylor close to my chest and let sleep take the both of us into blissful dreams.

Chapter 53

Taylor

The next morning after breakfast and while Mom is trimming Bryan's hair a bit to tame the longer-than-normal dark brown waves, a thought hits me, and I am ashamed that it didn't hit me sooner.

"Bryan, how do you feel about going over and seeing your grandparents?" I ask.

Bryan looks at me as Mom takes a snip of his hair, and he puts his right hand to the bridge of his nose and lets out an aggravated sigh towards himself. "I am a horrible grandson. I didn't even think about telling them I am okay." Bryan says with sorrow in his voice.

"We'll go over as soon as Mom finishes your haircut." I say. "Better to go looking as fresh as you can, right?" I add. He gives me a smile, and I give him a bashful wink.

"You can find the silver lining in almost anything, can't you?" Bryan asks.

"Yup. One thing though, I would keep this little stubble you have." I say while running my hand over the fairly filled in beard that he's starting to grow in.

I go upstairs and dress in a baby blue sweater and a pair of black pants, and I pull out a pair of dark jeans and a heather green three-quarter-sleeve shirt for Bryan to wear. When he comes up after his shower in nothing but a blue towel around his hips, he smiles at my clothing choice. He gives me a sound kiss on the lips before he slips into my bathroom to get dressed. Then we both leave to see John and Gail.

We walk across the street and have Bryan stand back past the door, so he is not seen right away. I smile at him as I knock on the door. After a few heartbeats, Gail opens the door, and her smile is bright and happy to see me. I walk in and gently shut the door, but leave it unlocked.

"You look lovely today, Taylor. How are you?" Gail asks.

John comes into the living room with a cup of coffee for him and Gail. "Oh, Taylor, I didn't hear you come in. Did you want a cup?" John asks as he lifts the mug in my direction.

"No, I'm good, thank you." I say with a smile. "Are you two up for a surprise?" I ask.

"What do you mean?" John asks as he takes a sip of his coffee and puts it down on the table along with Gail's cup.

"I think it's better if I show you." I smile and get up off the couch to open the door.

I hear Gail let out a sound that is half scream, half laughter as Bryan walks into his home and sits beside his grandparents on the couch. Gail instantly breaks down crying and goes from hugging Bryan to running her hand over his face and back again. John keeps his hand on Bryan's shoulder and gives a playful punch to his jaw because of the beard he now has.

"That looks good on you, son," John says.

"Thanks, Grandpa," Bryan says with tears in his eyes.

"Oh my. I can't believe it. Thank the Heavens you are alive and well." Gail says through her sobs. "You're not my little man anymore, are you?"

She asks as she also runs her aged fingers across his facial hair.

Bryan takes her hand in his and gently kisses her fingers like he's done for me so many times before. "I will always be your little man, Granny." Bryan says, his voice thick with emotion. "I'm just wiser now, I guess."

"You're battle-worn." John says, knowing that's what Bryan means, but just didn't want to verbalize it.

"Yeah, battle-worn. That's a good word for it." Bryan says.

After a few hours of talking all about what happened, both of us being sure to tell our respective sides, we leave John and Gail feeling whole again. Feeling that they didn't lose another part of their family.

Chapter 54

Taylor

Three and a half weeks later we are back to our old selves. And today, Bryan is getting dressed so he can go down to the agency to get his badge reinstated. He's still a little iffy about getting it back when I'm not, and for the first time, I'm ready to go before Bryan is.

"Babe, you know I'm ready to go before you are?" I ask as I see him sitting at the desk in my room. "Just get what you need and let's go." I say, running my hand over his left shoulder.

"Okay. I guess I'm stressing a little." Bryan says as he takes my hand and gives my knuckles a light kiss.

"You'll do fine. They just want to make sure that you're okay to be back in the field." I say reassuringly.

"I still wish that you would try out." Bryan says with a sly smile.

"Right now, let's worry about getting you squared away."

As we head downstairs, we see that Dad has made waffles and air-fried chicken for breakfast. I make Bryna eat a little something to hopefully calm his nerves.

"I believe in you, Bryan. And I need you to protect my daughter if she gets tangled up in things like she does on occasion." Dad says while giving us a warm smile.

"Dad, I do not get tangled up in things. I go in full force." I say with a smile.

"That I can agree with." Mom says while giving me a smile.

After we have breakfast, we walk toward the front door, but Mom stops us and pulls Bryan in for one final hug.

"You will do great."

"Thank you, Kathy. I appreciate you and Tom for believing in me." Bryan says.

"Are you saying I don't believe in you, Bryan Alexander?" I ask, trying to sound serious, but my smile gives me away.

"Oh, I know you do, Sweetheart." Bryan says as he pulls me toward him and gives me a sound kiss on the lips.

I knew my picking at him would change his attitude this morning. He lets me go, and I wipe at the lip gloss to smooth it over my tingling lips while trying not to look in the direction of my parents, but I feel their, or at least my father's stare on me.

"Duly noted, Babe." I say, still a little flushed from his spur-of-the-moment kiss.

Bryan finally opens the front door and walks outside first to make sure everything is okay before he extends his right hand, signaling me to follow. I take his hand and close the door behind me. He walks us to his truck, opens the passenger door, and helps me in the seat, just like old times. He gives me a loving smile and a wink as he closes my door.

As he gets in the driver's seat, he takes a cleansing breath and looks over to me one more time before he turns the engine over. The engine roars to life, and the idling motor makes the cabin shake ever so slightly. I take his hand and give it a little encouraging squeeze.

"Let's do this, Bullet."

As we pull up to the brick building, I think back to when I entered these halls a few weeks ago to get my own badge reinstated when I thought I lost the one I love most, and now I am supporting the same person in getting his back. We get out of the truck, and as Bryan opens the main door of the agency, we walk in with his arm around my shoulders, and we see Mark and Lexi waiting on us by the large staircase.

"Hey man, glad to see you back on your feet." Mark says as he extends his hand to bring Bryan in for a man-hug.

"Thanks, man, for everything." Bryan says, but his words say more than he can express.

"No biggie." Mark says like these last five months weren't Hell on anyone, but the worry lines near his eyes tell a different story.

"Bryan Evans, we are ready for you." Says an older woman in a navy pinstripe suit and a clipboard close to her chest.

"Don't get into any trouble while I'm gone." Bryan says, looking at me then to Mark.

"Trouble is my middle name, you know that." I tease.

He smiles gives me a quick peck on the cheek and walks off with the woman. After a few minutes of silence, Mark breaks it, and I notice a sly smile on his face before he speaks.

"Have you ever thought about at least trying the testing for fun?" Mark asks.

"Mark, you can't try it for fun." I say like a mother scolding her child.

"I think I can have someone override that. What do you say?" Mark asks with a mischievous gleam in his eye.

I look at Lexi to see her reaction, and while she is shaking her head and rolling her eyes at her boyfriend's words, she shrugs at me and just smiles. Saying it's my choice.

I look at Mark for a few seconds. "Alright, I'll try it for *fun* and that's all." I say, my tone firm on the word fun.

"Great." Mark says with a big smile.

Mark walks me up to a plain, black metal door, and we walk through it, Lexi staying behind and gives me a thumbs up and a small smile of good luck. On the other side of the door, I see a platform waiting for me, beckoning me closer. Mark hands me a gun, and I look at it for a second. I instantly remember the day I shot Phil, and I shake it out of my head. It's his own fault he's dead.

"There are only practice rounds in here. So, you can shoot and not hurt anyone." Mark says, as if reading my thoughts. "When you're ready, walk on the ledge there."

I look out at the spotlight at the end of the walkway, and I take a deep breath, and I walk over to it.

"State your name." A deep male voice says over a loudspeaker.

"Taylor Sparks." I reply, my voice surprisingly steady.

I hear a switch thrown, followed by an electrical buzz as the testing ground begins to light up before me. Scaffolding, ramps, tarps, and ladders are scattered about to make the terrain difficult to traverse. I see several targets, some that need defending and some that need subduing.

"Begin when you're ready." The male voice says again over the loudspeaker, making me jump at the random announcement.

This is just for fun. Do your best, but this will go nowhere. I tell myself.

I rack the automatic pistol, and I start the *testing*. I see wooden targets pop up from the floor, and I shoot the threatening ones with ease, but one jumps up closer to me, and I almost shoot a posterboard kid. I take a deep breath and tell myself to look closer. I keep going deeper into the course, and I get a few more that pop up in front of me, and I react the way I need to. Shoot a bad guy or save a good one. But I get thrown for another loop when I feel a pair of hands on my shoulders.

The gun gets knocked away and my arms are pinned behind me, but I get out with my little trick. I wrap my legs around his neck, and I pull forward; he lets my arms go, and he tumbles over his head and on his back. I grab my gun and I shoot him in the knee where it would immobilize him.

"Good, keep going!" I hear Mark exclaim over the speaker.

"If you can hear me, Mark, I will kill you for this." I grumble.

All I hear is his laughing in response. *Laugh now, soon you won't be, buddy.*

I shoot a few more poster board targets. But then I get real ones. Kids, men, and women. Good guys and bad. When I see the kids, I hide my gun, and when I see anyone else, I just nod at them. Then I hear a girl scream at the top of her lungs in fear, and I see a freakishly huge guy holding her by the throat with his meat-hook-sized hand, and he's pointing a gun to her temple.

"Don't come any closer! If you do, I'll shoot her!" He yells.

The girl just cries out and looks at me. "Hey, you don't need to do this. Let her go, and we will talk this over." I say gently, keeping my gun low so I'm not as much of a threat at the moment.

"No!" He yells back.

"What's your name?" I ask.

"Joe." He snaps in reply

"Okay, Joe. Listen to me; you don't really want to hurt her, do you?" I ask.

While I'm asking these questions, I'm stalling so I can find a place where I can shoot him and make him release the girl.

"You don't know anything!" He yells, and he pushes the gun to her head, and she cries out again.

When he moves, I see my chance, his knee is in my line of sight and aim, and I fire all in a heartbeat. He drops the gun, falling to his knees as the girl runs behind me. I keep the gun trained on him, finger just a twitch away from the trigger. Then the lights suddenly come on brighter than they are, and the guy gets up off the floor a moment later.

"Nice job, cadet. Usually, I just get shot. Good job stalling." He says with a smile.

"Thanks." I say, feeling a shy smile play on my lips from his approval of my stalling attempt.

I look up as another light comes on over a door to my right, and I hear the male voice. "Exit through the door there."

I walk over and I turn the handle to exit the simulation course. I see Mark on the other side with a brilliant smile on his face, almost as bright as Cody's face on Christmas.

"You were amazing!"

"Thank you. But the answer's still no." I say simply.

"Taylor, do you know what the FBI would be like with you on the team? You could teach the rookies how to shoot like you. If we could have people shoot like you do, we would be way better than we are now." Mark says with so much energy it makes my head spin.

"Mark, let it go. Plus, I don't want Bryan to know about this."

"Taylor, you did a wonderful job. I always knew you were a good shot." Wayne says as he's walking over to us.

"Thanks, Wayne." I say. "Mark here is trying to get me into the agency full time." I say, eyeing Mark.

"And what would be so wrong with that? You're eighteen like your friends here." Wayne says, looking me dead in the eye.

I look at him and I realize that, whether I like it or not, I just tried out for the FBI. And guessing by the look on his face, I'm in if I want it. Wayne makes me walk with him up the staircase to his office, and I come out a few minutes later. I see Mark looking at me, and I can tell he's about to explode with excitement.

"Did you get it?"

"That's for me to know and for you to find out." I say, showing that my hands are empty.

"Oh, come on." Mark whines.

I shake my head, and I look down the hall, and I see Bryan walking toward me. "Did you get it?" I echo Mark's question toward Bryan, meeting him halfway down the hall.

"Take a look." Bryan says as he pulls me into his arms, and I rest my hands on his chest.

He hands me a leather wallet, and I open it up, and I see his badge in it. "Congrats, Babe!" I say with excitement.

I wrap my arms around his neck as he spins me around, and when he sets me down, he kisses me tenderly on the lips.

"Thanks," Bryan says as he pulls away. "You didn't get into any trouble, did you?" Bryan asks, eyeing Mark.

"No. Come on, let's go to my place and celebrate." I say, before Mark could even answer. "Mark, you and Lexi can come too."

Mark and Lexi smile at my invitation, and we walk out together, and we drive to my house. When we get home, I notice that Mom's and Dad's cars are both in the driveway, and I take a deep breath.

"Are you sure you're okay with me having my badge back?" Bryan asks as he's parking his F150 behind my dad's Accord.

"Yes, I am. I couldn't be happier." I say with vigor in my voice.

We walk in the door together, and I can practically feel the excitement radiating off him. When we walk in, Mom and Dad are on the couch in the living room watching a movie, and when they see all of us walk in Dad pauses the movie as we all walk over into the living room to join them. Bryan and me on the loveseat, and Lexi sits on the couch beside Dad and Mom with Cody on her lap, and Mark sits on the floor in front of Lexi's legs, leaning on them with his back to her.

"Did you get it back, Bryan?" Mom asks.

"Yes, I did. Your daughter is officially dating an FBI agent again." Bryan says with pride in his voice.

"Well, so are you." I whisper, though I'm not sure it was loud enough.

But it must have been because all eyes are on me. Mom, Dad, Lexi, Mark, Cody, and Bryan are looking at me with dumbfounded expressions on their faces.

"What did you just say?" Bryan asks slowly.

"So are you." I say again, this time my voice a bit louder.

"Ha, I knew it!" Mark says while clapping his hands together once.

"Now I know who talked her into this," Bryan says, giving Mark the evil eye.

"Taylor, you really got your badge back?" Mom asks softly.

"Yeah," I say, and I pull it out and I show it to everyone.

"Annie, are you sure?" Bryan asks in both awe and with a touch of worry in his voice.

"Yes, I've never been this sure about something in my entire life. If you go out in the field, I want to be there, I can't stay home and wonder what's going on. To wonder if you will come home." I say as my eyes get misty toward the last of my words.

"Are we all partners?" Lexi asks.

"Yes, Lexi, I asked Wayne if he would sign us all on any case he gives us."

Lexi and I hug, and Mark gives Bryan a high-five.

"I can't believe we are back in business." Lexi says with a bright smile.

"Yeah, we are, and we're back and better than ever." I say with confidence in my voice.

Chapter 55

Taylor

After dinner, Mark and Lexi leave, and Bryan and I get ready for bed. I decide to get my shower first, and I am waiting in bed for Bryan to come up. He walks into my room with a pair of sweats on, and he slides in beside me and I snuggle up against his chest, and he wraps his arms around my waist, pulling me tighter into him.

"I can't believe you actually got your badge," Bryan says in bewilderment. "Did you really get it because of me?"

"Partly yes." I begin. "But the other part was I actually liked it. Deep down I liked being an agent with Lexi. And like I said earlier, I couldn't think about you leaving for God knows how long, and I'm just sitting here waiting for you to walk back through those doors. And I definitely couldn't handle someone knocking on my door and telling me that you were not coming back." I whisper.

"I understand the way you're thinking. I doubt I could handle it any better." Bryan says with understanding in his voice. "I'm just glad that we will be on the same case if one comes our way."

"One will come our way; it's just a matter of time. There is no 'if' in the FBI; it's 'when'." Bryan says.

"Well, *when* it does, we will be ready." I say with a wink.

"Yeah, we will." Bryan says. "What did they say after you were done in the shooting simulation?"

"Wayne said that I should teach the rookies on how to shoot and how to handle a hostage situation."

"And? What else?" Bryan asks in anticipation.

"Since he let me get my real badge, I said I would teach one class, so I told him all the rookies better be there."

"I knew he would eventually talk you into teaching a class." Bryan says with a laugh.

"I still can't believe that I am holding a real badge. In the past, I wanted out of the FBI, and when it came back for me, through you." I pause. "I thought, what the hell, if I can't run from the FBI, might as well be one with the people I trust the most." I say.

"Are you ready for this?" Bryan asks, rubbing small circles on my back.

"As long as you're with me and I have Mark and Lexi, yes, I am." I say. "There's no backing out now." I chuckle. "And I want to be there to help you and the others." I say as I glide my finger over the top of his broad shoulder.

"Alright. I know that you'll do fine. Just from some of the things I've seen you do I know you can handle yourself." Bryan says. "But that won't stop me from trying to be there for you. You are *my girl*, and I will do anything for you to make sure you're safe." Bryan adds while running his hands through my hair.

"So will I. And I will also do the same for Lexi and Mark." I say without hesitation.

"You'll make a great agent, Annie," Bryan says in a loving tone.

"Hey, I've been here before. I've just never been a real agent, that's all." I say.,

"Well, *I* haven't seen you as an agent. So, I don't know what you're capable of doing." Bryan says, but he's not even trying to hide a smile.

"Bite me." I say.

"Don't tempt me." Bryan says in a deep, sultry voice and scrapes his teeth over my earlobe, sending shudders down my spine.

I breathy laugh escapes my throat as I run my hand over his bare chest, trailing feather-light kisses along my invisible track. I hear him take a rattling breath as if trying to compose himself, and not act on the desire that I feel building beside me. I give a small chuckle as I settle back next to him and rest my head on his chest once more.

"Let me see your badge again." Bryan says after a few minutes.

I get up and I go over to my dresser, get my badge and I hand it over to him. He opens it up, and he looks at it for the third time tonight. "I'm so proud of you, Annie. For everything you've done. You thought I was dead, yes you fell down, but you came back with help. And you got your temp badge back to catch Phil and Daryl even though you got shot again in the process. But that helped you find me." Bryan says. "And I think without you being there when you were, I think I would have died for real that time. I don't remember being on the brink of death the first time; this last time I actually saw the light that I hear people talk about in the movies." Bryan whispers, his voice going dark. "And to hear that you shot Phil and you getting a real badge after all that to me is amazing. You are a fighter just as much as I am."

"I was just trying to do what I thought was right. And my thought was that *I* wanted to take Phil and Daryl down. That's why I got my temp badge. And yes, there was a good chance that you would have died that day. You were exhausted from that shot Mom gave you, and that's what Phil wanted. He wanted you to die that way or be too weak to fight him so he could finish it. And I'm glad I was there to take care of him and save you."

Bryan kisses me to try and lighten the mood, and I run my hand through his dark brown hair and down his chest. Whenever we talk about Phil or Daryl, I want to touch his scar and one of mine that now live both on my right side or the little circle on my left forearm, but Bryan said they don't matter anymore. They're just reminders of what we've been through together, and we will notice them less and less as time goes on.

"You two doing okay?" Mom asks while tapping on the frame of my bedroom door.

"Yeah, we're fine." Bryan replies.

"I'm glad that the two of you are back together now. I even told Wayne that the next time something has to be hidden like this, I am to get permission to tell the partners that the other is alive. Not just for you all but for all FBI. I would have to get permission from the other agencies to do that, but for the FBI now, I can. So, this *won't* happen again. And Taylor, I'm sorry that I had to keep Bryan a secret, but I couldn't do anything else," Mom says.

"Mom, it's okay. You were just doing what you were told to do. I don't blame you." I say.

She comes in and kisses me on the cheek and hugs Bryan. "Bryan, just take care of my daughter. I know that you two will be going off on some case sooner or later. Just please try to take care of her." Mom says.

"I will, Kathy. I think we have shown how much we care for the people we love." Bryan says.

"We'll all but Mark. He has yet to be shot. He doesn't love us." I say jokingly. "I'm kidding. He's a great partner and a great friend."

"Yeah, he is. And I have to remember to thank him for everything he's done." Bryan says.

"Even if you didn't agree with it?"

"Yes, because he did it for a good reason, even if it was off the charts." Bryan says.

Just then my iPad beeps, and Bryan picks it up and opens the video notification. "Hey you two," Lexi says when the feed loads in.

Lexi is lying with Mark the same way that I'm lying with Bryan. Both guys shirtless, and us ladies snuggled in so close you could barely get a piece of paper between us.

"This is weird." Mark says.

"So are you, but that's beside the point." Bryan snaps back with just a hint of playfulness in his voice.

"I think it's kinda cute." I say.

"So do I." Lexi says to Mark, giving him a light smack on the nose.

"Hey Mark?" Bryan says. "Thanks for all your help. I appreciate it."

"Any time, Bryan. You're my best friend and my partner. It's what we do." Mark says. "It's just I would expect the same in return."

"Count on it." Bryan says.

"Mark, Lexi, I want to thank you too. You helped me when I didn't know where to turn to. And we were able to take down those scumbags. And I honestly can't wait to see what case that Wayne will give us next." I say.

"Neither can we," Lexi says. "It will be so amazing having my sister with me! We are going to be the talk of the agency, I know it!" She adds with excitement.

"In a good way, I hope, Lex?" Mark asks with a sly grin on his face.

"Oh, shut up. At least it won't be us getting into trouble!" Lexi shoots back.

"Trouble is your middle name, Lex." Mark growls as he goes to nuzzle Lexi's neck, and she lets out a squeak of laughter.

"Bye, Lexi. Bye, Mark. We don't want to interrupt anything now." I croon as Bryan taps the disconnect button.

I laugh as I snuggle deeper into Bryan's arms, but he had other plans. He flips me on my back and pins my hands above my head, and he leans in close to my right ear. His breath a hot, gentle caress to my skin. My breath tightens in my chest at his boldness.

"I know another woman whose middle name is 'trouble.' I wonder who that is, hmmm?" Bryan rumbles.

At first, I am at a loss for words, but when his dark, sultry chuckle fills my ears, I feel a crooked smile bloom across my face.

"I don't know who you're talking about. I'm an angel. I don't get into trouble." I croon.

"Oh, Baby, just you wait. I'm going to show you just how much trouble you can be," Bryan says as he leans in, his lips brushing over mine tenderly at first.

Then he deepens the kiss as he rolls his hips into mine, his black sweatpants sliding against my pajama bottoms, and I can't help the quiet gasp that escapes my lips at the feel of him against me. Just as I am about to arch my hips against his, we hear a throat being cleared in my doorway. Bryan jumps off me and lands on the floor with a hard thud as my heart soars in my chest.

We look over and see Mom standing in the doorway with her hands on her hips, her right foot tapping the floor in an annoyed rhythm.

"I'll act like I didn't see anything since this is your first infraction. *But* don't let me catch you two again." Mom warns, but I see just a hint of sparkle in her eye before her face morphs into the stern mother I know she can be.

"Yes ma'am. I'm sorry, it was my fault. I started it." Bryan admits as he gives me a sideways glance to keep my mouth closed.

"Alright. Now go to sleep, you two," Mom says as she walks away, and when Bryan gets back into bed, I still see a sly smile playing on his lips.

"I never seen you jump that fast before." I laugh.

"Yeah. That's what happens when you get the shit scared out of you." Bryan chuckles. "Your mother really knows how to kill the mood."

"Well yeah. That's her job. *But* she gave us a loophole if you didn't catch it." I begin.

Bryan looks at me like I grew a third eye, but I only smile as I say, "She said, 'don't let me catch you two'." I watch as Bryan's face goes from shock to pure dark amusement.

"See, I told you. Middle name is 'Trouble'."

"Well, I gotta live up to my namesake, don't I? Taylor Allison 'Trouble' Sparks."

We finally settle into a restful slumber and await the next mission that I know will come down the line soon enough from Wayne. But until then, we will take each day we have as a calm blessing until the tornado of the next case comes barreling towards us.

———————————————

THE END

Thank You and Other Works

Thank you for reading my debut novel!

If you enjoyed *Everyone Has Secrets*, I would love to hear from you! Please consider leaving your review on Goodreads and or the location where you purchased this book!

Thank you again, and this is not the last you will see of Taylor and the gang!

If you liked this story, please check out my other books, which are available on Amazon as well as most online bookstores.

Other Works:

Everyone Has Secrets Series:

Secrets in Miami- Action packed racing ring- Touch Her and Die- Found Family

The Wolf Within Series

The Wolf Within- Paranormal Werewolf Romance -Fated Mates- Protective MMC's

The Protector's of Power Series

Fire and Water- Elemental Power System- Friends to Lovers- Enemies to Lovers- Side Character MM Romance

The Eagle Project Series
The Eagle Project- Ex- Military- Enemies to Lovers-Forced Proximity-Touch Her and Die-Protective MMC's-Secret Identity

See you in the next book, Readers!!

X.O.

B. M. Light